Alba Walking

in the Shadows

May we all carry a torch into the shadows.!

Denis O'Leary

Floricanto Press

Denis O'Leary

12-9-17

Floricanto Press

7177 Walnut Canyon Rd.

Moorpark, California 93021

(415) 793-2662

www. FloricantoPress. com

ISBN-13: 978-1977532084

"Por nuestra cultura hablarán nuestros libros. Our books shall speak for our culture."

Roberto Cabello-Argandoña and Leyla Namazie, Editors

Dedicated to the women of the world who live in poverty and take the responsibility for the deeds and laws of men. May justice serve all equally.

Alba Walking

Alba

Table of Contents

1. Birth   9
2. Death   11
3. Shadows   15
4. Headlines   18
5. The Morning Call   24
6. No Me Llames Oaxaquita   33
7. Frogs   35
8. The Radio   38
9. La Llorona (The Weeping Woman)   47
10. DNA of the Shadow People   51
11. A Face from the Shadows   58
12. The First Contact   61
13. Three Questions   70
14. Old World War II Black & White Movies   75
15. The Accord   83
16. Another Victim   88
17. Running Interference   102
18. The Teacher, the Unitarian, and the
    Homeless Reporter   104
19. Press Conference   110
20. Mixtecos and Hollywood   115
21. The Article   125
22. Delays   130
23. Culture and the shadow people   137
24. Fast cars, women and Jesus   141
25. The Donald   149
26. Courtroom Thirteenth and the Nun   154
27. Jury Duty   165

28. Drop dead date   173

29. Innocent   178

30. Alba   191

31. Friday the Thirteenth   253

32. FaceBook and the Experts   267

33. Safe Surrender Baby Law   286

1. Birth

Dim silhouettes project from the crescent moon light. A sound. What happened? Shadows offset from the few clouds in the sky, a breeze. A breath. Mud.

The 101-Freeway running through the agricultural area of Ventura County between Camarillo and Oxnard is quiet, only broken by a hum with an occasional passing car or truck running the ribbon of road. The night of May 20, 2012, is like most in the coastal California area just north of Los Angeles. The groomed strawberry fields lay dormant since dusk and the tools of the fieldworkers wait for dawn.

A pathetic scream into the darkness brakes the silence. A whimper. The mother groans. She falls to her knees. Panting. The cries continue and are loud, but from across the field they are drown out in the open space. Fifteen, twenty minutes pass. Breathing, cries, then exhaustion. A newborn baby's cry. The first breaths of a new life now overlap the pants of the woman, crying by both.

The woman strains to see the infant from the shadows of the Moon overhead. The light reflects off the blood, the afterbirth. Silhouettes. Mud. The mother already on her knees collapses forward. Flowers to the edge of the rows, in bunches. Strawberries hanging down to the dirt in the raised lines of white wet plastic. A bird squawks as it is disturbed in its sleep. A newborn baby cries.

What happened?

Minutes, perhaps hours. The woman turns to walk away. She looks back, stops, and listens to her breath, to the baby's gasps, the soft cries. What happened? She looks at the moon, turns away, takes a step, looks back again and runs.

How could this happen? It must have. The baby.

The mud. The body. The questions.

Why did this happen?

2. Death

Monday, May 21, 2012

As the purple daylight brakes over the strawberry field at the El Canto Farms, the first workers arrive six to a car at the edge of the field. The cars form a line to the side of the dirt road. As the workers step from the cars steam comes from their mouths as it collides with the bitter, frigid air. A radio from one group is telling a joke in Spanish and inviting those who are listening to stop at the radio station's van at Gonzalez Blvd. and Victoria Avenue in Oxnard for steaming hot coffee and donuts. Another field too far away to take advantage from this group of workers. Clouds streak in red now and a few rays of sun over the nearby hills mix with the contrails of today's early flights. A worker points and tells another in Spanish to start picking from the first rows. The men and women separate, two to a row. Each takes a side to pick. The workers become random spots of color in one small corner of the vast rows of the large field.

Grabbing a strawberry box from a stack on the back of a flatbed truck, another group of workers each walk to a spot between the rows, strawberries drop over the sides of the white plastic strips awaiting their hands. Box in one, metal cart with one flimsy wheel in the other hand. The workers step down into the rows, bow their backs to reach down at their starting spots. Box on the one wheeled cart, both hands carefully grasp a strawberry each. Grasp, pull, and place in the container, grasp, pull and place in the container. Both hands work at the same time, eyes scanning for the next group of strawberries. The day begins.

Picking strawberries is as picking up pennies. The wages are too low for the American high school or college student, but the American dream and the escape from violence, corruption, and even harsher poverty has brought the work force in waves to America and Ventura County for generations. Some workers can earn up to fifteen dollars, even twenty dollars an hour. The less experienced workers start off slower and rely on family participation to earn a living wage. It's hard, literally backbreaking work.

Family, colleagues, those who profit from taking advantage of others work side by side. Ten dollars for a ride to and from work, the driver can earn more, the passenger works off the ride with the first hour's work. Some room together, three, four, five families to a house. Rent is expensive. Some are single, sleeping in a corner, closet, bench, even under a trailer house, still, pay high rent. Others profit. Food, others profit. Sending half of what remains to family in Mexico, a fee in the United States at the check cashing business and another fee upon delivery in Mexico. The farmworkers are always looking out for robbers at both ends, immigration, police, la mafia, and drug dealers.

Men and women with blue jeans, some women have layers of skirts, all have large bandanas wrapped around their heads, over their noses and falling past their chin with another wrapped around the ears and the back of the neck. The sun, dust, pesticides, and anonymity of not having papers, this covering allows for survival.

Invisible people. The laborers who pick the fruit are

invisible to outsiders, invisible amongst themselves, shadows in the shadows.

The eyes of the workers see the red strawberry, the stained hands pluck the fruit, gently place the correct amount in the clear plastic oyster shell boxes and show the best looking strawberries on top. Another box, bending, crawling, kneeling, and rising at the end of the box to get the next box. Sun up early in the morning to seven o'clock today, sometimes sun set. Six days a week, sometimes seven.

The first hour is bowed back reaching down, bending over to reach then walking forward clearing each plant of its ripe fruit. Starting off is bitterly cold, layers of clothing are shed one by one as the morning sun rises and warms the skin. Stoop labor becomes kneeing labor, but this soon becomes uncomfortable, knees in the moist dirt, sometimes mud cakes on the clothing. Crouching is next. Walk forward, stand up to run and deliver a full box of strawberries and grab another empty box.

César Olivas, shovel in hand walks up the row checking an irrigation drip hose for problems. A rank up from stoop labor, César and a hand-full of workers are laboring around the pickers. He had started picking when he came from Mexico at fourteen years of age. Ten years later, he is a general laborer. Pay is a couple of dollars an hour better, but the routine is varied. This position of work includes standing now.

César finishes one section of the field and now has to go off to the side where the workers hadn't yet picked. Coming to the corner, he stops. Something catches his eye. Something is out of place. The day had flowed like most, the sun had risen, and the workers labored picking the fruit. Now, it is 9:30 in the morning, the fieldworker, Father of a six month old at home holds his breath. He contemplates with stupor: blood, a mass of tissue, a baby doll? A baby!

"¡Mira! ¡Venga aquí!" He yells to workers standing at the pickup truck about fifty yards away.

Some of the stooping workers look in his direction. They pause. Eyes peering over the bandanas now covering noses and mouths look towards the man who is pointing at the ground next to a patch of poppies bordering the rows of strawberries.

"¡*Un bebé*!" He shouts.

3. Shadows

Some have gathered, but another vehicle comes down the middle division of the strawberry field, dust following behind. Ventura County Sheriff Luis Silva pulls up to the area that is taped off by now. Some field workers are still in a group looking at the Sheriff's Officers taking pictures and writing in note pads. Farther down the rows, over a hundred field workers at work bend over collecting strawberries.

From the car, Silva looks around at the investigation site surrounded by a working agricultural business in progress. He flashes back to when he would go with his father, mother, and brother to the orchards. He had also been one of the workers at one point in his life. Summer work, backbreaking work. Silva takes a breath and opens the door of the car. Stepping out, the dust from the dividing road in the field kicks up. Silva walks towards the Sheriff Officers at the now marked off crime scene.

"Who found the baby?"

"A field worker. César Ortiz, when he was checking for leaks in the water line around 9:30 this morning." The detective answers.

On the ground, mud, white plastic over the rows of dirt, strawberries overflowing the foot-high rows and a patch of flowers growing at the end of each row. Strawberries. And the infant baby, after birth, dried brown blood with mud and ants streaming over all.

Three officers are unfolding a large white canopy to one side to shade the scene.

The baby boy has his eyes and mouth partially open. The baby appears to be perfectly formed, to have been full term. Arms and feet reach up towards the sky, or perhaps to the arms of a mother, as attempting to hold a father or anyone who will hold and give protection. The skin is blue.

At one side a few feet from the infant, investigators are pressing a strip of plastic into the soil around the marks found on the ground, and others are taking measurements.

"Are there any witnesses to the birth?" asks Sheriff Silva.

"No one has come out and said anything yet," responds the investigator.

"Was the baby born here?" Silva asks.

"It looks like it. The afterbirth is next to the baby. There are marks in the mud that look like the mother knelt overlooking the baby. There are hand and foot prints as well. Can't tell yet if there was more than one person. We will be making plaster casts in a bit." hypothesizes the Sheriff.

"Boy or girl?" Silva asks as he turns his back to the officer and looks out at the fields.

"Boy. We think full term. We just started interviewing the fieldworkers, but some don't want to say much. Others don't seem to speak much Spanish."

Silva looks around acres of strawberry fields broken up in sections with dirt roads and bordered with the orange of California poppies.

"What do they speak?"

Looking over the workers hunched over in the rows, a slight grin forming on his face.

"English?"

"Mixteco. It's an Indian language from Mexico."

"Can we get someone over here to translate?" Demands Silva.

"We called for help. We're taping the interviews as well; in case something slips by."

Another officer walks up to the two, "Names. What are we going to do about names?"

Silva looks out over a group of four ladies standing at the side. "DNA. Have the medics take saliva samples from everyone here? We might get the mother, father or a relative of the baby. Somebody knows something. There has to be a reason the baby was left here. If it was random, we'll hit the dead end anyway."

He looks down at the baby, not blinking for several seconds and takes his fingers from both hands to rub his eyes.

"My God! Can't you get the ants off the baby?"

"Not yet. I know, I know." Silence for a good ten seconds.

"There is probably over a hundred workers in this field! How do we get the DNA of all of them?" says an officer intrigued.

"All of them. Before the workers leave and disappear into the shadows." Orders Silva.

"I will call the medics. But what if the laborers refuse?" asks an officer puzzled.

"Show them that it's just a cotton swab in the mouth. Take their names and a picture of each too."

"It will take all day."

Silva looked up to the sky, "They will be here all day. We have time."

4. Headlines

The headline is what people remember. The headline is what people know. In a few bold printed words or a couple of spoken words, opinions become valid. The paragraphs that follow are not important. There are headlines every day. If the general public reads the article, it doesn't add much information beyond the title. The headline sells newspapers and the public, split into conservatives and liberals see the headline through that frame.

We are also subject to a 24-hour news cycle. It is a competition to get the news out, and in some social circles, you are ahead if you have the pulse of the news. Unfortunately, events are often complicated. The first reaction does not tell what happened, it tells that something did happen, which satisfies the news cycle of the moment.

This evening's local television news doesn't add much to the information. A 60 second feed from the strawberry field, "Tragedy" used to describe the event. The concrete that is 'fact' is set well before the viewer, the public knows what happened, what may have happened. An evil person left a new born innocent child to die.

A life is lifeless. A baby. A newborn. Yes, a mother has to be involved. The devil of a mother who left her newborn drop from her body and walked or perhaps ran away, leaving the infant to die.

The father? Perhaps the father isn't involved at the scene

in the strawberry field. He could have been there. How could the two who formed the new creation coldly turn their backs and not comfort the infant? How could they walk away from the baby's cry of life?

Flesh tone, hair color will soon divide the story from sympathy to fierce anger. Light skin, blond: a victim of a victim. Thoughts of an abused teenager, a youth abused by a monster. Sympathy.

The baby had been found in an agricultural strawberry field. There is a population that would instinctively point to illegal immigration as being the target of their already established hate for this community. A baby is a precious gift from God to many of these God fearing American Christians. A baby could also be an 'anchor baby' in the racist, (always claiming to be a non-racist) rant that people only do things to become American citizens and in turn become takers, without giving anything to the American Christian fabric.

Too little information is known. The Sheriff's Department doesn't even want to release if the baby was a boy or girl yet; the investigation could have used this information. A baby is dead. That's all that is known to the public, all that is needed.

Nothing happens in a vacuum. There are other things happening in the nearby communities of Oxnard and Camarillo, California as in the world that can influence public perception and the investigation.

Oxnard, California is the largest city in Ventura County with close to 250,000 people living in the mostly agricultural community. Seventy per cent of the residence of Oxnard are Latino. Most can follow their roots to Mexico, but the waves of immigration go from just arrived to generations established in this community and country.

Politically, Oxnard is weak as compared to the other smaller cities in Ventura County. Because of immigration status, most of the adult population in Oxnard cannot vote. Turnout on Election Day of those who can vote has been historically low. Other cities in Ventura County, although smaller have a higher per capita income and better voter participation. Oxnard is often overlooked or purposely passed over in many political actions.

Oxnard has a history with the farm labor movement. Labor leader, César Chávez started in Oxnard with the Community Service Organization in the late 1950's, well before he joined the Filipino fieldworker strike and brought together what would later be called the United Farm Workers. As labor has had organized representation in Oxnard, organized farm companies have won most battles and often cut organized labor victories short. As when César Chávez first called fieldworkers to unite, many of the people who opposed labor action by the common worker were Latinos who were better established in the different agricultural companies: Latino versus Latino, Mexican versus newer Mexican.

Ventura County as a whole is very conservative, but I tell people that Oxnard is Haight–Ashbury. Oxnard not only has a very high Democratic representation, but service organizations have been able to provide the information, services, and protections that many political agencies could not provide.

El Concilio (The Council), had been the organization by leaders of different civil rights organizations bringing them together and for many years had provided educational, legal and practical services to the community not ready to form a line in front of a government office to ask for help. The sitting President of El Concilio had also become for better or for worse the spokesperson for the Latino community. In recent years though, El Concilio lost some of its clout, but La Hermandad Mexicana, the League of United Latin American Citizens, Clinicas del Camino Real, California Rural Legal Assistance and the United Farm Workers had collectively filled the vacuum.

The fresh wave of immigrants would almost always need to find out what services are available and who to go to for those services. Unfortunately, and perhaps it is human nature, but many who had come before would not only not extend a hand to the next arrivals, but in some cases take advantage of the newer wave of humans.

Too often I had been told the joke about the crabs in the bucket. A fisherman is on the pier and has collected a good amount of crabs. He throws them into a bucket. Another person comes up and tells him that he should cover the bucket because the crabs would be making their escape from the open bucket. "No, it's not a problem. Have a look." And he is true to his word; the second one crab is about to climb over the lip of the bucket another pulls it back in.

I consider this more a commentary than a joke. I had seen the same in our community for far too many times.

Oxnard and its surrounding community is over seventy-percent Latino. The new waves of Latino immigrants feed into the hard working agricultural labor force. It also gives opportunity to those who want to gain by the force as well as an opportunity for those who want to support and strengthen the community.

Another community in Oxnard is the Afro-American community. With a history of sitting at least one member on the five-member city council in the past, there were also two sitting African-American elementary school board members in 2012. African-American civil servants included the Chief of Police, Chief of the Fire Department and City Manager. The community of only two percent of the total Oxnard population is well represented, and the African-American population seems well united and well represented with amongst other groups a local chapter of the NAACP.

Notably, the Asian community is six percent of Oxnard's population but does not seem nearly as politically vocal as other demographics in the city. There have not been any elected Asians in Oxnard for many years.

On the other direction of the field where the baby was found is the city of Camarillo. This community with mostly street names in Spanish is also mostly Anglo, and financially better off. Camarillo is much more affluent, and even though smaller in population it is politically more empowered. Conservative, the community tends to lean Republican, and many from the community are vocally opposed to undocumented immigrants, to the point that legal American citizens of Latino origin are often targets of the "they are all illegal aliens" banter.

Many a letter to the editor in the local Ventura County Star newspaper would be expected to come from this part of the County opposing anything that smacked of Oxnard or Mexican. Code words and direct outrage often are brown and white. The newspaper blogs and opinion section of the Ventura County Star would surely pronounce the guilt and love to all.

The baby was found in an expansive agricultural area between the two cities. The 101 Pacific Coast Highway runs like a ribbon connecting the two cities. Los Angeles is an hour to the south and Santa Barbara an hour up the coast to the north. The mother of the child could have been from anywhere and could have retreaded to anywhere.

The event comes as a blow of sadness, soon to be forgotten. A crime? A tragedy? All had the same response at the time: It was sad to hear that a new born baby is dead.

If this had been of a mother who was blonde haired, blue eyed and young, it would have been sad. Having been found in a strawberry field, the other possibilities came to mind: Latina.

5. The Morning Call

Before the gates open outside and students are allowed on the grounds, I start my day as most junior high school teachers do, in the teacher's mail room of Rio Vista Middle School, Oxnard, California. The death of the baby is the furthest thing from what I have on my mind this morning. I have seen and forgotten about the evening news the night before. A sixth grade teacher, I come before the students enter the campus to see if I have any notices in my mail box on the wall. Other teachers are coming into the room looking in their boxes as well and leaving. My cell phone rings. Strange. I don't recognize the number.

"Good morning."

"Good morning. Can I speak to Denis O'Leary?"

"Speaking."

"My name is Sheriff Luis Silva; I'm with the Major Crimes Division."

My heart stops with cell phone to my ear. Standing, I look down at my feet. In the split second that follows I take note of where I am and wait for news that could change my life. My wife? One of my three sons? Thoughts pass in my mind in the fraction of a second, but it seems much longer.

Hind sight, Sheriff Silva could do nothing else, and the next line is surely part of his life. As if he were reading my mind for that second, or perhaps he heard an audible gasp of air, "Don't worry, all is fine with your family. You're O.K."

I sigh to myself and listen, "Have you heard about the baby that was found dead in a strawberry field yesterday?"

I remember having seen the news on KEYT channel 3 and reading the headlines in the newspaper. I hadn't read the article.

"Yes," I pause, "how can I help you?"

"We think that you might be able to help us. We think the baby is Mixteco. It was born full term and left in the same place it was born. We think the mother may have been a victim. We thought that maybe you could help us find her."

Standing there in the teacher's mail room, a few fellow teachers walk around me. I am talking to an investigator about the mother of a left for dead baby, handbag with computer and papers, on the floor leaning on my leg at my side. I look up at the clock, twenty minutes before I will be in front of my sixth graders.

"What can I do? You know that I'm a teacher." I paused a second, "Do you think I know her?"

"Could you help us locate her? We think that there is a strong possibility that she is Mixteco and we know that you work with that community. She could be a victim." "Do you think she is still around here?" I ask.

"We don't know."

I listen with my mouth partially open and giving full attention to the unexpected conversation.

"She could have been a prostitute. We know that when the prostitutes get pregnant, the pimps sometimes sell off the baby. She might have tried to get away. She could be young. I think she may need medical attention."

I listen carefully. I ask myself if the mother could be a teenager that I may have had in one of my classes.

"I want to help, but can I get back to you in twenty-four hours. I need to think about this and talk to my wife."

Sheriff Silva gives me his phone number and asks me to call him back either way. I agree and step out of the room towards my classroom. Sixth grade long division in Math and plate tectonics in Science. It is difficult to not think about the morning conversation during the day.

At home, I call three friends, all with the League of United Latin American Citizens. I am a member of the civil rights organization and had even taken some leadership at the regional level. Each of the three have the same answer to the possibility of helping look for the mother: that I would be a snitch, spy and never be trusted again in the community. I was an elected elementary school district Trustee; it would be political suicide.

They are probably right.

I am always in a balancing act of sorts in LULAC, and with the many other duties I take on in the community. I am not Latino. I am not only fluent in Spanish but had fought many times for issues concerning the Latino community. It seems strange to some, and I have many times heard that I am trying to pretend to be Latino. I shrug it off.

I had gotten into politics in 1990 with the fieldworker movement at my first teaching job in Lindsay, California in the Central Valley when mothers came to me asking to speak to their husbands. A freeze had dehydrated the beautiful oranges on the trees and unemployment was widespread almost overnight. The husbands did not want to accept charity, not even food supplies that different churches and organizations had offered.

I do speak to a room full of fathers the next night. Simply, we talk about responsibilities. As a father, they had the responsibility to look after their family. I ask them to set aside macho-ism and allow their family to get by this hard time. I ask that they take the food being offered at this moment and to return the charity to others in need when they are on their feet, and others are down. Simple enough, but it diverted the crisis and got me started in advocacy.

By the time that Sheriff Silva called, I had worked with Dolores Huerta and the United Farm Workers on two farmworker contracts in Ventura County and helped bring LULAC back to the region after an absence of many years. I had been known most for my openness to discuss education issues for the Latino community. I had also been accused of politically shooting from the hip too often, though I would disagree.

Propositions 187, 209 and 227 had all passed through California, and all had won. Prop. 187 would have denied all public services to undocumented persons. Medical services, labor protections, well fair, child service, and public education would be denied all undocumented persons in California. Prop. 187 passed in 1994 with 59% percent of California voters approving the measure.

I was one of many who spoke in our opposition of 187 over the next five years and had celebrated its legal defeat in 1999 when then Democratic Governor Gray Davis withdrew the appeal in court, killing the bill. I was surprised when late one night I found out about the legal move when a local newspaper reporter called to ask my reaction.

Proposition 209 came to the ballots in 1996. It was designed to remove any affirmative action from public employment and public education. It passed with 54% of the vote and effectively blocked many minority students from entering colleges and universities.

Proposition 227 came in 1998. Titled "English for the Children" I almost signed the petition some months earlier to get it on the ballot. I was a bilingual teacher in Santa Paula's Isbell Middle School and was also Ventura County's President of the California Association for Bilingual Education, (CABE). The person at the grocery store entrance asked if I wanted children to learn English in schools while he held out the clipboard with the petition.

Up to the campaign that led to the vote to repeal bilingual education in California, CABE had been a teacher advocacy group that shared nice lesson plans to help in the classroom. Now I found myself talking on radio, TV and to the newspapers trying to get as many "No" votes as possible. I traveled to Sacramento several times before and after 227's passage to argue of the damage this proposition would cause.

I had fought for Latino rights more than I, and many recognized leaders would have thought. I never considered myself a leader. I only had the nerve to take a step when others asked me to be careful.

I taught in Santa Paula, California and had become well known as an advocate. Appreciated by some as well as hated by others. My letters in the op-ed section of the Santa Paula and Ventura County Star newspapers gave me an outlet and also often made me stand out.

I was asked by several people if I would think of running for city council only to see surprise on their faces when I answered

28

that I didn't live in Santa Paula. One day, walking to visit a friend at his shop on Main Street, I was stopped in my tracts when an elderly gentleman sidestepped in front of me. One more step and I would have walked into him. He looked up at me with a finger in the air, "There are no racist in Santa Paula." Then he took a step to the side and walked on.

Towards my end of my teaching in Santa Paula, I received over the time of about a week, three unsolicited phone calls, all from superintendents in different Ventura County school districts. Would I think about working in their district? I found out later that the superintendents of the different school districts in the county would meet once a month. Apparently my Santa Paula superintendent had bad mouthed about me, and the reaction by the other superintendents was in my favor.

The third call I got was from Gloria Quintana. Now the Superintendent of the Rio School District, I had worked with her before on the issues of bilingual education. I had no desire to leave Santa Paula. I enjoyed the staff and especially the migrant student community and their families, but I hung up the phone and looked at my wife saying, "Maybe I should go to the Rio School District. It's a nice, quiet district and the population is about the same as Santa Paula." Also, my commute would be cut into less than half the miles I had been driving at the time.

Almost immediately after landing in El Rio, I found myself leading LULAC as the District Director and also witnessing a political move to get rid of Superintendent Quintana.

A list of about a dozen charges had been brought up against the Superintendent who had hired me. About half seemed to concern legal matters which I could only be a witness, but one, in particular, struck me. She was accused of hiring too many Latinos! In writing!

I supported Gloria Quintana in general, but as District Director of LULAC, I argued with friends that I and we couldn't stay silent on this. I was warned, and rightfully so that I was also an employee of the district and that this could be very bad for me. I responded with, "Had this been an African-American superintendent accused of hiring too many African-Americans in writing, would we expect the NAACP to stay silent?"

I stood up and took many blows. Quintana finally was fired and after a long legal battle was awarded 1.3 million dollars because of a Brown Act violation by the school board while letting her go.

A Brown Act violation occurs when a governing school board takes an action without proper notice to the public. Simply said, a minimum of a twenty-four-hour notice has to be made public before a vote can be taken. School Boards often have a degree of violations that occur and usually rectify the issue by placing the same item on another agenda and voting on the matter again. As easily as this could have been fixed, the school district leaders decided to continue the issue in court and appeal their loses several times. Each time the district lost, and the verdict was repealed the sum went up.

Gloria Quintana had won the court battle, lost her job and I was standing in a work place with a big target on my forehead.

One day I was teaching in a class looking at the clock, needing to use the restroom. As a teacher, I have to call the office, ask for a person to come to the class and wait for the replacement to arrive. We joke about how students who normally don't seem to pay much attention in class, are very much in tune to the whisper into the phone by a teacher asking for a restroom break. Later in the day, I was accused by administrators of going on the break to call the press! They even gave me the option of confessing because they said that they had technology in place to pick up cell phone conversations. Of course, they were bluffing, but I stood my ground. I couldn't even use the restroom without hearing this trash. I also wondered what was going on that they felt was worthy of the press knowing.

Towards the end of the long Gloria Quintana and LULAC case I had run and lost my first election for Trustee in the Oxnard School District and about a year later been selected to the board after one sitting Trustee had passed away.

I had worked very closely with the Mexican Consulate over the years. Over time I got to know members who worked at the local consulate and was asked to help distribute books donated by the Mexican government and help organize community events such as legal representation for the DREAMers.

In May of 2010, I was invited to go to Mexico City to attend a series of meeting in the Foreign Ministry concerning how the Mexican Government could better serve its citizens in the United States and Canada. I was one of twenty educators who had been asked to attend. Most were Mexican-American themselves, but about half needed translation into English during the meetings.

I learned how the Mexican government was willing to offer hundreds of millions of dollars to help in the education of their citizens, but that no American government official was interested in accepting the funds. The debate of "illegal immigration" stood in the way and taking funds to support education was seen as accepting the immigrants that half the American political system wanted to symbolically or figuratively get rid of.

During a visit to a small reception at a museum in Mexico, I stood with a few educators at a glass box with an old book opened inside. Wax seals and ribbons lay next to signatures on the old text. We asked a host what the book was and when he told us that it was the Mexican copy of the Treaty of Guadalupe, my colleague jokingly asked if he could borrow it. "I only want it for a week. The people in Arizona would be very interested in this. Please. I only need it for a week." We all laughed.

The Treaty of Guadalupe was signed in 1848, ending the Mexican American War and in doing so giving the United States ownership of Texas, California, New Mexico, Arizona, Nevada, Utah, Wyoming, and Colorado. It also gave American citizenship to Mexican citizens who lived in the new territories, protected ownership of property and allowed the culture and language to continue. Like most treaties of this era, the provisions had mostly been forgotten.

6. *No Me Llames Oaxaquita*

In 2012, several weeks before the call from Sheriff Silva, I was approached by several high school and college students who belonged to a youth group of the Mixteco/ Indigenous Community Organizing Project, (MICOP). The five or six smiling students came with a proposal for a resolution on anti-bullying of Mixteco students in our schools. The students wanted to know if the Oxnard School District or any school district for that matter would be interested.

I remember about fifteen years earlier having been in a crowded meeting at the United Farm Worker's office in Oxnard and one worker having stood up to announce that a Mixteco work squadron had started working in one of the many strawberry fields in the area. "They're going to take our jobs away from us!"

It seemed as another wave of immigrants who would be grateful to their employers and opposed to the benefits sought by generations of past workers with the union. Yes, an element of racism also was very obvious within the numbers who all had come from Mexico.

Now, these students come to me from a self-help community organization to support the Mixteco community with an anti-bullying resolution for the schools. *"No me llames Oaxaquita"* (Don't call me little Oaxacan) called for respect of the now estimated 20,000 plus in the community of Ventura County and a panel to review any bullying or discrimination in our school system.

The students seemed surprised when I told them that I thought that the school districts would warmly accept it. The resolution first went to the Oxnard School District and the students made their presentation. They told about bullying that came from Spanish speaking students from Mexico as well as from some teachers. Their parents had suffered these degrading actions and name calling in Mexico and now in the work places and fields of California. The students wanted to create awareness and a safety net in the schools. It passed in the Oxnard School District with a five to zero vote in favor and the following month passed with the same margin in the Hueneme School District and the Rio School District. The Oxnard Union High School District did not want to consider the resolution saying that the high school district already opposed all forms of bullying.

With the "*No me llames Oaxaquita*" resolution I was introduced at several functions as 'an expert' on the Mixteco community. Truth be said, I only considered myself as an expert in that I knew that they existed.

MICOP representative Gustavo Román and I were asked after the passage of the resolution to talk on a national radio network on Radio Bilingüe to discuss the anti-bullying resolution. I was surprised at the interest from many parts of the United States to get a copy of the resolution to present it to the different school districts in other parts of the country. We also spoke to the *LA Times* and local papers. Most surprisingly to me in this time was the phone calls from life long civil rights advocates from LULAC and the NAACP who asked me how long this has been an issue. "Since Cortés landed in the new world," was my answer.

7. Frogs

I speak with my wife in the evening about the phone call from Sheriff Silva. Her first reaction is something like, 'What are you getting into now? Let someone else take care of this.' Viviana has always been the smart one in the marriage.

I met my wife while I was an exchange student in high school to Santiago, Chile in 1979. I would return while in college during my summer breaks, finding that I would learn more about politics in two months in Pinochet's Chile than in nine months of study at Cal. State University, San Bernardino. We dated, too often via mail (well before the internet) and in short visits to her country. We married in Santiago in July of 1986.

Viviana learned much about the United States as I grew into a political advocate, but she also was apprehensive to advocacy because of her experiences under the Pinochet dictatorship. Teachers were an especially vulnerable group.

Working with the poor and the masses, teachers too often became community spokespersons and leaders. Too often they were found lying in a field with a bullet to the head after being declared missing for a few days. Viviana had difficulties with my involvement in social justice at times.

"Did you talk to the others?" Referring to my co-conspirators from LULAC.

"Yes, I did. They think that I would be a *sapo*." (sapo = frog = spy).

"Why do the Sheriff's want you to do their job?" We are in the kitchen putting things together for dinner.

"I don't know." I wonder if the investigation found something that would connect with me in MICOP, the UFW or my work at the Rio School District with the mother.

Viviana and I talk about finding the mother to not only catch her, but to offer health, and psychological support.

"Silva told me that the baby was born full term and had no signs of abuse. I can't believe that a mother would go full term with a pregnancy only to abandon it in the dirt."

"Women have given birth long before doctors came around; she probably will be fine." Viviana mentions.

Our own experience is one miscarriage very early into Viviana's first pregnancy and three premature deliveries which by the grace of God and much medical attention turned out positive. Pregnancy had not been a very pleasant time in our marriage. Now we are talking about how a full term baby was abandoned to die by someone else. There is a nerve that this personally touches with our family history. We have become stronger perhaps, but now I am asked to find a mother, a person who perhaps didn't value the birth of the child.

"I want to make sure that she has psychological help. There's no way that a person can go through with that and not be traumatized."

"Why you?"

The conversation goes well into the night. Calm and without Viviana's overt opposition, but notably concerned. "They will hate you. You have to think about the family. Will we be safe? They will hate us, too."

"We can also try to stop this from happening again." Even though I naturally had been leaning towards helping, this is the point of the talk that convinces us both to go ahead.

"There is a law called the "Safely Surrendered Baby Law." It allows mothers to give their babies to a fire station or hospital within three days, no questions asked. I can ask the Sheriff's Department to mention this law every time the case comes up. We need to let mothers know that there are options." After a great discussion and much reflection, there is quiet for a time from both of us. Viviana agrees.

The next morning, I call Sheriff Luis Silva. I tell him that I would agree on the condition that the Safe Delivery Baby Law be mentioned in all the Sheriff Department's releases while we search for the mother. He agrees as well.

Silva talks about how the investigation thought that the mother could have been a victim. I am concerned that the mother could be a young teenager or immigrate who did not know that they had options. Also, we talk about the possibility that the mother is a prostitute. I am told how often when the woman becomes pregnant the baby would be put up for sale. "Maybe it was a case of the deal going wrong."

I tell Sheriff Silva that I would also want to make sure that if he finds the mother that she receives medical attention, psychological attention and proper legal support. He agrees on these three points.

I finished the conversation by mentioning, "Who knows, if the mother is found I may be supporting her against the police department." We agreed to talk shortly, and I said that I would start making contacts right away.

8. The Radio

The thinking was that the mother may have been just passing through the area or probably already left to where she feels safe. Action. I need to take the first step fast. I need to get my message in order and take the step.

I have an in with radio. I have been helping my friend David Cruz with color on a radio show in mornings a couple of times a week. David had been on TV news with NBC in big markets like San Francisco, San Antonio, and Los Angeles.

A good solid news reporter. I met David Cruz while ending our area's first César Chávez march. Like first times for any event it was small and even though I was one of the organizers, admittedly poorly organized. The gathering at Plaza Park in Oxnard got a lot better very fast. The couple hundred marchers turned the last corner, and I saw David Cruz. I recognized him because of the main of hair and his TV profile. At first, I was thrilled that he would be interviewing us for the evening news, but found that he was on his own. "Do you need an M.C.?" he asks.

Over the following years, David Cruz was active in not only the César Chávez celebrations but just about every other local Latino function. Now away from KNBC channel 4, David is starting up with a radio show in the morning with local Radio Lazar, KOXR La Mexicana.

The shows are in Spanish, and I invited myself as co-host often. The show is from six to eight in the mornings, and we spend most of the time looking at our lap tops looking for current news to pass on to the listeners.

The show seemed to catch some popularity, but I knew that David Cruz was still volunteering his time to reboot his options. Spanish language radio can be a great medium, but in my point of view, it is wasted too often with off color jokes and mariachi music. This show covered news, events and quite often criticisms of the same Latino community that was listening. "La voz del pueblo" (The Voice of the People) filled a void within the listening public.

The first place I go is on David Cruz's show. He had built a following over the year. We both know that people are interested in this format when fieldworkers started calling from the fields! Some also criticized David's motives. It is a sure sign of success in the Latino community. We would remind each other of the crabs in the bucket when this was said.

David is not keen at all on my goal of looking for the mother. He believes that she would never be found and that I am working for the wrong side. Just the same, he lets me be on the air to talk about my search and the information about the Safely Surrendered Baby Law.

I was on KOXR on May 24, May 30 and June 5. I

know that David and another co-anchor Mauricio Reyes speak of the search for the mother on other occasions as well.

My message is: "I am trying to contact the mother of the baby found in the Nyland strawberry field outside Oxnard. I am concerned for her health, mental status, and wellbeing. I have secured doctors at Clínicas del Camino Real and the Ventura County Medical Center who want to offer their services."

I also negotiate with David Cruz that I would include, "I am not with law enforcement. I am a teacher. The Sheriff's investigators do want to question the mother. A child was found dead, and this is not acceptable in any culture of the world."

We speak of the Safely Surrendered Baby Law. California had passed the law some ten years earlier. It allows mothers as a last resort to give their new born to a fire station, police station or emergency room at a hospital with no questions asked. As long as the baby did not show signs of abuse, the child is cared for future adoption, and the mother is allowed to go free.

In this case, the mother did not use the safe surrender of a baby option. We presume that the mother did not know, or was somehow forced to deliver the baby in the dead of night and forced or chose to walk away. How could a person feel a baby grow inside her for nine months and walk away? Did she expect that the baby would survive and be found? Did she know that she had options before and even after the delivery?

We are focusing on the Mixteco community because this is where Sheriff Silva asked me to look. We also know that this is the community who needs the most attention at the moment. Fear in the Mixteco community had been passed down over the generations since Spanish blood infused and took over what is now the Spanish speaking world. Mixteco and other indigenous peoples of Mexico and Central America had been looked down upon, marginalized and left to a world of hard work, few opportunities, and poverty.

The radio show and this topic focuses on including the Mixteco community in the conversation, not preaching to it.

I find it interesting that some callers to the radio and people who would approach me in the street or stores would

40

tell me how baby abandonment is common. The theory is that a mother would deliver the baby in the countryside because in many parts of Southern Mexico there is no medical attention or means to receive medical services. A mother would leave the baby and come back twenty-four hours later to see if it is strong enough to survive before taking the baby in and taking care of it.

I had a flash back to my wife's grandmother Marina. She was delivered on a clipper ship off of the coast of Peru in the 1900's. I remember Abuelita Marina coming up to Viviana and me shortly before our marriage and asking how many children we wanted to have. We had never talked about this between the two of us, a question that concerned grandmothers much more than the bride and groom. I was at a loss for words, but Viviana said rapidly to please, "Two or three."

A smile and Abuelita Marina held our hands in hers' shacking them up and down, "Then you should have six or seven in case a few die."

It was a true life expectation for Marina and every woman of that generation in Chile. Why shouldn't life have been different in Mexico? And today? What is the mother's reality today?

On May 30, the local ABC affiliate, KEYT channel 3 calls me in the morning and asks if they could come out to interview me for the evening news. I ask that they come at my lunch hour and am to meet them outside the school parking lot on the sidewalk. It is an important issue; I cannot be in any way representing the public school district with this issue. The district is not interested that I publically speak on any issue, but knowing that they have accepted that we will disagree on this point.

I had gotten to know reporter Tracy Lehr a bit over the

past few years. She worked at an office not far from my school which made me an easy interview as long as we got our schedules right.

Tracy Lehr and her cameraman Sean arrived at the school and first went to the front office to ask for me. I, in turn, get a concerned call from my principal. She tells me that the TV news is at the office and that I had been told before not to bring in the media during work hours.

"We are to meet during my lunch hour." It was only five or ten minutes away. The principal at the school had dealt with my relationship with the press in the past. Mostly she seemed annoyed that I would be involved with something other than the daily lesson and school district benchmarks for students that would be dropped on her desk.

I come out the gate after taking my students to the line in front of the cafeteria for lunch and leave the grounds for the interview. I tell the reporter about how I am concerned and that I want to extend medical help and counseling to the mother. I speak for about two minutes, knowing that what I say will be cut down to sound bites of a few seconds each. I give my cell phone number and ask that it shows on the screen.

Waiting for the evening news, I hope that I don't sound stupid and look at the phone, ready to get crank calls and maybe by luck a lead. The interview looks good, and the tight shots leaves to the imagination that I am at school. That is a good thing; I truly don't want to mix my campaign in this matter with my work as a teacher.

The sad news of the death of a baby is announced again and a picture of the strawberry field shown. I am introduced as a school district Trustee who is helping the Sheriff's Department looking for the mother. My five second clip shows me saying that I am looking for the mother and I have people at the ready to offer medical, psychological and legal services. The news channel continues with information about the Safely Surrendered Baby Law. At the end of the thirty-second segment, they place my cell phone on the screen. That sends shivers up my spine, but it is necessary.

The news ends, and I look at my phone. It doesn't ring. At least I am not going to get every crank caller or gad fly's opinion in my ear. About a half hour later the phone does ring. I hear Spanish in the background, and the phone hangs up. I had the return number on the phone; I call that number: no answer.

Could it be a person that could help?

I don't expect a positive response from the English language TV service, but the community message needed to go beyond looking for the mother.

I pass on the number left on my phone to Sheriff Silva and later find out that it was more than likely a wrong number.

I don't know if any of this will get any results, and if it does, if we do find the mother, would it help her?

I start getting exasperated gestures over the next month or so. "Why are you trying to help a baby murderer?" seemed to be the common theme. People I know well, people I know casually, the principal I work under, I could see who the Christians were now.

For some in the community, the baby who they had once complained about as being an "anchor baby" is now a precious lost soul. This is as it should be, naturally. The discussion of anchor babies and "illegal immigrants" is one way of dehumanizing the human beings that are not wanted. Unfortunately, it takes a loss of life for this community to change its tone, unfortunately as well just for a very brief time.

As a School Board Trustee, I am an elected official. The superintendent of the school district (who in fact is hired by the Trustees), comes to me and gives what is probably very reasonable and sound advice: "You are an elected official, a community leader in education. You shouldn't be coming close to a baby killer." Sheriff Silva calls me a couple of times over this period and tells me that the investigation is continuing and that he feels that they will find the mother. I don't hold his optimism. He also calls I feel to confide in me his emotions in dealing with this issue. Any father, family member or spectator would have the same feelings. The void left in who did this and why it came about are very overwhelming.

I am not too concerned about the print media. I need this message to get out orally.

On June 5, 2012, I am allowed to take time away from my teaching and rush over to the neighboring city of Ventura. KUNX radio has a "Mixteco Hour" that the message would be translated from Spanish to Mixteco. I know that my target audience may be more likely to be listening or to pass on the word to others. Surprisingly, my employer also changed, at least officially, its tone. I am sure that the KEYT Channel 3 news interview helped.

I had already been on the radio in the morning with David Cruz on KOXR; now I am leaving at my lunch break to Ventura to be on the Mixteco Hour. Radio studios are normally small, but this seemed more like a walk-in closet. Two radio hosts, one translating everything into Mixteco and three other guests besides myself in a small room with no windows.

I am the second person to be introduced and able to bring up my subject. Needless to say, the others had their mouths open. One is there to sell gym membership, another selling used cars, and the third is selling some make-up. I think that I may not have helped their sales this day.

Rushing back to my school to teach two more classes, I listen to the station in the car as listeners are still calling in to give their opinions of who the mother is or where she could be. No leads are called in, and the salesmen try unsuccessfully to change the subject.

I also hear the used car salesman try in vain to get people out to his lot. Again, the Spanish radio format, in my opinion, is a great opportunity to advance the community and unfortunately is used too often by short sighted entrepreneurs, the crabs in the bucket. I had left my cell phone number again, but even though listeners were calling the station with their comments, no one was calling me with information.

Yes, by the way: I would have answered the phone while in my class. This is taboo in front of thirty twelve-year olds trying to learn. I did tell my principal about my plan that if an unknown call comes in that, I would take it. The phone call hasn't happened as of this moment.

I have my plan, and know my limits. I know at this point; my news cycle is ending. This is pretty much my last chance to get the plea out that I could expect that it may possibly helped in finding the woman. I later speak again on David Cruz's show and try to bring up the subject in the free Spanish and English weekly that comes out in the area. Vida newspaper has already published several articles on this matter.

I do give Manuel Muñoz credit for publishing his free bilingual newspaper for over thirty-three years. These publications come and go but he seems to have found the formula. Often he has taken up the causes that I would hope he could get out, and at times he saw fit to not publish. Vida newspaper just the same is required reading in several cities in Ventura County and an asset to the community.

Results: People tagged me with being a hero, civic leader, and on the other extreme a supporter of a baby killer. The baby killer minded people are the ones who usually step forward. 'Why in the world would I be trying to help a baby killer?' As if I were, somehow, in favor of infanticide! Apparently, the mother is better off in their eyes not found, in the darkness of the shadows, cursed and condemned. Nevertheless, she cut nerve of the issue and what may come up from more details being made public may cascade into other non-convenient subjects.

9. La Llorona
(The Weeping Woman)

As a school teacher in mostly Spanish speaking immigrant communities, I have often witnessed a belief, customs or a fabric of the Latin American community. I have been fascinated with the history and perhaps the real life dramas that shape the lives of my students, their parents, and the community.

Having taught for twenty-six years, I have probably learned as much or perhaps more than I have taught. I admire the effort, the heart of the communities that I see. Simply, having entered the environment of the Latino community, having learned the language, I have been able to be a part of the rich culture, the family, struggles and yes, the negative underbelly of the people who have lived in the shadows for many of us in the United States of America.

Again, as a teacher, I have had to use any resource I can find to make a daily connection with my students and often with their families. One of my favorite resources, one of my favorite books I have come across is *"Stories That Must Not Die"* by Juan Sauvageau.

A collection of folk tales from Mexico and the Southwest, the bilingual text captivated not only my interest but over the years that of my students. In 1992, I had the chance to meet Dr. Sauvageau at the CABE conference. I was surprised that I was not the only teacher to consider this book a gem.

Dr. Sauvageau was elderly when he came to the conference. A very tall man, his mustache was recognized by one teacher in attendance as Dr. Sauvageau being the model for the pencil drawing in the book of the *Devil in the story*, "The Devil takes a Bride."

The author, a native of Quebec, Canada was a Professor at the University of Colorado in the late 1970's. He took on the project to travel for two years throughout the Southwest and Northern Mexico. He explained that he would travel alone. His audio recorder was a large suitcase and target was to listen to storytellers.

Arriving in a village, he would go to a church, post office or general store which also had the post office. He would ask if there was a good storyteller in the area for his project. Nine out of ten times he was told about an elderly man who usually lived over the hill somewhere.

He would knock on the door, introduce himself and say that he was told that the person was a good storyteller. Could he record some of the tales? He was never turned down.

Electricity hadn't come to many of the parts he visited. Entertainment would be the families of the area getting together around a campfire. Food, a guitar, singing, and the storytelling.

Ghost stories, cowboys, and Indians, family life and comedy, the stories entertained as well as giving the elder member of the community the opportunity to teach the children. Sauvageau told us that he would not consider a story for his book unless he heard the same, or similar story in at least three different regions. Naturally, even the same story would be told differently, and that is where his personal touch came in authoring his book.

By far the most popular, the most told story that he always heard at every location was "*La llorona.*"

The story can be told in many ways and tells of different eras. I have heard that the story comes from the pre Columbian Aztecs of Mexico, others tell of colonial Mexico and I have heard several current versions that are said to have happened even in Ventura County.

This is the story of a woman who fended for herself and her infant children. She somehow had been scorned by the father of the children and whether she had once been of status, high society, or dirt poor from the beginning; now she fended for herself and her offspring.

She believed in a God and Heaven. She believed that somehow she could succeed, but life was hard and miserable. The mother of the children one night fell asleep and dreamt that her children could be in Heaven. She somehow followed up her dream by throwing the children into the river. Happy that she had followed through with her motherly duties of caring for her children she went back to sleep.

With the first light, the woman woke and looked for her children. She soon realized what she had done. She jumped into the river, crying out for her children.

And even today, if you are up late, you may still hear the cries of La Llorona as she looks for her children. If a child is out alone, they too may be mistaken for the child by the ghost of the good mother who is still looking for her infants.

Are we now looking for the Weeping Woman, "La Llorona" who has left her child to die? Culture is not an excuse. But I must recognize that the mother had a belief system, a culture, a reason.

Forced upon her or acted out, the baby was left to die.

There is a reason for culture. Mortality rates, survival and religious norms, the story has an infinite number of tellings. Around the campfire, the story conveys the fear as well as the message of "get to bed and don't wonder around too late at night children."

Are we looking for a ghost?

10. DNA of the Shadow People

My window for being a community spokesperson to try to help find the mother has ended. I haven't been able to help find the mother, but still I am having people coming up to me to ask about the Safely Surrendered Baby Law and how a good Catholic boy could be trying to help a baby killer. Where did I go wrong? What could have my sixth grade teacher, Sister Mercy have done differently?

Over the next two months, Sheriff Silva would call me a couple of times. I would apologize for not being able to help, and he seemed to be optimistic that he would find her. "I think we'll find her," he would tell me at the end of each conversation.

One of the concerns that she needs medical attention is pretty much ruled out. Had the mother needed any attention, she already received it or has already suffered her fate. I am sure that the mother would still need some counseling or psychological help. How could a mother carry a baby full term, feel the baby move inside her, go through natural labor and walk away from the baby in the mud? Yes, this is I am sure a long term issue. She will face the judgement of her conscience at some point in the near or distant future. Is she a murderer, or victim?

Silva questioned this as well, and I thought that he would call to release his feelings on someone who would and could listen. He and I still talked about the possibility; maybe we are hoping that the mother is a victim. It would be much easier to connect with a victim mother who we could support than a murderer who needs help.

It is August now; I am out of school on summer vacation. No worries of teaching and working on this issue from another Universe. Sheriff Silva calls me to say that the DNA taken at the field from over a hundred fieldworkers has found a match to a close female relative to the mother we are searching for. He tells that the match is either of the sister, mother or the aunt of the person we are looking for. I am amazed that he or science made such a connection.

Of concern again to me is how did they take the DNA samples. Were the fieldworkers told that they could refuse to give a sample? Did the fieldworkers know how their DNA could probe into their lives? Into their family tree? I didn't know these things. I'm pretty sure that the fieldworkers didn't know.

The match that they had come up with may have thought that since she was not the person who gave birth and left, that they would not match what the police were looking for. I would have thought this. Apparently, DNA can now go deep into a person's family history. Siblings, parents, uncles, aunts, and grandparents.

I am happy to hear that some match has been made, but did the mother or sister realize that a connection could be made or did they think that it would only prove that they were not the mother of the child left to die?

I question if this was legal. When dealing with the shadow people who are undocumented to live and work in the United States, who are often under-educated, did they know they had the right to say no? Did they know that they had a real option to walk away?

Silva also says that he had the name and address of the DNA matched relative. He gives me the address and asks if I could pass by the house some day and relate any details that I could gather.

The house was in the South of Oxnard, near Harrington Elementary School. This detail catches my attention because the monthly Mixteco community gatherings would meet at Harrington School. I had known about the meetings for a few years before I was invited to attend. It wasn't that I was unwelcome by the organizers (MICOP), but it was believed that the Mixteco families that gathered could be scared away if they saw any Anglo Americans hanging around.

When I was finally invited, these meetings reminded me a bit of the stereotypes of the Christian charities of years past. Women and children would gather, packing the cafeteria. The small children would make Fruit Loops necklaces while the mothers and grandmothers are seated at the school lunch tables and talk. The organizers would give from the stage information about rights or services. Translated from Spanish to Mixteco I was surprised that the languages did not sound anything alike. I could only pick out the words that reflected modern technology. New words. This was the language that Cortés heard when his conquistadors arrived at the coast of the Aztec lands some five-hundred years ago.

The mothers would listen to the speaker over the talk from the children to the side of the cafeteria. I was also asked to speak in a couple of these meetings, talking about the relationship the parents should have with the teachers and schools of their children. "Come forward and present yourself to your child's teacher. Ask questions and listen to the answers." I asked that the immigrant parents own their child's education. Perhaps they could later defend their vision for bettering their lives in other forums as well.

At one meeting, the local medical clinic parked their motor home on the asphalt of the playground and offered Flu shots to all at no cost. The clinic asked me to go to the streets around the school to ask the fathers who were in their cars and mostly pickup trucks by themselves waiting for the meeting to end. Few men would go inside the cafeteria for the meetings, and few accepted the flu shots. The common theme was that they all sat alone in the driver's seat and had the same soccer game from Mexico blasting out the open windows in Spanish.

After they gave the public information, the mothers lined up to accept bags of food. Many women would be holding their infants in the roboso wrapping around their upper body, breastfeeding while they would gather the plastic bags of food in a free hand. The population was young; many mothers had three or four children under five years of age. In a few cases, an older son or daughter would walk down the line, and as I handed the bags to them, they would be surprised when I explained that they should help their mothers carry the food.

Of greatest interest in the food lines was to get a ticket to go to a small room off to the side of the stage and receive a box of diapers. This was a true value and convenience to the underpaid immigrant family.

Had I seen the mother in a past meeting? The DNA showed that the person lived only a short walk to the school. Did the family walk down the line accepting backpacks with school supplies or food? I was driving down the street where the family lived. Fifty some year-old houses, some well-kept, others the color of dust over the faded color of years past.

Driving to the address I was given, I wondered if I would see the person outside or peering out a window of the house. All I could see is a large jolly jumper in the front yard with kids running around. A couple of cars, nothing fancy or new. A plant hanging near the screened front door, the door behind it open, surly to let the kids in faster as they ran about. I called Sheriff Silva to tell him that a birthday party was going on and he laughed and said that he knew. Naturally, the Sheriff's Department is also staking out the house.

"We saw you pass by." He chuckled. Here I am nervous to drive by and look and in an unmarked car is off to the side, they are apparently starring at the family!

I now am interested in the case more in a justice mode. I had always said to myself and to anyone who asked, "I am not working for law enforcement." Now I know that the authorities are a step closer to finding the mother and getting some answers to what happened and why. Could she still be a victim? Did the mother take off to parts unknown? I now think that the family may lead to a disappeared mother that we were interested in finding.

About a week later Sheriff Silva calls again. "We were wondering, would you think of knocking on the door and asking for the mother we are looking for?"

It is an interesting question, and in the end, he seems to answer it himself.

He continues, "We would give you a bullet proof vest and have officers standing by." He pauses, and I can only think of the innocent good seminarian that was shot to death years ago in a sting operation back east in some police action with officers standing by. It takes only a couple seconds of silence, and Silva continues by answering his question himself, "No. We can't do this."

It sounds like he wants me to correct him and jump in, against his and my common sense and say, "Sure, I will do that!" It would look good in the movies!

An interesting idea that could be a spectacular ending to this stage of the search and I tell my wife about it. "You said no, right?" She looks at me with the look of "You fool! I hope you didn't say yes."

I woke up that night with a dream of making contact.

I am standing there at the door. What would I say? What could I say if I actually went through with this contact plan? And who would answer the door? Would they have a shot gun?

The next day Sheriff Silva calls me up again. This time he asks if I could speak to Sergeant Steve Green about the case. We set up a time, and a few days later I have Green sitting in my living room.

In full uniform, a big man, Sergeant Green takes a seat in a chair in my living room and has a note pad opened on his knee. I am glad that I am working on the same side as law enforcement on this one. It seems that Green is sizing me up a bit as well as telling me his thoughts of the case. He is in tears at a point, talking about the baby, covered in mud and motionless at the side of a row of strawberries in the field. I am sure that Green is a father as well. He tells me that he wants to find the mother. He wants to know if she is a victim if she was somehow forced to do this and if she needed help.

56

Then he comes out with something I had heard before, "We would like to know if you would think of knocking on the door and asking for the mother? We would back you up. We would give you a bulletproof vest..."

He almost beat Silva in finishing the script, without missing a breath, "No. We can't do this. It's not a good idea."

I sit in my living room, face to face with a poster officer of law enforcement in a chair not six feet in front of me, my mouth open, wondering if he wanted me to jump up and offer my services, offer my life. "It is a bad idea," I said. "What good could come from knocking on the door?" I can imagine looking down the mussel of a rifle, or perhaps blank stares from a family member or the same mother we are seeking. "OK, I give up?" What could I expect? I am a teacher!

"We will find her." Sergeant Green tells me.

"I wonder if she is still in the area," I tell him. "Going to the door could only tip her off to run further away than she may already be."

Green gives me his card and thanks me for my help up to the moment. He also plants a seed hoping that I would come to him. I tell my wife again about the 'knocking on the door scenario' and how Green withdrew the idea before I could even tell him that it was crazy. Viviana agrees and mentions that they probably wanted me to go along and offer to take the dangerous step.

11. A Face from the Shadows

Again on September 27, I find myself in the "cabina" of David Cruz's radio show on KOXR. We remind listeners about the tragedy and the search for the mother and for the answers to what happened and why this came to be. David and I along with many friends have tried for years to set up a safety net of information that could help people in need. This one got threw the net.

It has been a time since I had mentioned the subject to the general public, at least those who are listening to a Spanish radio station. David is at the controls across from me with a large table in the middle which takes up most of the space in the room. I have to imagine the radio listener outside, perhaps listening from home or in the fields of the area. There is only one window in the room, and it faces out towards the station's hallway. A large poster reads KOXR in very large letters and La Radio Mexicana beneath takes up one wall. Random posters spot the other two. David Cruz is very professional, and even though he has told me of his reservations many times in pursuing this case, he is very professional in the delivery.

The lesson for the day is repeating once again the opportunities for medical attention during a pregnancy. Our audience, many undocumented are hard to convince.

Contrary to common belief to many anti-immigrant patriots in our community, the undocumented worker and their family does not report to the welfare office once they step foot on American soil.

The best we can do is put the message out once again. We both know that this will not get directly to every person in our community, but the information will get to some circles.

I often tell people that I could stand naked in an intersection, waving my arms in the air, yelling and lighting myself on fire but only a limited number of people will take notice. I can't expect everyone to get my message or care for that matter.

We do not mention that the family has been located, and even though it's tempting to debate the use of DNA on over 100 fieldworkers, we will tackle this issue another day. In fact, I look forward to that debate. It could even be an important issue in a future court discussion if the case every gets to court!

It is another month before I get the call.

While at the counter in my kitchen, preparing for Thanksgiving dinner the next day, my cell phone rings in the evening. It is Sheriff Silva. "We got her."

"You found her? Where?"

"We picked her up a week ago on false documents charges. We stopped the car she was in."

"Do you know it was her?"

"We are waiting for DNA tests to come in before charging her. We haven't questioned her yet, but it's her." Silva answers.

This news hasn't hit the newspapers yet, and won't until we file formal charges. Silva asks me not to share the news yet.

"What is her name?" I ask. This is a goal. A name of the person. I know that it is too early to get other details.

"Alba Flores Zapata," Sheriff Silva forcefully responds.

I ask that he repeat the name as I write it down on a napkin the second time. Finally, a name for the mother we were tracking.

Alba Flores Zapata, twenty-years old. She is single. She was living with her sister. She is at the Todd Road County jail. Silva tells me how he is concerned that she won't get a good attorney.

Santa Paula's Todd Road jail is holding her in lieu of one million-dollar bail for the charge of having fake identification.

Silva asks, "Can you look around for a good attorney to defend her?"

"I will ask around."

"Don't do anything yet. Wait until this is public."

Public defender Pat Rawson was chosen to represent Alba Flores Zapata on the lesser identification charge, but no charges had been filed yet in the death of the infant.

It worried me that a public defender would not give the time or know the background of an indigenous Mexican to give a good representation. I tell Silva that I would do what I can to try to find someone. But first, I was asked to wait until DNA results confirmed that Alba was the person we were after. That would come a week later.

12. The First Contact

First contact with authorities is an important moment. Language will be questioned and presumed by all sides in the future. Does Alba Flores Zapata speak Spanish fluently? Is Mixteco her first or only language? Does she speak any of the other indigenous languages from Mexico?

An investigating officer sits down with Alba shortly after booking. He asks in Spanish if Alba speaks Spanish.

"*Sí*," Alba answers straightforward.

"Do you understand English?" asks the officer.

A pause, "*Nada*," she says. "Do you speak any other language?"

"Mixteco," she clarifies.

"Do you read Spanish?" continues inquiring the officer.

"Yes. I learned to read in school," she explains in Spanish.

The officer places a paper on the table facing Alba. It is a document explaining a prisoner's rights and it is printed in Spanish.

"Can you find the word '*derecho*' (right) on the paper?"

Alba looks over the paper and places her index finger under the word on the first line.

"Can you find the word '*abogado*' (Lawyer) on the paper?"

Alba looks again and finds the word further down on the paper. She points again at the word.

"Can you find the paragraph that talks about your right to a speedy trial?"

Alba looks again, takes a breath and scans the document. After a good half minute, she points to a section of the document.

"Yes. Can you read it back to me?" requests de investigating officer.

She slowly reads it, but with no difficulty.

Spanish at this point is the language of contact for the following interviews. It is apparent that Alba does not understand technical legal vocabulary and the context of much of the legal jargon. Both will have to be explained to her in the future. Alba gave up her first indigenous language in the school she sporadically attended for the Spanish she had to learn until she was ten years old.

I am aware that when a person confronts danger, no matter how fluent they may be in a second or third language, they think of two things: their mother and in their native, first language.

Facing murder charges in a foreign country, I would want to communicate in my native first language. For the better convenience of the legal system, Alba had graduated to her second language of Spanish.

Sheriff Silva calls me again to ask if I could help in finding a good attorney. He also points out to me that he still is holding the baby's corpse as evidence and that the child deserved a proper burial.

I had only once briefly met Luis Silva, and I could tell that his father role would drive much of our phone conversations. There was a trust, and he seemed to expect that I could work miracles in my evenings after getting off from being a teacher.

He and I talked about sitting down and having lunch someday to get to know each other a bit better. Despite only briefly having looked each other in the face, trust was a must with such a serious matter that we are confronting.

Oxnard is lucky to have one of the ten Mexican consulates in the state of California.

The Mexican Consulate had also been informed and I set an appointment with Consul General Edmundo Correa to discuss the matter. The consulate is trying to make contact with the family as well to see what they would like to do.

The remains were not released yet, but all from outside the family wanted the right thing to happen. I know that the Consulate deals with repatriating the remains of loved ones. This would be the route I would expect to go, but the case isn't to the point of releasing the body just yet.

The news of finally finding the mother goes public on local TV and in the *Ventura County Star* newspaper on December 27, 2012. The headline is "Police finally find, arrest alleged mother of baby found dead in farm field." The Sheriff held Alba for just over a month, but withheld any questioning until after the DNA test permits filing charges of murder against her.

The family shortly after the first news had come out made the statement that they did not know about a pregnancy before or after the birth of the child. I question that they did not know. The El Canto Farm is a good seven miles from the family home. Did she drive herself to and from the field?

Other questions would come up later, but I am not in the position to ask. I will have to rely on time and the authorities to address these questions.

I am interested in seeing this person in jail myself. What is she like? Can I tell by looking at her if she is a killer? I am concerned that she is somehow a victim caught up in the mix.

I am having a hard time getting a referral to an attorney. Still the information about the case is not complete. She is a field worker from Mexico with false papers in hand. She left a baby to die. I presume that there is no money in the family's coffers to pay for a good attorney. I know several attorneys, most are in education law and the ones who deal with immigrants are not allowed the time to follow the process of a long murder trial. The other issue is the money. Pro bono is great, but in reality, it is the attorney who is paying for pro bono.

My friends in LULAC are worried that I got caught up in a no win case. Baby killers are on the bottom of the totem pole even amongst criminals. A Mixteco baby killer would have few friends, and the prejudice on the street would cloud the starting point of objective help.

From the time that I got word that the woman, Alba was found, I want to look her in the face. I know that I can't grab her by the shoulders, shake her and yell 'Why did you do it?' But I want to see what she is. Perhaps standing near her somehow I could become the mind reader that I wish I could be. Somehow I could get the impression from how she speaks, how she looks or who she is to get the impression of what happened.

In February I get another call, this time from a friend at the Mexican consulate. She tells me that the family tells the consulate's legal counsel that Alba did not want to have contact with the Consulate. On the other hand, the Mexican Government could only make contact if invited. They were very surprised that the family had said no. "Nobody ever says no."

"Could you see Alba Flores Zapata in the jail and ask if she would want to speak with us?"

Now is my chance to answer some of my questions. My chance to look the woman in the eye. Was she a victim?

Was she a 'Charles Manson'?

I make the point that I will be asking four questions if I could. Had Alba received medical attention? Was she receiving some form of psychological help or counseling? Was she satisfied with her legal defense? And did she want to speak with a representative from the Mexican Government?

Would Alba even want to speak to me? I may not even get the chance to get close to her to ask. I am fluent in Spanish but know nothing about the Mixteco language that she surly speaks. What if I can't communicate with her? And then she could just say she didn't want to speak with me.

On February 15th, 2013 I leave my school at 3:30 and drive towards the Todd Road Jail between the cities of Ventura and Santa Paula. Uninvited, not knowing not only if I would be allowed to see Alba, but that she may not want to speak to me. I had seen the jail from the 126 freeway but only now find out that there is only one road leading to the facility. I also get frustrated because I also find that there is no direct exit to the jail from the freeway. Having made a large loop around the area on surface streets, and coming to a dead end that was not connected, I finally am on the long road that seems to only point towards the jail in the middle of agricultural fields.

The sign at the door says that I am not allowed to bring my cell phone into the jail. It makes sense. I walk back to the car, put my phone in the glove box and go towards the door again.

Inside I read signs poorly written with grammatical errors in Spanish about visiting. A family is at a center windowed section speaking with a woman in Sheriff's uniform. They go towards metal detectors to the side, and I walk to the window.

"Hi. Can I help you?"

"I hope so. My name is Denis O'Leary. I'm here to see Alba Flores Zapata." I put my driver's license in the coin slot wedge under the thick bullet proof glass.

The officer looks at my license.

"Are you an attorney?"

"No..." I responded.

I get a puzzled look.

"You're not family." She smiles.

"No."

Silence for a couple of seconds.

"What church are you with?"

"Well, I'm Catholic," I said nervously, "but I was asked by the Mexican Consulate to come and speak with her."

"Do you work for the Mexican Consulate?" she inquires.

"No." I categorically said.

The look I get in return is not one that is saying that I am going to get any closer.

"I am a school teacher. I was first asked by the Sheriff's Department to help look for her. Now I am asked by the consulate to ask if she wants to be contacted by them." I explained clarifying my role to her.

"Who was the person at the Sheriff's Department you worked with?" she persisted.

"Detective Luis Silva, Special Crimes Division," I said something she could use. Not the way I had planned the conversation for the last couple of days.

She writes a few things into the computer to the side and hands me back my license.

"I can't say if she will speak with you, but go up the stairs, down the hall and she will be at window A-3."

Success! At least in this part. I had tried to rehearse what to say to Alba to introduce myself, but now I am already flustered with the easy part!

I walk to the metal detectors, place my keys and coins in a box to the side. I look at the young Sheriff at the entrance.

"Do I need to take my belt and shoes off?"

"No. You're free to go." She answers.

I walk up the stairs, make a left and go up another set of stairs. To the right now is a double door. Through the door, there is only one way to go, turn to the right. I look down the longest hallway without windows I have ever seen. A few doors on either side. No windows or signs on the doors. What seemed to be one-hundred yards is only broken up by a camera from the middle of the ceiling every twenty to thirty feet. At the end, the doorway opens up on both sides with booths divided up in concrete cinder block walls. A single stationary metal seat at each booth looking into the window. A chair on the inside facing out and both sides have a phone hanging on the right of the seats.

Looking for window three, I find it is still empty. I stand back to wait. Other windows have what looks like husbands and wives speaking into the phones. One woman has a child in her arms while she speaks.

After about five minutes a small woman in an orange overall comes through the booth, I am waiting and she looks at me, and I take my seat. We both pick up the phones only for her to start looking at her wrist band. I start reading the instructions next to the phone. I needed to wait for her to dial a number. (The instructions were only in English.)

She smiles. I put my phone on the receiver again and wait until she motions that I can pick it up.

She is the killer of the baby that we have been searching.

"Hello. My name is Denis O'Leary," I introduced myself in Spanish:

December 2011, Michoacan, Mexico: The woman gives her mother a hug. The street is mainly dark with a single street light illuminating a small patch half a block down from the house.

"I will write when I get to María Guadalupe's house *mamá*."

"God bless you and protect you." the elderly figure raises her hand and makes the sign of the cross on her daughter's forehead.

Tears and the woman picks up a bag from her side. A man places another bag in the back of a pickup truck parked at the edge of the dirt road. He gets into the driver's side, and the woman walks around and sits with her smaller bag on her lap.

"Are you sure that you have everything?"

"Yes, I think so. If God wishes, I should be with María Guadalupe in a week." The conversation continues into the dark on the way to the town some two hours away stopping at the bus station.

The bus station is small, benches lining one side of the room and a counter with a sole attendant at the other.

After waiting for a family to get their tickets, the young lady takes her bags in hand and steps up to the man.

"Where are you going?"

"North."

The man looks up from his counter.

"North?"

"The United States. The border."

"A bus is leaving in 30 minutes for Mexico, DF. You can transfer from there to any point north." The man writes out the ticket.

"Name?"

"Alba Flores Zapata."

"Going alone?" he asks.

Alba placed her hand almost without thinking on her stomach.

"Yes."

13. Three Questions

"I was asked to talk to you." I expectantly said to her in Spanish.

The small Mixteca woman looked at me without saying a word. I don't even know if she speaks Spanish. Maybe she doesn't understand what I am saying. I am sure that my name surely sounded like noise, and she surely won't remember my name. What I say in the next couple of seconds would build a relationship or end the contact.

"I am not a police officer. I was asked to talk to you by the Mexican Consulate." I further explained attempting to ameliorate any fears.

I know that I have no guarantee that this woman would want to talk to me. She looks at me with no expression on her face.

"I am a teacher." I continue to expound.

"A teacher!" She repeats softly.

I had made contact. Her eyes show interest and perhaps trust enough to talk.

"Yes, a teacher. I teach twelve-year-old boys and girls in school." I elucidate.

This seems to have broken the ice. Honestly, there is no reason that Alba needs to talk to me. She is here for the ride. I come to her, and it appears that she is being polite at first, but being a teacher seems to spark a conversation between two strangers from two different universes.

"What do you teach?" She curiously asks.

"I teach mathematics and science this year. It changes from year to year." I specified.

I don't want to force myself on her as well. Who knows what she is thinking at this point, but I don't know her state when she walked away from the crying baby on the ground either.

Am I speaking with a victim, or with Charles Manson? The innocent person in jail too often depicted in the Mexican *telenovelas* or a crazed murderer?

"I am a teacher. I work with the Mexican community a lot, and I was asked at one time to try to see if you needed help. To try to find you." I said.

I don't know how I was going to get past the introduction, but I want her to know she has options.

"I was asked by the police to help look for you. I am not a police officer. Now I was asked to come by the Mexican Consulate to talk with you if you don't mind." I continue to spell out my role.

The twenty-year-old woman looked like she could fit in with the thirteen or fourteen-year-old girls at the junior high. She smiled and nodded. She seems to want to talk to anyone and I am sitting on the other side of the glass from her at this moment.

"Where did you learn Spanish?" she asks me.

"I went to school in Chile. I am from the United States, but I studied a year in Chile. I met my wife in Chile." I want to get as much out as fast as I can before she reconsiders, cuts me off, turns around and walks away.

She is very interested in where I teach.

"Do your students speak Spanish?"

"Yes. A lot of my students are from Mexico. But I teach

my classes in English." I pause, "Do you speak another language also?"

"Yes. Mixteco. Do you speak Mixteco?"

"No. I wish I could. Several of my students speak Mixteco, too."

She smiles.

"I have four questions to ask you. You don't have to answer if you don't want to. Do you mind?"

I am very conscious that I have a phone to my ear and that the woman in the orange jumper on the other side of the window is not the only person listening.

"Have you received any medical attention?" I ask.

"Have you seen a doctor?" I insist.

"No. No one speaks Spanish here. I was given some aspirin for a headache. I had to point."

"Is that all that has happened?" I incuriously ask.

"Yes, they gave me some aspirin for my headache. My stomach felt bad too."

"Have you been able to speak to a psychologist?"

"No."

"Any counseling?" I specify.

"No. I have been by myself."

"Have you spoken to an attorney?"

"For about five minutes in the courtroom. The attorney didn't speak much Spanish. She said that she would come back to me to talk, but I haven't seen her yet."

I pause a moment. Alba seems to be enjoying the conversation and seems to be more at ease in answering the questions.

"I was asked by the Mexican Consulate to ask if you are interested in talking with a representative from the Mexican government," I stated.

"By all means! Yes, I want to." She pauses again. "But with one condition, that we have no windows or telephones. I want to talk with them." She enthusiastically says.

"I will let them know. Is there anything you need?"

"Yes. You're a teacher. Can you ask if I can have some English classes? I don't understand anything they say, and I would like to learn to read in English. Can you ask?"

"I will. I don't know who I need to ask, but I will find out."

"I will pass on the word to the Consulate. Would you mind that I come back sometime to see how you are doing?

"Sure."

We hang up and nod again to each other. The woman who we had been looking for could have been any polite person walking down the street. She looked like a fourteen-year-old. I wanted to have asked her why she did it. What was her past? Who else was involved? I had experience with knowing that people were listening from my years in Chile during the dictatorship of Pinochet. Even when calling from the United States, if I had asked about anything political, click. I would not be able to get a call through for another couple of weeks.

I had to keep my information to myself until the next day. I went to work, taught and at 4:00 was able to drive to the Mexican Consulate just a few blocks from my home. When I arrive, my contact, Soledad Urias is in the parking lot heading for her car. I park my van, get out and walk towards her. I let her know that

Alba does want to talk to someone. She tells me that she thought that this would be the answer.

I could see that the situation stood out. I would think that any person in a foreign jail would be claimer to speak to a person from their country, or for that matter any person who could conceivably help them get out of jail.

Alba's family had declined a meeting, which seemed odd. Alba came to attention when I, a stranger to her mentioned the possibility.

Then another person came out the door. I didn't expect to be conducting my hot information like this, in the parking lot, standing between a couple of cars angled next to the exit of the side of the building, but it worked. Soledad introduced me to Silvia Nieves Ochoa, the legal counsel at the consulate. We hadn't met before, and Mrs. Nieves seems surprised and very skeptical.

"What church are you with?" I keep getting this question!

"I'm not with a church."

"What organization are you with?"

"I'm working on my own. I'm a school teacher, but the Sheriff's Department and even the Consulate have asked me to help. I'm on my own."

She doesn't seem to be keen to what I have to tell her. She seems more interested in who I was than what information I have to share. Apparently, the three people from the Mexican Consulate who had asked me to speak with Alba Flores Zapata didn't include the one person who worked on legal matters.

14. Old World War II
Black & White Movies

After that weekend I get a phone message call from Silvia Nieves the next Monday. Could I come by to speak with her at the Consulate at the end of my day?

Apparently, I am more welcomed this time. I don't blame Mrs. Nieves; I am apparently a complete surprise to her. My contacts reached out to me without consulting with her before, but it brought results.

Arriving at 4:00, I introduce myself again, this time in her office. Mrs. Nieves tells me that she is very happy to hear that Alba wants to speak with the consulate.

"It was very strange that the family said that she wasn't interested. Nobody says that in her situation."

"I would think that the first thing that I would want to do is get in contact with my government." I suggest.

"That's usually the case. But we have another problem."

I remember thinking, *What now!*

Mrs. Nieves looks out the window. The American and Mexican flags are at eye level from the second floor office. Juan Soria Elementary School is across the road. "Ventura County is the only place in the United States that we cannot speak to a Mexican national without an attorney from the District Attorney's office present or having the conversation taped."

I look at her with surprise and a grin, "There must be a county in Mississippi..."

"We consider this a violation of the Geneva Convention. Could you help?"

"I don't know what I can do, but I can try to look into it."

I had only heard about the Geneva Convention from old black and white World War II or Vietnam War movies.

I thought that this was only for prisoners of war.

She also asks if I could make contact with Alba's cell mate.

"Esmeralda Martinez was arrested over a year ago." Mrs. Nieves explains. "She was arrested after her eleven-month old son had died. The police forced a confession out of her, and now her husband has disappeared. She has no family and I am certain that she is innocent."

"What happened?"

"The baby was sick. They even took the baby to the emergency room the evening before, and the baby was cleared by the doctors to go home. The next morning, they found the baby dead in its crib." She related.

"Was the baby treated at the hospital?" I asked.

"No, they checked the baby and said that everything was O.K. The police interviewed Esmeralda and convinced her that 'She should have done more, that it was her fault.' The distraught mother agreed that she should have done more to save her only son, and Esmeralda was arrested." "Does Esmeralda speak English?" I insisted.

"No, she speaks Spanish, but her first language is Mixteco. She was crying and tricked into a confession by the police. I am one hundred percent sure that she is innocent."

"So you think that it was crib death." I clarified.

"Yes. She has not had any visitors. I have seen her twice, and she has a public defender, but can you see her? I am sure that she would like to talk to somebody who is not an attorney." She explains.

"I will see her. Would it be appropriate that I ask about the services she has received?" I answered.

"By all means."

Now I have two Mixteco women with dead babies. I had a Geneva Convention violation to look into, and I am a full time junior high school teacher who could only get on the phone in the evenings. My wife just shakes her head and asks what I think I could do.

"Who knows? I need to make some calls." I retorted.

That evening I call a friend who is an attorney and a termed out California State Assembly-member. Pedro Nava had helped me in the past with advice on how to go about with the search for Alba.

I ask Pedro Nava about the Geneva Convention. "Yes, the Geneva Convention is the standing guideline for foreigners in prison anywhere in the world. Did they ask you to help them with that?"

"Really? Am I now working on a world court issue?" I ask. It seems funny. "What should I do?" I wondered aloud.

"You could go to the Secretary of the State, Hillary Clinton, but first maybe you should contact someone with the County government." He informs me.

In the meantime, the consulate started work on getting

77

proper documents to the family of Alba to allow them also to visit her in the jail. They had not been able to enter the prison for a visit, and now the family seemed interested in speaking with the Mexican Consulate on this issue that was now in their interest.

It seems that an agreement was made to not ask about their immigration status. Before my visit to Alba clarified that the message from the family was off, it seems now that the family wants just to stay low. I am glad to see that the consulate is trying to help the Zapata family in what they can.

The family had already spoken to the newspapers, saying that they didn't know about the pregnancy before, during or after the birth and refused to say more. They were selective in speaking with the Mexican Government, but now they could at least support their family member.

The Sheriff's Department is surely interested in turning a blind eye. Taped phone conversations from family could glean new information that interrogations may not. The family is walking a very fine line, as is Alba.

I go again to the Todd Road Jail, this time to see Esmeralda. The attendants at the front desk remembered me from two weeks earlier. They seem a bit surprised that I know about Esmeralda. She had been in jail for a year already, and the news had been forgotten.

"Who are you with?" The officer asks. .

"The Mexican Consulate asked that I come and see her. I am a teacher; I don't work for them, but they asked if I could help." I respond.

The man who is just listening the first time I came by for

Alba was now at the window punching in my information from my driver's license into the computer at the side.

"Good. Esmeralda hasn't had any visitors. It has been a long time. I hope she wants to talk to you."

Esmeralda is very different from Alba in many ways, but she also has the eyes of a deer caught in the headlights look. Alba was more willing to see where the conversation would take her as we spoke.

Esmeralda is in her early thirties and though also short, of a thinner build than Alba. Again, I don't want to interrogate this woman on an open telephone, but I wonder what the true story is. In time all would be said in court.

"Hello, my name is Denis O'Leary. I am a teacher, but the Mexican Consulate asked if I could come by and talk with you."

Esmeralda had a hard time with my name, trying to repeat it a couple of times, but she seemed to have been told by Alba that a balding white guy had come by to talk with her.

"There are people at the consulate who believe that you are innocent."

"I am innocent."

"I was asked to come by to talk with you. Can I ask a couple of questions about how you are being treated here?

I incisively ask.

"Sure." She responds matter of factly.

I got pretty much the same answers from Esmeralda as I did Alba. Both claimed that communication was poor, but after Esmeralda had been in jail for a year she now has a cell mate that not only speaks Spanish but her native Mixteco as well. She told me that she has only one uncle in the United States who lives in

Texas and she presumed that he did not know what had become of her. Esmeralda talked about her desire to go back home and live with her mother.

"I just want to stay and help my mother. She is getting older, and I know that she could use my help. I don't want to be here in the United States. My place is with my mother in the fields around the house," she tells me. Esmeralda asks me if I have ever been to Mexico.

"A couple of years ago I was invited by the government to go to Mexico City to talk about education. A lot of meetings in a couple of days. I wasn't much of a tourist. I also would go to Tijuana when I was a kid with my family."

She smiles and gives me the same answer as my contacts while in Mexico City.

"Tijuana isn't Mexico."

"That's what everyone from Mexico tells me." We both laugh.

After the visit, I ask a good friend, Margaret Johnson-Spring if she would be interested in visiting the ladies. Margaret is a religious person who seems to take on social issues without proselytizing to those she meets. Most importantly, the seventy-year-old is a woman. I am sure that Alba and Esmeralda would feel much more at ease and be much more open with Margaret than myself.

Margaret would soon meet with the ladies almost every Thursday after that. They soon started calling her "*Abuelita*" or 'Grandma.' Alba would see Margaret and her family for her two visits allowed in a week. Esmeralda would get only Margaret but seemed very satisfied.

Margaret also starts bringing others to visit with her as

well. She brought in the Clergy Council to the topic of seeking fair trials for both ladies.

The moral support from the Clergy Council, which represent most all denominations, is reassuring. They tell me how. I start to get people coming to me and asking about Alba and Esmeralda. I am skeptical at first. Many people are still asking why I am supporting a baby killer. They don't even know about the second woman. Even the news that she was a rape victim that fled from her rapist and Mexico did not seem relevant to these people. A fair trial would be fair only if it found her guilty. How could I be supporting a baby killer? It continued.

Margaret would pass on to me her conversations and later would show me letters and drawing the ladies made and had waiting for her at the front desk. They looked like traced Disney coloring book drawings, the letters to Margaret showed a connection to the outside world and gratitude for Margaret's friendship.

Margaret would also deposit small amounts of money in the ladies' accounts to allow them to buy small items in the commissary and to buy stamps for letters. Later I would find out that this money could also be used to make phone calls out. The recorded calls generated on the ladies' part could be of interest to law enforcement as well.

I am surprised to find out that Margaret had never visited a jail before. I had expected that she may have visited people in the past as part of her ministry. I appreciate her time and interest greatly. I know that Margaret is not preaching to the ladies. It seems to be a good friendship that the ladies need to remain tied to the world outside of their situations.

Margaret would tell me with a grin and twinkle in her eye,

"You got me into this."

I also visited Esmeralda a couple of times more. She tells me of her desire to help her mother. She wants to return home. Her intension is to stay away from the horrors she experienced in the United States. We do not speak of her son; I never want her to say anything that could be used in her favor or more likely, against her in the court case to come. I would ask my basic questions about medical attention, counseling and legal representation.

Nothing had changed on these counts.

We did have one full belly laugh when I made reference to my balding. Esmeralda bent forward she laughed so hard. I don't mind that the laughter was at my expense, I am balding as my sixth grade students like to remind me often. There is no getting around it. For these few seconds, Esmeralda isn't in jail, she is laughing.

I would learn over time that the ladies could never receive classes in English. Because of the nature of their charges, the two are not to be considered safe in the general jail population. I passed on this news as well. Both seemed to understand and take this in stride.

15. The Accord

On March 15, 2013, I come to visit Alba Flores Zapata for the second time. I let her know that the Mexican Consulate had an issue with the County jail system and that I had made calls and was trying to see if we could resolve the issue. I wonder how many other persons were denied a confidential meeting with a representative from their government.

It seems to be a natural request. An American in a Mexican jail or anywhere in the world for that matter would be banging on the bars to get someone from the US Embassy to talk with them.

Alba is very religious this day. She is very happy to see me, and I can see that she is interested in talking. She tells me how she is asking that God would protect her and asks if I could pray for her. It seems natural that a person in jail finds God or puts more faith in God. I tell her that I will, but I am here more for her practical civil rights that I could do something about. Prayer is in another category, and I humbly don't think that God or the saints are going to make Alba's life better because I pray for her.

I am a religious person, I think. I also don't want to give false hope beyond my ability to help. Friends laugh when I tell them that I am a pessimist. When they tell me that I'm not, usually accompanied with a chuckle, I'm asked, "Then why do you do what you do?" No answer.

"Have you received any medical attention?" I ask.

"No," says Alba.

"Any counseling?" I persist.

"No one." She says.

"Have you spoken to an attorney?"

"I was supposed to have spoken with my attorney, but nothing happened." Alba explains.

I look behind Alba, sitting on the stool with phone to her ear. The small booth is the size of a larger telephone booth. The door behind her is glass, and I can see a walkway that leads to the door and metal railing that separates this level to a lower pit with Sheriff's Officers working at lit control panels and another series of doors behind them.

I have no idea what the Officer's functions are at these controls or computers. I can imagine that this is a central station in the prison, at least for this area. The official reminds me that someone is listening to the conversation, and in some part, our conversation will be recorded.

My side of the window is open. I have people walking back and forth as they look for their loved ones or clients in the different petitioned booths. Children play behind me, while their mother or father speak to the loved one in orange.

I tell Alba that many people were talking about her. Her head turns a bit as if this took a few seconds to understand. I say that many people don't want anything good to happen to her and others were very supportive. I tell her as for myself; I wanted her to have a fair trial. She thanks me for my help. She also thanks me for helping her family to be able to meet her.

It takes some phone calling, and I joke with my wife Viviana and a few friends in the process that I am well over my head, but I have an appointment set in the office of Ventura

County Supervisor John Zaragoza. Invited is Sheriff Chuck Smith and Silvia Nieves Ochoa of the Mexican Consulate.

We meet on April 19, 2013, in the main office of Supervisor Zaragoza. I know that I had gotten the Sheriff Department's attention when I see Sheriff Chuck Smith himself in full uniform coming towards the office. Smith is the elected County Sheriff and the top person to represent the department. Up until that moment, I was afraid that I would meet with someone further down the chain of command.

I am also soon concerned when at first the legal-council for the Mexican government is not present.

It is not a gotcha type meeting. I don't want to beat anyone up, and it seems to be just that. We sit around a coffee table, sofa on one side and chairs on the other three, and picture books on the table of Ventura County. We got down to business.

We sit down and I am asked to explain the issue.

"Thank you for coming. I asked that we get together because the Mexican Consulate brought to my attention that they are not allowed to make contact visits with Mexican nationals without a representative of the DA's office present."

Then the door opens. Silvia Nieves Ochoa comes in. Thank God. We all stand up again. Introductions and I start over.

"I have been informed by the Mexican legal-council that the Consulate is not able to have a contact visit with Mexican nationals in our county jails without having a representative from the District Attorney's office present or having the interview recorded by the Sheriff's Department. The Mexican Consulate believes that this is a violation of the Geneva Convention." We all look at each other around the sofa and chairs pulled up to the coffee table in the office.

A few of us start talking to the person at our side; all with the same idea. The Geneva Convention seems to be something not expected at the county level.

Mrs. Nieves continues. "We have tried to speak with Mexican citizens in the county jail system and are not allowed to speak with them in confidence. We believe that this is a violation of the Geneva Convention."

Supervisor Zaragoza looks at the Sheriff and explained that this is why he called for the meeting.

"I don't know about the legal status of the Geneva Convention, but what is the Sheriff Department's policy with a prisoner speaking with a consulate?"

Sheriff Chuck Smith reminded us that he had been voted into office only the November before and that he has not heard of this issue coming up until now. He asks if he could make a phone call to ask what the policy is. He goes to the side of the room and dials someone from his office. It seems that he was put on hold by the person on the other end for some time. I'm sure they were looking for the information.

He spoke almost in whispers, and as much as I would like to hear the conversation, it was impossible to tell from his tone of what was going to happen.

Finally, Sheriff Smith comes to the group again and sits down. "I can say that there was never a written policy preventing the consulate to speak with prisoners in private. I promise that I will look into this."

And that is how the meeting ends. A couple of weeks later I hear from Silvia Nieves that the Consulate can sit down with Mexican citizens without supervision. She thanks me for the help.

We took an obstacle out of the way, and it never hit the newspapers. We cleared a Geneva Convention violation between two nations, and I can only hope that this will serve to protect and bring justice to many people in the future.

16. Another Victim

August 2011, Michoacán, Mexico.

Alba arrived at her house. It is late, and she tries not to wake anyone in the house. She was crying, unkept and nervous. She had been raped. She could not speak of it. Her rapist is a relative. A provider for the family. She would not be believed. She would not be believed. She keeps silent.

A couple of months pass, and Alba is vomiting. She is pregnant. Wanting to get away, go away, Alba decides to go to the United States. She hasn't seen her sister in several years, but she and her husband had made a good life in America. Oxnard, California.

The consulate meets with Alba and many others are in the now allowed contact visits. The consulate is still concerned. I am asked to come by the consulate to talk. In May of 2013, several things have happened.

Silvia Nieves asks me. "Do you know that Alba was raped?"

"I heard. Is it true?" I query.

"Yes. It was her brother-in-law's brother." She elucidates.

"Will he be arrested?" I demand.

"She doesn't want to sign the papers." Ms. Nieves states.

"Can you do anything?" I ask.

"Not until she officially accuses him. I let her know that she has up to ten years. I also told her that it would help her case and may even get her out of jail."

I give my opinion. "I bet she doesn't want to upset the family. The men are the money makers." I relate.

"Probably. Her mother has already disowned her. She doesn't want anyone to mention her name. But we have another problem."

"What's that?" I eagerly inquire.

"Her family has paid $10,000 for a private attorney." Says Nieves.

"$10,000 for an attorney on a murder charge?

That's a drop in the bucket." I clarify.

"I don't expect him to do much to help her. She needs her public defender, he has been working on the case already and now this new attorney will need to start from scratch. Can you talk to her?" I amplify.

"I can try, but her family has been taking up her two visits a week. I will have to go early and try to beat them in line for the visitation." I said.

The attorney's name is Timothy Ruby. I can't find out much about him except hearing that the police department knows about him. I had to read between the lines.

The concern is originally that Alba should get a good private attorney. Public Defenders are known for being over worked and too often ineffective. Now, the idea that the family put together $10,000 which I am sure is a lot of money on their part to hire an attorney seemed out of place. One attorney told me that $10,000 would pay the first of several investigators in a case like this. I am to expect the bare minimum.

The summer months pass with Margaret visiting the two ladies at the Todd Road Jail and telling me about how happy she is with the public defender of Esmeralda. The Public Defender is said to have been contacting experts on the Mixteco culture. It seems that she is far ahead of the curve.

On the other hand, Alba's family was taking up the two visits and communication through Margaret came to a standstill.

September was coming, and we had heard that both ladies would have their court dates a few days apart from each other. The plan is for Margaret to attend and I would try to make the hearings after my school is out, for about the last hour of the day.

Margaret calls me to say that she found out that Alba's case is to come up the following week. It comes as a bit of a surprise to us in that we had expected that it would be a couple of weeks further down the line.

I have had hoped to speak to Alba's attorney before the case starts. I want him to know of the possibility that he may want to at least talk to me before the case starts. I may be the best witness that she can have. I know that before the Sheriff found Alba and after her arrest that she was considered a possible victim by law enforcement. It isn't much, but I know that Alba doesn't have much going in her favor.

I find the number for attorney Timothy Ruby on the internet and call. I mentioned my connection with the Sheriff's Department, the Consulate and in that, I had spoken to Alba a couple of times. To my surprise, we set an appointment for the evening before the trial is set to start.

I come to his office a couple of blocks from the Ventura County Government Center, where Alba is to be tried. The office is on the ground floor of an older complex of attorney offices, chiropractors and dentist offices. Walking into a small waiting room with a love seat on one wall and a door leading to the main office with stacks of papers and files everywhere. Mr. Ruby greets me and walks me in.

A woman sits at a desk only a few feet away from where we sit, partitioned with stacks of books, papers and files with papers almost falling out of them. Stacks of books mixed with files and the odd loose papers are in almost every spot around the room. Two old chairs face each other in the middle of the room. We sit.

Ruby is a tall man. Elderly, he is somewhat unkept, and his clothes seem naturally wrinkled. Mr. Ruby fits the filing system he had apparently organized over the years. The woman is at a keyboard with large monitor TV in front of her. A large long haired white cat lay on top of a stack of papers behind the monitor. This cat looked like a lion of sorts, and the smell of old papers, dust and cat litter box on another smaller table made apparent that the cat had been around quite a long time.

Mr. Ruby asks me how I got to know about the case, but before I could start his cell phone rings, he picks it up, says "Hello" and hangs up by accident. It happens a couple of times, showing me that the disconnections when I had first called him had nothing to do with a bad connection. When he is able to talk he first shuffles through a stack of business cards with a rubber band around them and finally finds the AAA card he is looking for. He passes on the phone number from the card to the caller.

Back to me, "So how did you get involved with this case?" he asks.

"I got a call from Officer Luis Silva asking if I could help get out the word and look for the mother of the baby found in the fields."

"And you have done this before?"

"No. I am a teacher, but I have also worked with different civil rights groups. The Sheriff contacted me, and I went on the radio and TV to try to see if we could help find her."

"Did you get paid?"

"No. Never came up and I never asked." This was the first time that even the possibility had crossed my mind.

"I wanted to contact you to let you know that the Sheriff's Department always considered Alba as a potential victim."

Seemingly not interested in my comment of being a victim Ruby continues, "Did you find her?"

"No. Alba was picked up several months later. I knew about the details when the Sheriff was getting close, they even asked once if I could go to the door with a bullet proof vest and ask for her, but I didn't find her."

"You were duped by the Sheriff's Department." I ignored that.

"I know that there may be no witnesses that you can call on. I wanted to make sure I came and spoke to you before the trail in case I could be of help."

"It's a simple case," he tells me. "We plan on arguing that Alba was not allowed to be interrogated in her first language. She didn't understand everything that was being asked."

I look at Ruby, a bit surprised that he is sharing this with me. "She speaks Spanish. I spoke to her twice. Her Spanish is not academic quality, but it is good."

"You spoke to her? Where?"

"In the Todd Road jail. Twice. The Mexican Consulate asked if I could make contact with her. Her family first said that she didn't want to speak to anyone, they said that this was very unusual. We even straightened out a Geneva Convention problem with the jail so the attorney from the consulate could speak with her."

"What did she tell you?"

"I had a few basic questions about how was her treatment. I asked if she wanted to speak with the consulate."

"Did she tell you anything about the case?"

"No. I know better to ask. I was curious, but not over a wire tapped phone. I'm not going to ask."

"We are going to ask why they didn't have a translator in Mixteco. I'm going to keep it with that," he repeats.

I thought for a moment. Here is a person who is unkept, paid very little to work on a murder case, and who has called me a dupe for working with the Sheriff.

"That's a good argument for a college debate, but you are not going to get a majority of a panel of jurors to agree that this is a good reason to let a woman who left her baby to die, free." We both sat up in our chairs a bit closer to each other.

"We can win on that. They should have had an interpreter."

It is quiet for a moment. Our voices are calm, but I could feel the tension in the room rise.

"Do you speak Spanish?" I ask.

"No."

"Do you have an interpreter?"

"Yes."

"In Spanish?" I ask.

We look at each other eye to eye again for a few seconds without talking again.

I continue, "So I am on the jury. I see that you argue that a woman who left her baby to die in the mud should be let free because she didn't understand the questions in Spanish and that she needed a Mixteco interpreter. Then I hear the person translating what you say to her in Spanish.

What am I supposed to think?"

"What do you think we should do?"

"Ask about the legality of taking over one-hundred DNA samples from many people who are undocumented. Did these people know that they had the right to say no, or that it could lead indirectly to the mother of the baby? To Alba?" I'm talking faster now.

"Mention that she was a victim of rape."

"Did she tell you that she was raped?"

"The Sheriff and the Consulate told me. Hell, she could get not only off on the charge but get a Z visa to stay in the country as well! She's a victim."

We both stood up, and he took a step to the door. I turned and followed. In the smaller waiting room outside the path of books and door, there is a young teenage Latino boy with his mother sitting on the love seat. Hands folded on their laps they both look scared.

As we pass through the door and into the waiting room, Timothy Ruby speaks again. He is walking next to me. I can't believe what he is saying, and he seems to time it as we approached the outer door. "She's guilty anyway, so who cares. She'll get life."

I am amazed, and want to run back into the room and tell the mother and her son who are waiting on the love seat to run! Run away fast! I don't. I pause outside the door and walk slowly out towards the parking lot.

The next day Alba is in court. Margaret and I expect the case to start, but we also guess that it will take a few days to select a jury. I decide to go to work that day, but I call Margaret during my lunch break. I had planned to head over to the Ventura County Government Center to sit in on the court around 4:00 if they were still in session. Instead, Margaret gives me the news that the case has been delayed. She gives no details, but we will get together in a few days.

Alba had been in court, seeing Margaret from behind a barred off section away from the public seating. The attorney Timothy Ruby was late. The judge was not pleased that he was not present and delayed any proceeding for a couple of hours from the given starting time in the morning.

When Timothy Ruby did appear in the courtroom, he had two translators with him. Apparently, he had looked for and with time gotten a Mixteco translator to come with him as well the Spanish translator. Ruby looked shaken.

You don't make a judge wait.

Ruby ignored Alba when he walked in, passing her and apologized to the judge. He then asked for a continuation of the case to allow more time to prepare. It was granted. Ruby was ready to walk out of the courtroom when the judge raised his voice.

"You have a client who wants to speak with you."

Alba looked as she was trying to figure out what was going on and perturbed at the same time.

Mr. Ruby walks towards Alba with his translators and speaks with her for about five minutes before turning to leave again.

Passing from the bar to the seats, Margaret introduced herself to Mr. Ruby.

"Hello, my name is Margaret Johnson-Spring. I am a Unitarian minister, and I have visited Alba several times in jail. Is she OK, today?"

"She will be fine." Mr. Ruby replied, looking towards the door.

"Will you be ready for the next court date?"

"She's guilty, and she should do forty years," Ruby answered and walked out of the room. Margaret watched with astonishment as well as three attorneys who were waiting for their trials who overheard. Margaret composed herself, smiled towards Alba, raising her hand and waved as Alba waved back before she was taken away.

A couple of days later Margaret and I meet to talk about our concerns without at first knowing what Timothy Ruby had said to the other. Within twenty-four hours Mr. Ruby had said the same thing with different words to the both of us. The Mexican Consulate had been concerned about Mr. Ruby, and we both had grave concern now as well.

We decide to go to Alba and let her know what we had both been told by Mr. Ruby. I also speak to Silvia Nieves at the Consulate and Pedro Nava to ask what options we might have.

Alba could be defended by whoever she chooses. I understand that, but I don't feel that she would stand behind her representative if she knows what he had said, to two different people on two separate occasions!

On September 20, 2013, Margaret and I visit Alba at the Todd Road Jail together. This was the first time we had come together. Margaret is recognized much more readily by the guards at the front desk than I. They joke about seeing her again. She had made the trip once a week since the beginning of the year. This is only my third visit to Alba and would turn out to be my last for quite a long time.

We walk down the corridor, both talking about the length of this windowless, long hall. Margaret asks me to try to explain the situation; my Spanish is better than her's. We both had talked about the situation. We hope that Alba would on her own accord change her representation to the public defender.

Margaret has spoken to the Public Defender of Esmeralda and is very excited that the attorney seems to be looking into the culture and talking to Esmeralda. She also has told Margaret that she knows about Alba's case and would be very interested in defending Alba as well.

Coming up to the windows at the end, Alba is waiting for us this time. Margaret sits down and picks up the phone. I stand to the side and share a smile and wave with Alba.

"How are you today?" Margaret starts. I could only hear our side of the conversation.

"Yes. I came with Denis to talk with you."

They speak about letters that had been written and that Alba's family had visited.

Then I am handed the phone. Margaret stands and allows me to take the stool. I put the phone to my ear. "Hello, how are you doing?" I ask.

"I am OK. How are you?"

We speak pleasantries for a moment, and I start my planed beginning. "I want to let you know what we have been told, but I want you to know that you are the one who needs to decide what to do. I want you to take your time and be the person who decides what to do next. Do you understand?"

Alba smiles.

"I spoke to Timothy Ruby the day before your hearing. He didn't seem too interested in your situation, and at the end, he told me that he thought you were guilty and who would care if you got life. The next day he said pretty much the same to Margaret in the courtroom." Margaret nods.

"We think you may want to consider Esmeralda's Public Defender. She has been working a lot on the case and is reaching out to see if she can be found innocent. She also has told us that she would be happy to defend you as well."

I repeated several times that I wanted Alba to take her time and make the decision that she thought best for her. "I know that your family has hired Mr. Ruby and I think you should talk to them."

We talk about what the postponement means. Alba, like anyone, would in her position want to think that she could have already been freed from jail to go on her own.

The next trial date is set for another four months away. "Now," I tell her, "You do know that if you change attorneys right now, it could delay your trial again?"

"Why?"

"Because the new attorney would have to study your case, interview experts and prepare for the trial."

Alba tries to ask me what I wanted her to do a couple of times.

"What do you think I should do?"

"I think that you should take some time and think about it. You need to talk with your family. What will be best for you? I don't know how this is going to come out."

She asks to speak with "Grandma" (Margaret) who takes the phone as I stand up and she sits down again. Margaret tells of the same story of what Timothy Ruby had told her while they spoke on his way out the courtroom.

"I am very concerned," Margaret tells her.

"How would I change attorneys?" Alba asks.

"You would need to fill out some papers requesting to drop your attorney for a public defender." Margaret had the papers in her hand and raised them to the window. Margaret asks if she could hand the phone to me again because my Spanish is better. Alba nods again and smiles.

I take the phone back.

"I don't want to promise you anything," I tell her. "My concern is what Mr. Ruby told me. Having a great attorney still, might find the court saying that you are guilty and deserve a long time in jail." Alba looks at me motionless. We wanted to come to you because we thought that you should know what he had said."

"You both have been very helpful."

"I have always come here to ask if you are being treated fairly," I tell her. "I don't know what the outcome will be. You may lose the case no matter what, but I want you to have your rights, and I want other woman in the future who are raped to know that they have rights too."

This is the closest I come to talking directly about the events of her case. Again, I am always conscious that we are being taped.

Alba for the first time since I had seen her face became emotional. She stands halfway up. "Yes!" she said with a tear coming from her eye. I could also see in her face, 'Yes! You got it!'

"I want to change my attorney. I want to sign the papers."

I thought 'No!' but I didn't come out with the word.

"You should think about it. You should talk to your family."

I truly didn't want to be in any way to make the decision for her, even though I think it is best. Truly, I don't want to be responsible for whatever negative result that could happen. We have no way to know how this would end. This is real, not a hypothetical story, but a life, future lives!

From the beginning, I am convinced that she had left her baby. Full term, a victim and baby killer at the same time. What is the goal? I could only think 'justice' is the goal. For the moment, she needs a representative who would not tell a complete stranger that he was taking a case that he didn't care about because he thought that his client was guilty.

The family had put together $10,000 which I'm sure is a lot of money for them. On the other hand, it is a drop in the bucket for a defense attorney who is taking on a person with murder charges. They also paid in advance. Bills are paid already.

It had occurred to me that the family may have had gotten everything they wanted. Timothy Ruby could defend a neat little argument that Alba's first language is Mixteco and that she did not understand the questioning in the legal realm in which she was caught up.

Questions of 'Who helped you? Who didn't help you? Were you raped? Who took you to the field? Who took you home? Who helped you after leaving the baby? These questions would have directed questions towards the family, perhaps others. Another layer of responsibility. Possibly other crimes and convictions.

"She wasn't questioned in Mixteco" is a nice contained

response to being caught. Clean, and probably impossible to convince a majority of a jury to use to offset murdering a baby and to set a person free.

Margaret and I speak to Alba a bit more before our forty-five-minute time expires. Margaret would get the papers to Alba and contact the District Attorney who is representing Esmeralda Martínez.

We watched Alba stand and turn towards the door

in her phone booth on the other side of the glass. She raises her hand as she steps out the door. We turn and walk towards the long hallway. It is a good time to talk about what happened, but we are both in thought as we leave the prison.

17. Running Interference

September 29, 2013

The lunch bell rings, but I don't have to tell my sixth graders that it is time. They had already put away their books, and I have the twelve-year-old students in two lines outside the room ready to walk to the cafeteria. After dropping them off into the lunch lines, I walk a little beyond to the door to the teachers' lunch room. Sitting down I take out my cell phone. I have a message. It is Mr. Timothy Ruby.

"I know what you did! She told me! You pulled a fast one! You had her sign that paper!" Ruby's message was yelling over the phone. "I forbid you to talk to my client again! If you do, I will get a court order against you talking to her! Do you understand! You are not to talk to my client again!"

One other message was also recorded: "Hello? What..." It is Timothy Ruby a second time, seemingly still not able to understand that he dialed me back a second time. Oh well.

I call up Margaret to let her know of the message Ruby left on my phone. He had spoken to her as well. It was much less abusive, and he did not tell her to stay away.

We both consider the call strange. I am concerned that Alba had just become marginalized by her attorney and her family.

Apparently, though, Margaret is needed in Alba's life. Margaret was not told to stay away. She is "Grandma."

I decide not to press Timothy Ruby. He had the right to say what he said. I can only hope that he turns into Perry Mason at this point. If Alba is being harassed in any way, it is from her family. The love of a family I believe is holding many secrets and I am afraid that a fair trial for Alba has taken a back seat to a safe escape for the family's actions.

18. The Teacher, Unitarian, and the Homeless Reporter

I walk into the office in the Mexican Consulate. Mrs. Nieves sits at her desk and as I say hello she immediately takes the ringing phone. In Spanish, she spoke about transferring the body of the loved one on the other end of the phone to a village in Mexico. Hanging the phone up, she commented, "Monday's are always lined with making arrangements after a funeral. They add up over the weekend."

"I would not have thought that the consulate would do that."

"We take care of our citizens. There are many details to take care of that people don't think about until it needs to get done." She turns and looks my way.

"I spoke to Alba Flores Zapata and the D.A.'s office. She took pictures of the baby with a cell phone."

"What!" we both just look at each other for a few moments.

I sink in my chair, "What does this mean?"

Monday, May 21, 2012: Moon light, a few clouds, a breeze. Mud. A whimper. A baby's cry. It was the first breath of a new life. The mother groans. She falls to her knees. Pants. The cries are loud, but from across the field, they drown out with the occasional car or truck passing on the freeway. Fifteen, twenty minutes pass. Breathing, cries, exhaustion.

The woman strains to see the infant. Mud. Flowers.

Strawberries. A bird squawks as it was disturbed in its sleep. A baby cries.

The woman looks up at the baby. Still breathing hard, she pauses for several minutes. The baby is crying, flailing his arms and legs upward. His small hands grasping in the air. Alba reaches into her pocket, takes her cell phone and looks at the screen. She points at a button, presses it and points the cell phone at the cries, at the baby.

She takes several pictures. They don't show the cries. They don't show the pain, the breathing. They do show the mud. They do show the small fingers grasping.

As daylight broke over the strawberry field at the El Canto Farms, the first workers walk six from a car to the edge of the field. Steam coming from their mouths in the cold. Clouds streaked in purple, red and a few rays of sun over the distant hills.

The court set the case to begin for Alba on October 9, 2013. We had little time to figure what Margaret and I should do if anything. Can we try to help someone who doesn't want helped?

We get together at my house to ask each other, who we should talk with. The Mexican Consulate is also concerned, but Alba has every right to decide who should represent her.

We have several options. The first is to step away and not visit the subject again. I should have run away from this a long time ago. A teacher, not only an elected official but an elected official for an elementary school district. I had gone to our televised school board meetings expecting questioning of why I was supporting a baby killer. The meetings had come and passed, and I had only heard these words in conversational voice from my boss, and a hand full of strangers in the street. Cutting my losses would be politically correct now.

Margaret is not running for office but holds her weekly "Occupy Oxnard" gatherings at Plaza Park, (La Plazita as we know it) in Oxnard since the Occupy Wall Street movement had started a year earlier. Margaret would have city councilpersons, city commissioners, and community members meet with folding chairs in hand and talk of how to make America better.

We both decided that we need to continue supporting Esmeralda Martinez in what we could. We also decide to continue pressing Timothy Ruby to give a good defense. Hell, maybe we could push him to turn out to be a great attorney.

A press conference!

We decide to hold a press conference outside the court to call for a proper defense in the Alba case. We also will write letters to the court asking about Mr. Ruby's the statements made to us about his thoughts of Alba's guilt.

We need a media person. If all else fails, we need one person to bring the issue to the media.

You can never accurately guess how great or little attention the media will give on any given issue in the community. Reporters are assigned for an event or topic in part to what is economically feasible for the company. Newspapers, radio, TV, are all investment companies when you get right down to it. Will it be worth the time of the reporter to attend a news event?

The court date is set for October 8, 2013, but having a conference on the same day would not bring our objective to the front. We want to say that we expect a proper defense by Timothy Ruby for his client. We need to call for the conference the day before so he and others could hear about it the night before or read about our concerns while they are preparing to leave their homes on the same morning.

Our person to get is Sean Justice. A freelance writer, Sean is a great writer, be it for two free weekly magazines, one in English and the other Spanish. The VCReporter has a good circulation in the county and Vida Newspaper covered the dense Spanish speaking areas of Oxnard, Ventura, and Santa Paula.

I met Sean Justice a few years earlier when he was covering the political antics of the Superintendents in the Rio School District. Even though Sean worked for the two free weekly papers, he seems to have written the best articles of the day on that subject.

A bit unkept and ragged at times, I didn't think much of it. Many reporters are. He is a good writer, friendly and he will listen to us.

I remember at one school board meeting in the Rio School District that Sean seemed a little more anxious than he should. He came up to me, "I have to leave soon, could you fill me in later of what happens?"

"Sure, you have something going on?"

"No, I don't have a ride."

"Oh. If you like, I can give you a ride."

Expecting to be dropping Sean off at his home or office, where ever that might be, I was later a bit surprised when he asked if I could take him to the bus station.

"I can take you to your home if you like?"

"That's OK. This is fine."

It took a few more lifts before I confirmed to myself that Sean Justice, my best go to reporter is homeless. The shelter is a block from the bus station.

So the best defense team that we can put together to protect a Mixteco woman who delivered her baby in a strawberry field and left him to die was a junior high school teacher, a good intentioned Unitarian in her seventies and a homeless journalist who writes for two free weekly newspapers!

The date of the trial is coming up, and though the crime had appeared in the papers and on TV the couple of days after finding the baby and later a blurb was out again in the local media when the mother appeared, beyond the headlines there is little known. Everybody has an opinion; nobody knows what is going on with the facts of the case.

We need to get the word out.

Margaret and I decide that we need to try to get the story out and Sean Justice was our go to journalist. The daily newspaper was not interested in anything other than a result of an event such as the trail. We wanted to argue that beyond the headline of a baby being found dead in a strawberry field that there were issues that cloud the contempt felt towards the mother of the baby.

Sean checked with his editor at the weekly free magazine, the *VCReporter* and got her interest in writing an article on the case. *The VCReporter* would often pick in-depth subjects to report on, and to the editor's delight, these would often scoop the daily *Ventura County Star*. Sean Justice started the interviews that expectantly included all sides of the issue.

The idea is to get an article out before the nearest court date, but we soon find that isn't going to happen. No problem, an article, any in-depth article would be welcomed in time. Sean would call me up and ask a couple of questions and finish with, "I'll get back to you."

Margaret and I both write letters to the judge. We write

separately, both telling of our concerns with the statements Mr. Tim Ruby had said to us individually. Margaret hand delivers her letter first to the judge's office at the Ventura County Government Center. She later calls me up and tells me that she is stopped. It made sense; anyone could claim that their attorney isn't representing them well. She learns that the Judge would not even be forward the letter and that the secretary would send a form letter stating this.

Just the same, I come in two days later with my letter. Knowing the dead end I am facing, I don't expect much, but the clerk and secretary in the office lobby give me their attention. They ask what I had to do with the case. I'm sure that being the second person in a couple of days catches their attention.

I go through the drill. "I am not an attorney."

"What church are you with?"

God bless all these people with churches who must keep our court system and bureaucrats busy. "No, I am not with a church."

The puzzled look...

I tell of my motives and involvement. The Sheriff's Department and later the Mexican Consulate.

The ladies explain to me the same they had told Margaret. Surprisingly they do ask for my letter. I expected the form letter that Margaret eventually receives but I do not get my form letter. On the other hand, the secretary does give me the address and process to write to the California State Bar Association.

We both write to the Los Angeles address of the California State Bar Association as well.

19. Press Conference

Margaret and I are trying to do what we can to progress the possibility of a fair trial for both Alba and Esmeralda. We meet on a rare occasion, usually working on the ever developing plan by phone.

More and more Sean Justice becomes our first contact. We know that he is working on his article, which seems to be taking a long time and has passed a couple of key dates that we had wished it might have been released. Sean is in the loop, and we know that whenever it appears, it will help.

The next court date is a couple of weeks ahead now. Margaret visits Alba again and is asked to show me a letter she had been given by the prison staff from Alba.

Margaret comes over to my house in the evening. She, Viviana and I sit in the living room, and first Margaret shows us the drawings both Alba and Esmeralda had given her. They were of Disney characters drawn on oversized white postcards and looked as if traced from coloring books. Messages and words of friendship written in beautiful cursive loops. "*Abuelita*" was the key word. Margaret is very respected by both, and I believe considered a "grandma" by both.

The penciled letter is written with basic Spanish grammar, but it is very clear. Alba asks that we do nothing that would cause her to be in jail longer.

Now twenty-years of age, Alba loves her family very much. She follows the family into her defense because she loves them. I don't blame her to ask for silence from anyone away from her family.

Margaret is loved and appreciated as well. Tim Ruby wants me not to see his client; he said nothing of Margaret. Alba is afraid that I am to cause her being in jail longer, she doesn't mind Margaret. In a sense, it was planned this way. From the beginning, it was better that a woman with a knowledge and strength in religion support Alba and Esmeralda. I, a white male am not going to be able to comfort and make the connection with the ladies as Margaret can.

Alba had no family to see her when I first introduced myself. Margaret came at a time that her family was not able to see her due to the lack of documents and now they are filling the two weekly visit spots most of the time. Margaret would at times wave at Alba as she passes their booth as she goes to visit Esmeralda who never had family in the area.

Margaret and I would follow the changing panorama of the cases. We both agree that the focus is slipping away from defending Alba to preventing another child to die due to the lack of information about medical services and finally the Safely Surrendered Baby Law.

Having an attorney who throws the case for profit is not going to prevent mothers from abandoning their infant children to die in the future. Allowing Tim Ruby to argue a language issue when he doesn't have a Mixteco translator is not going to serve Alba in a jury case.

We decide that we will have a press conference the day

before the next trial date to argue that Alba needs a full defense that includes her actions and those of others around her. We hope that we will push if not force Mr. Ruby to do his job.

A press conference is announced for Monday, October 7, 2013, in the court yard at the Ventura County Government Center. We call around and originally have a handful of local civil rights leaders willing to speak. These speakers seem to disappear as the date comes closer.

It is going to be Margaret and myself. I take the day off from teaching. Something that I rarely do. We wait in the courtyard between the two Government Buildings at the Ventura Center. I have contacted the press and know that Sean Justice will be present. Margaret had picked him up from the homeless shelter in the morning. We wait.

As the time comes close, the fear of no one is showing up gives way to a reporter from the *Ventura County Star*. A group of friends who were starting a local TV cable channel and a phone call from KEYT Channel 3 saying that they would cover our issue but not be sending out a reporter to the press conference.

Margaret and I each hold an eight-by-ten-inch photo of Alba's mug shot. It is time, we call everyone together, and at that moment we see the KABC Channel 7 van pulling up to the curb. We got the Los Angeles network!

Susan Templeton of the *Ventura County Star* writes a brief article giving an over view of the case and how I was calling "for an informed judicial process in Alba Flores Zapata's case."

We discuss our concerns that her rape would not be brought up in the court. Templeton calls me up later in the day to ask how I know she had been rapped. I answer that the Sheriff's Department and the Mexican Consulate Attorney informed me of the rape.

"So you don't know for sure," Templeton asked.

"No, I wasn't there. I didn't witness the rape." It's all I can answer.

Good question. I think I gave an appropriate answer.

October 8, 2013

I am at Rio Vista Middle School in my sixth grade classroom and plan on sending texts and making calls in the day. Margaret picks up Sean Justice again. There is also a couple of the local cable TV channel friends who want to ask the judge about videotaping the court case.

The judge sits down and looks forward. The prosecutor's table has three people standing. Alba Flores Zapata is off to the side, behind bars in a white painted cage; the bars are strips of metal, angled in a way that I believe that the judge can see the defendants much better than those of us in the public section. Her defense table is empty.

"Has the defense come and stepped out?" the judge asks.

"Not that we know of." answered a member from the other table. The bailiff nods to confirm what the prosecuting attorney has said.

Judge Jacob B. Strauss looks towards a woman seated to the side.

"Can you try to contact Mr. Tim Ruby to see if he had an emergency and to see when he may be present?"

"Yes, your honor."

The judge stands up and leaves through a side door.

Judge Strauss comes into the court a couple of times after that. The attorneys for the prosecution are present. The judge is visibly upset. From my little knowledge in the court process, I know that you don't make the judge wait.

Two hours pass. Tim Ruby steps into the court and is told to come forward to the bench. The judge does not appear to be happy.

Tim Ruby goes back to the table and promptly asks for an extension. The case is now delayed until February 11, 2014.

Later that night I speak with Margaret who is sure that the press conference shook Tim Ruby. People were asking what was happening in the case. We shed light. Even though we are disappointed that Ruby was late and then granted an extension, perhaps the extra time will be put to good use and give a better result.

20. Mixtecos and Hollywood

The *Mixteco/Indigena* Community Organizing Project or MICOP is the group to get in contact with when you want to help the Mixteco population in Ventura County. I would have good conversations with Carol Bright, the Development Director, and Gustavo Roman, the Executive Director of the organization about the indigenous community in general and specifically the cases of Alba and Esmeralda. For a group that wants to aid and spread pride, two cases of child death are not a brochure advertising topic.

A nonprofit organization with a Board of Directors and potential grants in the waiting, MICOP isn't likely to take up the cause for Alba or Esmeralda. Set on not only supporting the culture and needs of some 20,000 plus Mixtecos in Ventura County but selling to those who are not Mixteco, the new peaceful people who have recently arrived to our neighborhoods.

Gustavo is Mixteco himself and concerned for the ladies as well as the image of the community. I never want only to expose the negative of a people, but this topic continues through different conversations at different encounters. For better or for worse, the subject is a raw nerve that connects truths and stereotypes into a real news item.

Yes, I had heard from many people in different settings that the dark side of the Mixteco community includes alcoholism, incest, and rape. Not themes that anyone would want to fly from a banner about their people.

Families often live in one roomed homes in Mexico. Little privacy and intimacy is allowed. I cannot say that these terrible vices are the norm. Rumor and stereotypes have always been rampant about the indigenous community in Mexico.

One needs not look any further than Mexico superstar movie actors María Elena Velasco in the role of la India María and Mario Moreno as Cantinflas. Both considered cinema silver screen superstars and national heroes, both portrayed the negative stereotypes of indigenous Mexico.

Poverty is a truth in the indigenous community. Services are sparse, and in many rural pueblos, the community traditionally has fended for itself.

Where I have seen mostly women come forward in the MICOP meetings, it is the men who take the political lead in Mexico and the United States. Men have traditionally led meetings of representation or duties.

The Mexican Federal Government for all its bravado has little practical control in the southern regions as well as the northern states of Mexico. The drug cartels have taken over much in law enforcement in the region. There are villages with no young men! They have been killed or forced to leave, often going to the United States to make money to support the family left behind or brought with them.

The negative stereotypes often come from the Spanish speaking Mexican community. While on the radio and even once while sizing a suit, I hear how Mixtecos have more than one wife. I would ask Gustavo if this was true.

"No."

"It's a bad rumor?"

He looks at me with a smile, "Who could afford more than one? It would be tiring."

But then we would have the conversation that sure; there are some cases of men taking more than one wife. Well, we can say the same in the United States with the Mormon communities in Utah.

Rape and incense is a very raw nerve. It is in our American culture as well. No, it seems to be unacceptable in the indigenous society as it is in the mainstream Spanish speaking society of Mexico, or for that matter, in the mainstream American society. All will admit that it does happen.

The taboo to accuse a male family member of a sexual violation not only can mark the victim, but take the male offender out of financial circulation. Alba was denied her mother's support. Esmeralda's husband left for Mexico abandoning his wife and may have taken justice in his own hands.

MICOP in one of its probably most effective campaigns has held an annual Indigenous Knowledge Conference at Oxnard College since 2013.

I decided to go to the conference in 2014 and again 2015.

I have been called an expert on the Mixteco community. I answer that I am only an expert in that I know that they exist. It is also a great opportunity to get some expertize because I am still expected to defend the community as an expert whether I accept the title or not.

Most conferences that teachers attend are for teachers and attended by only teachers. The Mixteco subject attracts not only educators but also law enforcement, health care workers, social services, journalists and the general public. It is very refreshing to see the wide range of interest. It also shows the vacuum of understanding towards this indigenous community.

I go with friend, Michael Rhodes who is a great sounding board for me as the events surrounding Alba and Esmeralda develop. Michael tells me that he is a retired movie and television show director. I think "retired" is solely out of modesty.

We first met by his insistence to contact me. Michael Rhodes had 'retired' and had the time and gumption to license clips of current movies that students would recognize. He put these clips together with a general question: If you were in this situation, what would you do?

Michael apparently had quite a lot of success with this nonprofit project, and he wanted to see how he could better direct it to the Latino students. He insisted on contacting me by phone message, e-mail, and written letter. I expected he was just another salesperson who thought that School District Trustees could purchase items by their own accord.

One day I answered the phone, and it was Michael Rhodes.

"Yes, let's meet."

"Are you available now?"

"Sure." and I give him my address.

Older than I, Michael sported a Stetson that reminded me of Indiana Jones'. This hat though had a glow about it that it was worked into shape from experience, not purchased that way.

We shake hands, and Michael says, "Before we get started, I have to tell you a story."

I am thinking that now I have to sit through a story before I tell him that I have no money to buy anything.

"I have started a project called 'Film Clips.' I have licensed clips of current movies that kids will recognize and pose questions to help in character building."

Sounds interesting, I think. Every teacher has thought about doing this, but this man had the know it all to get permission from the movie industry.

"I wanted to see how I could better get this to the Latino community and I heard about a conference in Miami. I asked if anyone could direct me in the way of connecting Film Clips better to the community. I was told about a conference in Milwaukee a couple of months later and attended it with the same question."

"I was told to meet with Christina Rodríguez in Los Angeles. She is the granddaughter of César Chávez and works for the foundation with his name. She liked Film Clips and told me that I needed to speak to Denis O'Leary in Oxnard, California." He starts laughing.

"I have been looking for you all over the country!" he says. "I live about a mile away!"

He showed me the DVD's with his clips, and I was impressed. My wife, my mother-in-law who was visiting for a couple of months from Chile and I later transcribed the closed caption into Spanish for the series.

Michael Rhodes is an interesting man with an interesting personality. I see a very Christian man in every sense of the word. He made a career of directing wholesome TV shows and movies. Little House on the Prairie, a few Hallmark Hall of Fame editions including Heidi, the movie Romero and as I introduced him to a friend once who is a Trekie: one episode of Star Trek! Michael laughed and said, "Oh, everyone has done at least one Star Trek!"

"Sure, in your world of friends!"

Michael has been encouraging when others were on the verbal attack.

Once I slipped on the phone, I had just found out about the cell phone pictures Alba had taken of the baby. "How could this fit into Alba being desperate, a victim without options?" I said that "Alba was guilty, but to what extent?"

"She is a victim." He was a bit upset. "She needed to step back to believe what happened, what she did. I'm sure that a good psychologist would agree that she acted that way because a disconnected event had occurred that she couldn't believe had happened."

"Yes. Alba needs to go into trial with the belief that she didn't do what she did on purpose."

Alba never had a psychologist or counselor of any type. I insist that had she been a blond haired, blue eyed 19-year-old who was raped and left to fend without knowing of her options, that she would have been afforded help immediately. Only she knows how she has handled the fact that she left a child, a newborn to die.

Michael and I meet at the MICOP Indigenous Knowledge Conference. There is an opening statement in the Performing Arts Center at Oxnard College, then breakaway classes in different parts of the community college campus.

There it is: Mixteco birth practices! A class on the practices in Mexico! Michael and I bee line it to the class. We are the only men in the room that holds about forty in all. Margaret also arrives later for the opening event but is seated on the other side of the room now with us.

Social workers, healthcare providers, law enforcement, introduce themselves with their names and occupations.

"Denis O'Leary, teacher."

"Michael Rhodes retired movie director."

"Margaret Johnson-Spring, divinity ministries."

We are an odd group in the room. The instructors are Carol Bright of MICOP, Dr. Claudia Iturrigaray, a university professor from UCLA and a local Mixteco mother. We get right into the subject.

Mixteco communities are often very remote, and services, as well as money for services, are sparse. Families often live together in small houses. Privacy can be an issue with intimacy. Couples often sleep in the same space as children and other adult relatives. Newlyweds do not necessarily have their own home or room to call their own.

As my wife told me when the case of the child who died in the fields first happened, women have been giving birth for millennium before doctors came around. Most women in this community will look for a partera, a woman who they trust to have knowledge in the delivery of a baby.

Usually an elderly woman, the partera will be contacted by the expectant mother ahead of time. The site of birth is quiet, often in the fields or countryside away from the village. This catches the attention of everyone in the class, but Margaret, Michael and I have different intentions of learning about the subject. We exchange looks at each other and mouth out our thoughts from across the room to show that this is important.

Alba as far as we know had no plan, no help in providing

information as to where to go for prenatal or delivery care. She went to a known field!

The *partera* or midwife takes the expectant mother away from people and the village in part because of the timidness in the culture. The husband may go as well. The role of the husband if he participates will be to hold the woman's arms from behind her back as she is in a sitting or squatting position.

The midwife will instruct in breathing and pushing to the expectant woman. At the time of birth, the midwife will reach her arms under the long skirt to catch the newborn baby.

"Why would the woman wear a long skirt?" asks a social worker.

"Modesty."

The social workers present in the class had a common question. Why did the Mixteco mothers they attend not to seem to be bonding with their babies?

Infant mortality. The lack of medical care and proper nutrition, the lack of practiced modern medicine or money to go to a hospital leads to a high rate of infant mortality. We know that bonding may take several months. The mother may still question if the baby will survive.

One aspect of the indigenous culture that I have had some painful conversations with people about is incest and rape. No person would like to claim that this is a regularly occurring situation in their community.

Not scientific: I have spoken to many people over the years that have told me that this is a problem. The remoteness of the villages, the overpopulation in living shelters and the abuse of alcohol would lead me to believe that this is indeed an issue.

The taboo of the subject, the male dominance in the family and community structure is too great, and suppresses the violence.

Rape and incest are taboo subjects in the United States as well. We have greater freedoms with issues concerning women, though progress is still needed. We in the United States have medical services more readily available, including many ways of receiving free services for the poor. We still have the same freakishly unnatural tendency to point a spot light on the subject.

Religion, religious people, and religious politics often eclipses helping sexually abused women in the United States. Immigrants in the United States are often kept at arms' length because of the politics of not wanting them in our country. Much of the same religious blinders exist in Mexico as in possibly the rest of the world. It is human not to want to accept that violations happen to women. It is easy to think that all families, all men, and women respect the norms of society.

I am not meaning to say that the Mixteco community is immoral. I do want to say that we must shed light on the problems that lessen the value of a woman and cheat the poor out of protections and life from the Mixteco community in Mexico and the United States.

Alba could have been hated for bringing an 'anchor baby' to the United States that would have caused the expense of thousands of tax dollars to pay medical expenses, not to mention educational expenses in the future. Alba was raped. She fled to her sister in Oxnard, California. She gave birth to the unwanted child in a field. Away from her home. Away from the community.

I raise my hand, "What if there is no father available?

What if the pregnancy was forces and not wanted?"

"Yes, that happens too…"

The mother will often go to the field by herself. Go where she can be alone, often at night. The mother will give birth. An established custom that the mother may leave the baby to the elements. Returning twenty-four hours later, if the baby has survived, God had intended for the mother to take the baby as her child.

It is amazing! Margaret, Michael and I are again looking at each other without talking. This is where Alba found herself! It gives background to the headlines that all had read. "Baby Found dead in the Strawberry Fields!"

21. The Article

The court date is coming close. In fact, we find out that Alba and Esmeralda are both scheduled separately for February 11, 2014.

I know that Sean Justice has finished his long awaited article. I had first hoped that it would have come out before the court date of October 2013. Now, months have passed, and I have had no contact with the ladies for several months.

Common ethics in journalism is that I do not know what Sean Justice is writing. I expect him to be thorough. I expect Sean also to be objective. In fact, I want to hear what Timothy Ruby or anyone else may have to say.

On February 6, 2014, the article comes out. A weekly paper, the free publication will be in stacks at different sites for seven days. This weekly is also placed in trays at the same courthouse!

The layout is fantastic! We got a front cover painting of a woman turned away looking over a strawberry field. Photos of Alba's mug shot along with Margaret and me at the press conference are also used. I am not thrilled by the title: "Language Barrier." This is not a matter of language, I believe this should be set aside from a language issue, but the subtitle helped: "Oaxacan immigrant, mother of newborn left for dead in Camarillo faces trial."

I am concerned with a couple of fine details that I believe are off a bit, but the article, for the most part, was accurate and very timely.

We did it! Days before the court date and we got out the story, part of the story of the woman behind the headlines and away from the knee jerk reactions of hate. Sean Justice, and publisher Brazil Murphy of the VCReporter not only scooped the daily newspapers and television, but they got it out the week of the trial!

Sean Justice started with describing Alba with a reference of the nursery rhyme about the little teapot : "She is short and stout." He continued that, "The twenty-one-year-old does not look like a woman accused of leaving her newborn child to die in a strawberry field."

He interviewed Gustavo Roman of MICOP, as well as Roseann Torres, an Oakland defense attorney who often represents non-English-speaking clients.

Torres was quoted in the article as saying, "Oftentimes our culture is that lawyers, doctors and teachers are so educated, they must be given blind faith, so these people will hire an attorney and say, he must know what he's doing."

Ruby offered little to the article because as he told Justice, his policy is not to talk to the press. He did state though that Margaret Johnson-Spring and I had our "own agenda."

Ruby reacts to the accusations of Margaret and myself that he told both of us of his client's guilt. Ruby flatly denies making the comment in the article.

"That is a lie, I never said that. I don't try my cases in public by volunteering my opinion." Ruby told the VCReporter journalist. I must say that I was very surprised that he opened his mouth to me.

I am not interested in arguing with Ruby about my agenda. I do admit I always try to form what others may claim is an agenda. I am not a rudderless boat in this storm. To claim that no agenda has prompted me in this case, would bade the question even in my own mind: why should I step forward? I do continue to state that yes, Ruby did tell me, "It doesn't matter, that she's guilty and would serve life anyway."

The article points out my conclusion that Alba was a rape victim. To be fair, Justice also pointed out that the Sheriff's Department did not conclude the same.

The article places the case in front of the public and hopefully will send the message to Ruby that the community is watching. I expect good work from his office.

22. Delays

The case is delayed once again! The next year brought both Alba and Esmeralda to courtroom number 13 several times each.

The cycle was roughly every two and a half months. They would usually be scheduled a few days apart from each other.

Margaret would usually find out through a meeting with Esmeralda, or Sean Justice would somehow find out and contact her. We didn't have much time to prepare or react to the news of the pending court date. Post the information on Facebook and call a couple of friends.

In what we would eventually call 'the fire drill' Margaret would go to the Ventura County courthouse at times with a few friends who had also accompanied her to visit Alba or Esmeralda in the Todd Road jail.

Arriving before the 8:30 in the morning start up time, she would sit and wait. Eventually, officers would escort either of the ladies into the cell to the side of the courtroom. They would exchange smiles and simple waves, and then the full attention from all would be directed to the proceedings.

Mr. Tim Ruby does not seem to be pleased that Margaret is in the room. At times he shows his displeasure with his expressions. He no longer speaks to Margaret. She and I would joke about what Mr. Ruby's reaction would be like once he sees me in the room.

Interestingly, where Tim Ruby told me that he didn't want me to talk with his client, he seemed to have gotten the message that Margaret was part of Alba's life. He had even criticized me as being a liar about what he had said about Alba being guilty but stopped short of saying the same about Margaret.

One by one, the trails of both ladies would be continued to another date. This happened some seven or eight times. Once the prosecution of Alba asked for the delay, but it was usually Mr. Tim Ruby who asked and was granted a continuation.

We had high expectations for the trial of Esmeralda. Her attorney had been to the MICOP conference and had consulted with professors from UCLA and other institutes about the cultural aspects of Mixteco life that could be used in court. The public defender, Ada Alberich would talk with Margaret while waiting for the judge to come to her case. We looked forward to the showing of how the two defense cases would contrast.

It wasn't to be. Ada Alberich, the public defender for Esmeralda Martínez, retired! We had little notice and no explanation. I can only hope that it isn't for health reasons. Another attorney is assigned. A pleasant gentleman, he has to start almost from scratch in learning the case and the cultural norms that Esmeralda had lived by.

Having been told by Tim Ruby not to speak to his client, my first natural response is to defy his demand and test him. Alba had isolated herself almost completely with her family taking the two visits a week. Even if I wanted to test Mr. Ruby, physically I would have to beat Alba's family to the visitor's center at the jail. And even if I wanted to beat the family in seeing Alba, she would probably not be interested in speaking with me.

I did visit Esmeralda two more times. The first was pleasant and encouraging in that Esmeralda seemed to be optimistic and living in the real world with her circumstances. Both times I go with Margaret who had become a regular.

I stand back from the booth at the beginning, allowing the two ladies to speak, only semi privately in that I can hear everything Margaret says clearly. A woman with a four-year-old comes up to me from the open visitor's section and asks if I am the father of David O'Leary. "Yes." I am a bit surprised.

"I worked with your son in the phone banks for CAUSE during the last election." The mother tells me that I have a very respectful and intelligent son.

"Thank you." Still surprised to meet someone who knows my son or anything about me here.

"You are a school board member, right?"

"Yes. For the Oxnard School District."

"Thank you for what you do."

I didn't want to ask, but she then tells me that she is visiting her daughter who got in a fight. It must have been more than just a fight because she was here her a couple of months according to the mother.

It is my turn to speak with Esmeralda. She tells us of her Uncle who lives in Texas. She hadn't contacted him since well before her arrest and her son died. She expected that he had no idea of the serious problems she is facing. She asks us to contact him and gives the name and telephone number. I later call. The gentleman didn't know about what had happened. He is interested in coming, but shortly after that, we hear about engine problems with his pickup truck. That is the last I hear of him.

Several months later I go with Margaret again to visit Esmeralda. This time I am completely thrown off guard. Esmeralda is scared to death to see me and shakes her finger as she starts talking to Margaret over the phone.

"She does not want to talk with you, Denis," Margaret says in a surprised and puzzled voice.

"Why?" Margaret asks Esmeralda with an exaggerated voice.

I don't know what to say, but I see the fear of God in Esmeralda's eyes. I walk away from the window and stand some ten feet back, leaning on the concrete wall.

I can still see Esmeralda, and she seems to calm down a bit as Margaret changes the subject from why she is reacting this way to everyday chit chat.

I look at the two talking and think about how I am surprised and think about how I could be offended. I think about leaving, but decide to stay. I talk a bit with an elderly gentleman who has a young three or four-year-old hanging on to his hand. He is waiting to see another grandson who is in jail for a year. The man with a cane tells me how he has taken over caring for the boys because his son and daughter-in-law have taken off.

The man is eighty-three years of age and is trying very hard to keep up with the little one. Not made any easier with a bad hip and back.

He also recognizes me from the school board and asks me my opinion about preschool. It is amazing the histories that our students bring to school with them. I wish that the teachers would know these details when they look into the eyes of the students on the first day of class. Perhaps we could make greater strides to educate the child. It truly does take a village to raise a child. Unfortunately, we too often separate education from social services. School Boards and City Hall should be addressing the same issues at the same time.

When Esmeralda ends her time with Margaret, Esmeralda places her hands together as in prayer and nods at me with a smile on her face. I do the same and Esmeralda smiles and turns to leave her booth.

We are shocked about what happened, and Margaret and I talk about it as we walk down the long hallway from the visiting booths. Esmeralda had acted this way once before when Margaret had brought an acquaintance with her who was also Mixteco. The college graduate of sociology had hoped to be able to speak in Mixteco with her but did not get the chance.

We can only come up with that Alba had passed on her fears of me as related to her from Tim Ruby. I am sure that someone has come up with that I am the cause of Alba still being in jail.

February 22, 2015

Viviana and I are invited to the ex-mayor of Oxnard, Manny Lopez's house to meet with civil rights leader Dolores Huerta. Manny and his wife Irma often have large gatherings with regional politicians at their large house.

Dolores Huerta is invited to give some words about her support for the candidacy of Hillary Clinton for President. I know that there will be many people coming to see Dolores, but I hold out some hope to ask her about possibly speaking publically about her support for Alba and Esmeralda.

Margaret is out of town, and couldn't make the gathering, but she agreed that I try to bring up the subject if I could.

At the end of the mariachi music and speeches from the

organizers of the event along with Dolores had ended I got a chance to sit down and talk with my wife, Viviana and Lori de Leon, daughter of Dolores. I bring up the cases, and she remembers that I had written a letter to them about the complex cases.

Dolores had been taking photos with guests and then came into the kitchen area of the house. Others followed her and offered some of the tamales that had been put aside for her. She sat down with Lori and me only to be asked several questions by others. Finally, Lori was about to mention our conversation.

Dolores is a good friend. I had worked with her several times over the years, including with two labor contract negotiations here in Oxnard. We became good friends when we were on the edge of a strawberry field speaking with fieldworkers. A car approached us on the same berm and was speeding up. The workers ran into the rows of strawberries. Dolores and I stood our ground. The driver hit the brakes and fish tailed to a stop just feet before hitting us. He took off, and we continued talking with the workers.

I told Dolores later that the headlines would have read, "Civil rights leader Dolores Huerta and another guy hit by car." We became good friends after that.

Our paths had crossed many times in Los Angeles and most notably in Milwaukee. At the national LULAC convention, most people knew that we were friends. I was asked to accompany Dolores for her three-day stay. She drove me physically and mentally exhausted. In her late seventies at the time, I had a hard time keeping up with her.

"I remember the case," Dolores tells me. "Are they still waiting for trial?"

"Yes. And a lot has happened."

"No one else would take this on. You are fearless!" Dolores tells me. "Denis is fearless!" she says louder for others away from the table to hear.

My wife smiles, "I wish he would stop sometimes." "He never will." Dolores answers.

Two months later I get a message from Lori to contact the Dolores Huerta Foundation and ask for the scheduler. Dolores is interested in coming to Ventura to have a press conference in support of Alba and Esmeralda.

Shortly it gets more interesting. Margaret has been taking more and more people to visit Esmeralda in the jail. Mainly religious people have gone to visit or have gotten into the conversation. Margaret invites me to a convent of some 20 retired nuns who at least some are interested in participating in the support of the ladies.

I joke with Margaret that I am a little afraid in that the last time I sat down with a Catholic nun, my knuckles were swatted.

Writing the letter to the Dolores Huerta Foundation, I try to keep the story short. I want to tell about the positive and the negative. It is Dolores decision if she wants to lend her name in defense of Alba and Esmeralda. I wait for an answer.

Later, the handler tells me that the meeting was going to be difficult. Dolores losses her oldest daughter and shortly after her brother. I still know that we have her support.

23. Culture and the shadow people

Santiago Ventura Morales was accused and convicted of murdering Santiago Ramirez Gomez, a fellow farm worker in 1986. Ruben had been stabbed twice in the chest and left to die in a strawberry field. The conviction was due to a misunderstanding on the lack of eye contact during questioning and the prosecution's use of fabricated evidence, including the use of a fake murder weapon. Only one witness, an undocumented person from Mexico, testified that Morales was the killer. The witness, Epifanio Bautista Lopez, first testified that he saw nothing, but changed his testimony after he was taken into the district attorney's office during a recess at the trial. Under cross-examination, Lopez then said that he was afraid of what might happen to him if he did not testify the way the prosecutor wanted him to testify.

Several days after the trial, four jurors, David Ralls, Patricia Lee, Sherien Jaeger, and Glorya Oppitz told the defense counsel, Lane Borg, that they had changed their minds about their jury votes and asked if they could do anything about it. The four were told that a verdict cannot be thrown out simply because jurors change their minds.

Three of these jurors formed a support group for Morales. They visited him in jail, sent him money, and wrote letters to the parole board asking for his release.

Morales's defense was hampered because Morales, a Mexican immigrant, did not speak English or Spanish, but spoke

Mixteco. The judge assigned him a Spanish interpreter. The interpreter tried to tell the judge that he could not communicate with Morales, but the judge refused to accept the idea that a Mexican defendant could not speak Spanish. Portland Oregonian newspaper columnist Phil Stanford wrote many columns outlining Morales's innocence. The Oregon Attorney General opposed Morales's petition for relief because his innocence was not a legal basis to overturn his conviction and release him. Four years after Morales's conviction, his lawyer established that another farm worker, Herminio Luna Hernandez, was the actual killer.

On January 4, 1991, the conviction was set aside due to the testimony of the new witnesses and the debunking of the forensic testimony, and because Morales had been denied his constitutional right to testify.

Morales was released from prison on January 9, 1991. Oregon Gov. Neil Goldschmidt pardoned Morales shortly after that, and the charges were dismissed.

Mexican immigrant sues after newborn seized by Mississippi agency

Mercury News wire services

03/12/2014

JACKSON, Miss. (AP)—A federal judge says a Mexican woman can proceed with a lawsuit against Mississippi's welfare agency and others accusing them of trying to wrest away a newborn girl she delivered while in the U.S. illegally.

No trial date has been set for the lawsuit, which the Southern Poverty Law Center filed on behalf of Cirila Baltazar Cruz in 2010.

The SPLC said Cruz—who spoke no English and little

Spanish—delivered her baby in November 2008 at Mississippi's Singing River Hospital in Pascagoula. Two days after the birth, the infant was taken from Cruz when the Mississippi Department of Human Services deemed the woman unfit, according to the lawsuit.

Cruz—who also could not read or write—had been interviewed by a hospital interpreter soon after giving birth. The interpreter spoke Spanish but not Chatino, a dialect indigenous to Cruz's native Oaxaca region of rural Mexico, the group's lawsuit alleges.

After talking with Cruz, the interpreter told one of the immigrant's relatives that Cruz was trading sex for housing and wanted to give the child up for adoption, according to the lawsuit. Cruz said in court papers that she tried to explain to the interpreter that she worked in a Chinese restaurant and lived in an apartment.

The SPLC argued in the lawsuit that the defendants deliberately failed to provide adequate language interpretation to communicate with Cruz, thus depriving her of the right to be heard and to challenge the allegations made against her.

Cruz was separated from her daughter for a year before her child was returned to her in 2010 after the intervention of the SPLC, a nonprofit U.S. civil rights organization that said it presses for immigrant justice, battles hate and extremism and helps children at risk.

Cruz and her daughter have since returned to Mexico.

In a ruling this week, U.S. District Judge Henry T. Wingate denied the immunity claims of two employees of the Pascagoula hospital and a caseworker with the Mississippi Department of

Human Services. Those defendants had sought immunity for the lawsuit under Mississippi's Tort Claims Act.

The lawsuit names the department, which is Mississippi's welfare agency, along with Singing River Health System and others. It seeks monetary damages and alleges the state officials conspired to deny Cruz and her child their constitutional rights to family integrity.

The MDHS has declined comment on the case. Singing River has said it followed proper procedures. The attorney general's office did not immediately respond to a message left by The Associated Press.

SPLC staff attorney Michelle Lapointe said in a statement Wednesday that Cruz will have her day in court.

She lauded the judge for letting the lawsuit proceed.

"This decision means that state officials cannot violate with impunity a mother's constitutional right to raise her child. Immigrant parents—like all parents—have the right to keep their families together. Fabricating charges against a mother to separate her from her child is egregious," Lapointe said.

24. Fast cars, women and Jesus

Margaret calls me in May 2015 to tell me that Esmeralda's brother was now living in Oxnard and that he and Margaret had gone together to the jail to speak with Esmeralda.

Despite the location, the encounter was a happy moment for both brother and sister. The 40-minute visit went by fast, and Margaret stayed out of the way.

A revelation came to Margaret from the brother that he had spotted Esmeralda's husband back in Oxnard. A week later Margaret mentioned the name "Ricardo Luna" to Esmeralda to get hand gestures and a shacking of the head by Esmeralda. Apparently, this was an unspoken name that she did not want mentioned on the tapes from visits in the Todd Road Jail.

Later in the evening, Margaret calls me.

"Denis, I think Esmeralda's husband has returned to Oxnard."

"Really? How do you know?"

"Esmeralda's brother mentioned this to me. He is on Facebook bragging about his nice car and women he hangs around with."

I punched in the name, and a Ricardo Luna came up from Oaxaca, Mexico now living in Oxnard. Besides the nice car, I could see several religious posts about Christ and following the message of Christ.

I also noticed that a local relative of this Ricardo Luna was a contact, or "friend" of mine on Facebook, a Mixteco university student I know. Three degrees of separation.

I call Margaret up the next morning to talk about the situation.

"I think we need to go to the police."

"Probably. Esmeralda seems to have wanted to protect him."

"The *telenovela* situation where the woman would even go to jail to protect her man and show her devotion." I don't know if this is truly the case, but the situation lends itself to several Mexican telenovelas I had seen over the years.

"Who should we call?"

"I think we need to go to the Oxnard Police Department. They are the ones who investigated the death."

"Do you know who would be involved in this case?"

"No. But we can bring the information up, and I'm sure that they would direct it to the right person."

It was a Saturday morning that we had the conversation, and Monday was Memorial Day. We decide to get together at 4:00 on Tuesday, in person and the Oxnard Police Department Headquarters.

Outside the station, I see several groups of about three or four uniformed police officers walking out of the main entrance of the headquarters and go to the corner. They seem to all go in the same direction. Tuesday afternoon: City Council meeting across the street at the City Hall. Oxnard has been rocked with the long suspected news that the budget is deep into the red. Now with a new City Manager and some time we know that the city will have to cut at least eleven million dollars and borrow sixteen million dollars almost immediately to survive in the short term.

The police officers are going to ask for no cuts from law enforcement. Jaime Tapia recognizes me waiting for Margaret to arrive outside the door. He is the Community Affairs Manager for the Oxnard Police Department.

"What brings you here?"

"I'm waiting for Margaret." She is on the Community Relations Commission for the city.

"Oh yes. Can I help you with anything?"

I think for a moment. "Yes. We want to speak to someone about a case we have been involved with for some time. We have some new information that we came about and want to pass it on. Who should we ask for?"

Jaime Tapia seems to know the case from conversations in the past with Margaret. "Is it the woman in jail for murder?"

"Yes. The one who lost her 11-month old son." The Oxnard Police Department worked on this case. Alba's case was out of the city and handled by the County's Sheriff Department.

"What happened?"

"We found out that the husband who took off before he could be questioned three or four years ago has returned to Oxnard."

"Interesting. How long ago has the case been open?"

"Esmeralda has been at the Todd Road Jail for three and a half years now."

"She is still waiting for a trial?"

"Yep. It's been a while."

"That's not surprising."

I wanted not to attract too much attention. Viviana is already very concerned that I, her or our sons might be in danger if it is found out that I helped pass on this information. Here I am, outside the Police Headquarters almost on the sidewalk next to the street talking about this with people walking by us.

"You should ask for Sargent Julie Raintree. She is in charge of family crimes and child crimes." Jaime Tapia pulls out one of his cards and writes her name and title on the back.

"She may not be in, but she would be the person in charge of that case."

Margaret comes up to us and says hi to Miguel. I explain to Margaret that I have a name to ask for.

"We knew that we may just give our information on to someone who could pass it on to the appropriate person. Now we have a person to start with."

Miguel went on his way to City Hall, and Margaret and I walk into the police station. Upstairs I walk to the receptionist behind thick glass. Four people are sitting in the waiting section of the small area, and I ask for Sargent Julie Raintree.

"Do you have an appointment?"

"No, Jaime Tapia gave us her name. We have some information on an old case that is of interest." I was still hoping to be somewhat discrete in public about calling out this name.

"Are you an attorney?"

"No." Here it comes I thought, what church do you belong to? Didn't happen!

"What is the case?"

We wind up not only explaining that case so she can look it up and give us a case number but telling her through the thin slot at the bottom of the thick glass the name of the person who we think should be questioned. So much for being discrete.

"Sargent Raintree is not available at the moment. The officer you should talk to is interviewing someone at the moment. Would you want to leave the information with me or would you want to wait?"

"We can wait."

"She is a very busy person, and you may want to make an appointment to talk to her in the future."

I look at Margaret who reads my mind. "I am retired, but Denis works and is very busy as well." "We will wait," I say.

We sit down next to each other and wait. In the

hour and a half, people have come and gone. They close the front desk at 6:00 and we are coming up on that time.

Margaret and I talk about police in general. I mention how my sons talk about how they think that I am anti-police because I voted against a police store front at one of the elementary schools in my district.

Margaret gets a phone call and talks to a person who apparently had gone to speak with Esmeralda and Alba along with her in the past.

"Yes, we are in the Oxnard Police headquarters. I'm her with Denis O'Leary. Do you know him?"

Margaret now starts telling her friend about why we are at the police station. I was truly hoping to be a bit more discrete.

"Yes, Denis O'Leary." Then she pauses. This is where it isn't best to only listen in on one side of the conversation.

"He's been chasing woman and talking about fast cars."

"What?" I look at Margaret with a grin on my face.

"No. I'm talking about Ricardo Luna. Margaret laughs and explains to her friend what is happening.

"That's how rumors get started," I say, and we both enjoyed the joke.

An hour and a half pass before we are approached.

"I was told that I can help you."

I am standing face to face with a woman with street cloths and no badge.

"Who are you?" I ask. She doesn't seem pleased that I ask.

"I am Sargent Julie Raintree."

"Oh yes. We have information about a person who we believe is involved in a case with a child's death."

"Didn't we make an arrest in that case?"

"Yes. Esmeralda Martinez is awaiting trial still. We have spoken to her several times."

"How long ago was this case?"

"About three and a half years ago."

"Well, if we made the arrest and she has been in jail that long that case is pretty much finished. She's guilty."

Oxnard's finest. We are standing in the hallway, and she is arguing that we are wasting her time.

"We are very busy and have only two people to work on all the cases in Oxnard. How did you get involved in this case?"

"The Mexican Consulate asked me to look into this case. They think that Esmeralda is innocent."

"The Mexican Consulate is usually wrong."

Margaret takes a step forward, "I have been seeing Esmeralda every week for more than a year. I think that she is innocent."

146

"I got involved in two cases after the Sheriff's Department and the Mexican consulate asked if I could help. I even solved a Geneva Convention violation after I got Sheriff Chuck Smith together with the Consulate. I asked Margaret to see the ladies because I thought that they would be more interested in speaking with an elderly woman than me."

"Did you hear what he said?" Sargent Raintree pointed at me while smiling at Margaret.

I got her attention. Wrong subject, but I got her attention.

"That's O.K. I'm 75. I could be his mother." Margaret seemed not to mind what Raintree took as a slip.

"We are asking that you check the files and see if this man was a person of interest."

"I can't share any of the information with you."

"We know that. This man is the husband of Esmeralda Martinez. He fled just after his child died. We think that he may have done it. Can you check it out?"

She pulls a business card out and asks the spelling of the name. We are done. A police officer walks by, and she attracts herself to him, and she turns and walks towards another door with him.

"Check out his Facebook page. It may help." We are done. I guess.

"Who knows if they will do anything?" I say.

"At least we can sleep knowing that we passed on the name."

"Yeah, the name of a person we think may be a baby killer who the police don't seem to be interested in because if they made an arrest, the case must be solved."

It is 6:30 by now. I walk Margaret to her car across the street and go to mine. We go home.

25. The Donald

June 14, 2015

Donald Trump announced from the Trump Tower in New York City that he is running for President of the United States. He will be one on a couple of dozen to announce his or her candidacy for the highest office in the United States.

Trump is a person who seems to have some star power for buying and selling properties. He has gone bankrupt and risen from the ashes several times. A character on a reality TV show, Trump plays himself as a judge to different personalities trying to impress him with their business prowess. As he makes his entrance, I'm sure that most America see this apparent announcement that he will run for President as a publicity stunt. It is also said that the people who gathered for the press announcement were paid $50 each to wear shirts and hold signs. The small crowd disperses before Trump even leaves the podium.

I see two things that stand out from Mr. Trump's announcement and that of his competitors at the time for the office. He got everyone's attention. The land speculator turned reality show entertainer hit the note of anti-immigration, anti-Mexican and rose almost immediately in the Republican Party polls because he was said to be saying what many were thinking but not saying.

TRUMP: "Wow. Whoa. That is some group of people. Thousands.

So nice, thank you very much. That's nice. Thank you. It's great to be at Trump Tower. It's great to be in a wonderful city, New York. And it's an honor to have everybody here. This is beyond anybody's expectations.

There's been no crowd like this.

And, I can tell, some of the candidates, they went in. They didn't know the air-conditioner didn't work. They sweated like dogs."

(LAUGHTER)

"They didn't know the room was too big because they didn't have anybody there. How are they going to beat ISIS? I don't think it's gonna happen."

(APPLAUSE)

"Our country is in serious trouble. We don't have victories anymore. We used to have victories, but we don't have them. When was the last time anybody saw us beating, let's say, China in a trade deal? They kill us. I beat China all the time. All the time."

(APPLAUSE)

AUDIENCE MEMBER: "We want Trump. We want Trump."

TRUMP: "When did we beat Japan at anything? They send their cars over by the millions, and what do we do? When was the last time you saw a Chevrolet in Tokyo?

It doesn't exist, folks. They beat us all the time.

When do we beat Mexico at the border? They're laughing at us, at our stupidity. And now they are beating us economically. They are not our friend, believe me. But they're killing us economically.

The U.S. has become a dumping ground for everybody else's problems."

(APPLAUSE)

"Thank you. It's true, and these are the best and the finest. When Mexico sends its people, they're not sending their best. They're not sending you. They're not sending you. They're sending people that have lots of problems, and they're bringing those problems with us. They're bringing drugs. They're bringing crime. They're rapists. And some, I assume, are good people.

But I speak to border guards, and they tell us what we're getting. And it only makes common sense. It only makes common sense. They're sending us not the right people.

It's coming from more than Mexico. It's coming from all over South and Latin America, and it's coming probably—probably—from the Middle East. But we don't know. Because we have no protection and we have no competence, we don't know what's happening. And it's got to stop, and it's got to stop fast."

(APPLAUSE)

TRUMP: "Islamic terrorism is eating up large portions of the Middle East. They've become rich. I'm in competition with them.

They just built a hotel in Syria. Can you believe this? They built a hotel. When I have to build a hotel, I pay interest. They don't have to pay interest, because they took the oil that, when we left Iraq, I said we should've taken.

So now ISIS has the oil, and what they don't have, Iran has. And in 19—and I will tell you this, and I said it very strongly, years ago, I said—and I love the military, and I want to have the strongest military that we've ever had, and we need it more now than ever. But I said, "Don't hit Iraq," because you're going to destabilize the Middle East totally. Iran is going to take over the Middle East, Iran and somebody else will get the oil, and it turned out that Iran is now taking over Iraq. Think of it. Iran is taking over Iraq, and they're taking it over big league.

We spent $2 trillion in Iraq, $2 trillion. We lost thousands of lives, thousands in Iraq. We have wounded soldiers, who I love, I love—they're great—all over the place, thousands and thousands of wounded soldiers.

And we have nothing. We can't even go there. We have nothing. And every time we give Iraq equipment, the first time a bullet goes off in the air, they leave it.

Last week, I read 2,300 Humvees—these are big vehicles— were left behind for the enemy. 2,000? You would say maybe two, maybe four? 2,300 sophisticated vehicles, they ran, and the enemy took them."

AUDIENCE MEMBER: "We need Trump now."

TRUMP: "You're right."

(APPLAUSE)

AUDIENCE MEMBER: "We need Trump now."

TRUMP: "Last quarter, it was just announced our gross domestic product—a sign of strength, right? But not for us. It was below zero. Whoever heard of this? It's never below zero."

As the lightening bolt flashed in the networks, activists and Mexicans in all parts of the United States reeled. Drug dealers? Rapists?

The vast majority of "Mexicans" are good, law abiding persons. I have met good people. Medal of Valor recipients, veterans, educated professionals, hard workers who quietly work close to the earth.

Yes, every segment of every society have for the loss of a better word, bad people. Now, the TV character has legitimized himself as a possible President of the United States in the eyes of many!

He would later spew off other hatful thoughts that only seem to increase his popularity. Even here in Oxnard, I have heard these thoughts repeated more openly. Trump would later call his followers "the silent majority" calling back to President Richard Nixon's description of those who brought him to office.

I would not want to be an accused murderer of Mexican heritage awaiting trial with this hateful rhetoric that seems to have hit a popular ear in our country. Alba!

26. Courtroom Thirteenth and the Nun

July 2, 2015, Thursday 8:30 in the morning at the Ventura County Courthouse, Court #13.

I am on summer vacation from school. A court date has come, and I am interested in seeing first-hand what goes on in Court 13.

I am happily surprised the night before that Viviana is not only off, but interested in attending the court hearing. She says what I was thinking, "She will only be told that the case will be delayed again."

"Yes, probably." I take time trying to remember the number of times the case has been presented to the court and how I told Margaret that I couldn't make it in the morning because of my work. The plan was always to run over to Ventura after school got out at 3:30 to catch the last hour or so.

We arrive to the County Building, empty our pockets and go through the metal detectors and head down the hall. Doors to courtrooms on one side and a glass wall looking out at the fountain under construction in the central plaza on the other.

I thought I had been to Court #13 before, but as I enter, I realize that I am wrong. I expected the ceremonial looking court room. Large rug tapestry with the state seal hanging on the wall behind the judge's bench facing the attorneys' tables, bar and the wood church like pews for the public.

Court room 13 is much smaller. The judge is facing a cage where the accused sit on two rows of benches with no backing. The cage is white flat metal strips with rectangular openings about two inches by four inches. The metal strips are also about a quarter inch thick and an inch deep. Only at the corner of the cage towards the public are the metal strips lined up to see the prisoners inside.

A muscular officer with a crew cut is at a podium between the door entering the room and the cage behind him. He appears to be the person I would want in a setting such as this to protect sanity if not physical threat in the crowded courtroom. This guard would soon set the rules for the room. An American flag flat on the wall to his side, a fist size Marine Corps insignia pinned in the middle of the flag.

I sit down on one of the metal rounded top benches for the public. As like for the prisoners, no back support. I had to balance myself as not to slip off. Nothing could be placed and left on these benches because it would be surly fall off.

The bar separated the public section that could hold maybe forty people if we sit closely and hold our breath.

About three feet between the benches from each other and the bar, one has to scoot back, move your knees to one side or stand up and tuck your stomach in to let another person pass.

About a dozen attorneys are standing on the other side of the bar. Various shades of blue, black and gray suits and business outfits for the men and woman flow back and forth as they seem to jockey for position. Papers or cardboard folders under most of the attorneys' arms. They would occasionally face the public area and call out a name.

I was waiting to see Margaret, but there is a mix of people, some waiting to hear their name and to find out what their next steps are and others who look like parents or wives of the men seated in the cage.

The red signs with white letters hanging high from the cage set the tone.

"Do not talk or communicate with prisoners in any way. Violators are subject to arrest per penal code section 4570 and will be removed from the courtroom."

"Look at the signs," I whisper to Viviana. "They are different."

The sign in Spanish read, "*¡Atención!*

Se prohibe que hable o que se

comunique con los presos. Según lo dispuesto en el art. 4570 del código penal quien lo haga podría ser arrestado."

No mention of being removed from the courtroom. Spanish speaking persons must think that arrest is the only option they face.

The guard yells out the instructions as well. He also states that we need to turn off our cell phones or turn them to vibrate. "Cell phones cannot be used in any way in the courtroom!" He paused, "No recordings, no photos!"

"No signals or gestures to the prisoners! No hats!"

I looked around and see fear. Respect for the rules, sadness for the situations the people find themselves in and fear treading into panic. A couple of mothers have their babies wrapped up in blankets and their arms. One woman is very pregnant.

Latino, Anglo, Asian and African-American. Babies, people in their twenties and others mature in their thirties, forties, fifties, and sixties.

Margaret enters the room. She comes with a woman who later would be introduced as Sister Gertrudes. I am thrilled! Finally, one of the Catholic Nuns that I had heard of and I am happy to know that is on our side.

Margaret wore her yellow t-shirt with the word "LOVE" and a heart in the center. Smaller lines above and below gave the name of Margaret's church. Sister Gertrudes, a retired Nun is not in habit but has on a thin white sweater over a simple floral blouse.

The public is whispering loudly to each other. Viviana and I are sitting in the second row watching the people coming in and out from the side door and the attorneys standing and walking around in front of us just on the other side of the bar. We can see the prisoners in orange long sleeve shirts and pants, but we cannot see Esmeralda. All seem to be men, and I imagine that Esmeralda is on the other side of the open door in the room feeding into the cage.

"Ladies and gentlemen, it's a really simple rule." The guard yells out. "You stop talking!"

I get up almost timidly and go to the guard at his podium desk to the side of the court, between the public entrance and the cage to his back. "Can I take written notes?" I ask, almost nervous that this ex US Marine and now correctional officer is going to break and put me in a choke hold.

"Yes, you can."

"Thank you. This is a first, and I want to follow the rules." I turned and walk back to Viviana to balance myself on the rounded bench. Margaret and Sister Gertrudes are sitting on a bench to the side of the group, backs to the wall.

"Attention, quiet, please. The honorable Judge Simpson is entering the court."

I am a bit surprised that nobody stands and Judge Samuel P. Simpson sits at his desk. Facing the cage and shifting to the podium for the attorneys, Judge Simpson goes through each of the prisoner's cases in a matter of 30 seconds to a minute. At times he would ask the attorney to comment, and a couple of prisoners were asked if they understand the instructions. Most if not all are continuations of a hearing date.

I must admit, I understand very little of what is going on, but am fixed on the words. Guilty or innocent, justice served or accusation in search of justice, this is real. This is peoples' lives being changed. Those behind the cage, those who are in the public section and those who are the victims who are not present, real life changing actions would change lives in what is being said.

People are coming and leaving as their case is spoken about between the judge and the attorneys. Margaret and Sister Gertrudes fill in the space next to Viviana as others had gotten up and left. We can whisper a greeting, and I learn the Sister's name.

"She is innocent." Sister Gertrudes said in a low voice.

"Yes."

"And Alba is innocent also." Sister Gertrudes seemed to need me to hear her say this. We are quiet listening for Esmeralda's case to come up.

"Esmeralda Martinez." The four of us sit at attention. We can see the mosaic of Esmeralda's face and black hair in the spaces open in the cage. I am impressed in how small Esmeralda is. The meetings in the prison were artificial, and she sat in an empty almost telephone booth size stall.

158

Now Esmeralda has others behind her, and the Spanish language interpreter as her Public Defender comes up to her from the outside of the white bars.

Almost immediately the judge and Esmeralda's Public Defender come to an agreement that a new date will bring her to this same court on August 8th. October 6th is also mentioned. The Public Defender asks the judge if he may speak to his client and the judge allows him to speak with the interpreter and Esmeralda. The judge takes the time to go through papers while the two are in conference with Esmeralda.

Esmeralda nods her head and talks back and forth with the lady who is translating what the taller Public Defender is saying. I take note that at one point the translator has her hand out at waist level, palm down and moving her hand side to side as if to say "kind of" or "more or less." I wish I could listen in to the conversation. I wouldn't want to have the years ahead in my life in the balance with an interpreter making gestures of "more or less" being the information I am getting.

Four or five minutes pass and Esmeralda turns and walks to the door at the wall in the back of the cage. Margaret is trying to wave or sit up. I can't tell if Esmeralda had seen us, but I wasn't going to try to get arrested. The four of us stand up, silently nod to each other and walk to the door leading to the hallway.

The hallway has people milling about. Talking in small groups, surly like us trying to recoup what had just happened or about to enter the courtroom. We are again introduced to Sister Gertrudes and now can talk. I ask Margaret if she knows why two dates were mentioned.

"I don't know. We will have to ask."

Viviana and Sister Gertrudes are getting to know each other a bit.

Margaret is happy to see Viviana. "I am glad that you were able to come."

"I wanted to see what Denis would be talking about."

"I told you that I had a surprise for you today," I tell Margaret.

"Sister, I am very happy to see you here," I say.

"Esmeralda needs our help. She is innocent. We need to be here for her."

"I'm glad to see you also because it answers all the questioned from my 'good' Christian friends who are appalled that we are supporting a baby killer."

"Oh, they don't know what they are talking about."

Margaret tells us that Sister Gertrudes has gone with her several times to the prison to speak with Esmeralda.

"That's great. Have you spoken to Alba also?"

"No. She is always with her family when we see her. Margaret has told me all about Alba's case too. She should also be freed. They are both innocent."

"Alba's case is harder," I tell the Sister.

"She is innocent."

"Denis is the one who introduced me to the two ladies. He had seen them and asked if I would like to meet Esmeralda and Alba." Margaret tells.

"I am not a woman. They needed the friendship of a woman who they could open up to better."

"I wish I spoke better Spanish." The three of us almost at the same time tell Margaret that she speaks just fine.

We are talking, and Margaret notices Esmeralda's attorney coming out into the hallway outside Court Thirteen. He is speaking to a client for several minutes not five feet from us.

Margaret gestures to the young looking attorney in the nice looking dark suit. He notices and asks Margaret if we would like to talk with him.

"Yes."

"I can for a few minutes, but give me a few minutes to finish up something here."

"Sure."

Margaret repeats to me of how impressed she has been with Attorney Kevin Taylor.

Introductions made, we learn that Taylor has dedicated most of his time on this one case. The Senior Deputy Public Defender, he inherited the Esmeralda case and tells us that he is hopeful that charges will be dropped.

Margaret and I jump on this in harmony, "With damages for being falsely arrested and held for close to four years."

"No, if charges are dropped there are no damages awarded."

I think that it may be better to go to trial then and win the case.

I introduce myself a bit more when Taylor asks how

I got involved in the case. After the story, I suggest that Esmeralda have a Mixteco translator instead of a Spanish translator.

"She speaks good Spanish, doesn't she?"

"Yes. It is basic, but if you were charged with murder, would you like to hear everything in your first or second language?" He nods.

"Besides, her cell mate also speaks Mixteco. What language do you think she uses most of the time?"

"I will look into it."

Margaret jumps into the conversation, "We have news for you."

"Oh?"

"We have found Esmeralda's husband!"

"You did? Where is he?"

"In Oxnard. He's all over Facebook. Esmeralda's brother spotted it. He's writing about how Jesus is protecting him and how he's driving around in fancy cars."

"Did you tell the police?"

"We did," I answer. They didn't seem to be too interested.

Margaret tells of the day that she and I waited in the Oxnard Police Headquarters to pass on the information.

"What did they say?" Taylor asks.

I look him in the eye, "The person in charge of family violence told us, 'She was arrested four years ago, she must be guilty.'" Silence.

"She couldn't tell us anything else in any case, but she looked at us like we were wasting her time. I don't know if they will look for him or not."

"Esmeralda wasn't married to him, was she?" Taylor asks.

"I don't know. He's her common law husband in any case." I say. Taylor nods again.

While ending the gathering in the hallway, Taylor changes the subject one last time. He wants us to know that Esmeralda doesn't want any media from us.

He seems to be directing this to me. "I don't think that it is necessary right now in any case," I tell him. "We'll wait to see what happens. Do no harm."

We all shake hands again, and Taylor has a brief conversation with Sister Gertrudes.

"Esmeralda is innocent." Sister Gertrudes reminds him. Taylor smiles and shakes her hand.

We see Kevin Taylor some five weeks later. Again in Court 13. This time he comes to Margaret and me sitting in the first row to say that he wants to talk with us later. My wife could not make this date, but Sister Teresa joins sister Gertrudes.

Esmeralda's appearance in front of the judge seems just as brief as the past appearances, but a couple of dates are said aloud.

'October 8' was mentioned almost as if it was more important that the September date mentioned.

"I think she has a court date," I whisper to Margaret.

"Oh?" Margaret says with some emphases.

"We need to talk with Taylor."

Outside Kevin, Taylor seems much more pleased to talk with us. He reminds us that he is dedicating most of his time to this one case.

"So, what is this October 8th date?" I ask.

"It's the drop dead date. The trial must start on or before October 8th." Margaret and I jump a little at hearing this.

"The only way that it can start after the eighth is if one of the attorneys are on an active case that is still in court. Then Esmeralda's case will start the day after the other case ends."

We can see the end in sight. Taylor also tells us that

Esmeralda has been in jail for just short of the record for a person without a trial charged for this kind of case.

"Not a record we want to break," answers Margaret.

Taylor then breaks the unexpected to us. "We located Esmeralda's husband."

"You did? Is he under arrest?"

"No. We spoke to him." Taylor paused as to look at our reactions. "Believe it or not, he said some things that help Esmeralda."

I later tell Viviana at home when I am recapping the day that the judge should have everyone turn their backs on Esmeralda and her husband so she could kick the shit out of him. Just five minutes, nobody would mind.

"He should serve four years in jail just because." We both laughed. The good news was that he seemed to have helped his wife. After leaving his wife and home the day that his infant son died, leaving his wife to suffer by herself, to answer the questions of the police and be in jail for four years, he now said something that could help! There is crime, and there is being a coward. The father of this boy left his wife to fend for herself in jail while he celebrated according to his Facebook posts that Jesus loved him while driving a nice car and bragging about his women.

27. Jury Duty

My son walks into the house with the mail in his hand. Without opening one of the letters he already knows what one is. "Dad! You have jury duty!

"Oh great!" I say sarcastically.

It seems that the Court has my name on their calendar. Every twelve months: jury duty. I am not always called, but a year ago I was the last person to be excused from the jury pool before a civil trial jury was sat. It saved me two weeks of being away from the classroom. It also came with a grown from the members who I sat with who realized that they would be listening to the case for the next two weeks.

Margaret, Viviana, and friends who know about the two ladies would joke about me or someone in the mix being called for Alba's or Esmeralda's case. "No! It couldn't happen." We would say to each other.

Two groups of jurors were called, and I am still in the large seating area at the Ventura County Government Center. The third group am called, "Denis O'Leary."

"Present."

I walk into court 23 with about forty other people. On the other side of the bar are two tables, each with a man in suit standing as we enter and take our seats. Next, to the younger attorney, a short Latino man stands, long sleeve shirt (a little large) and a tie hanging from his neck. The defendant.

I realize that the man is out of place and as the day goes on I see why. The jury pool of peers are mainly white citizens in their forties or fifties.

As the day goes on, I am still seated in the public section as the two attorneys question eighteen persons. The defendant in charged with attempted murder. We are told that it was not with a gun.

One by one, jurors are excused and replaced with a member in the gallery. The pool is for the most part willing to sit on the expected week-long trial. One woman has wedding plans and is told that she will be able to celebrate the wedding. One woman is the City Manager of Carpentaria; she eventually sits on the jury for the trial.

The defendant sits with white head phones, and two women take turns every hour or so sitting next to him and speaking into a small electronic box with a wire going below the table.

The fact that the defendant needs translation becomes a concern with the two attorneys. One of the attorneys ask one white male juror if having the translation would make him feel any more different about the defendant.

"Yes. He should speak English. He is illegal, and he should go back to Mexico."

The jurors did not receive any information about the defendant's legal status. The appearance was overwhelming for this juror. Yes, the man could have been trying to get out of being on the jury, but the all American, patriotic white man seemed to know a few code words better than most. He eventually was excused.

Language became the theme of the day. The judge stated that one juror who was of Cuban decent and had moved to

Ventura County from Miami, Florida, less than a year ago could only consider the testimony in English. She was asked if she could ignore the first person testimony in Spanish during the trial.

"It would be difficult. Spanish is my first language. I would have a hard time ignoring the words."

Another man who looked Latino was asked the same. "I'm fluent in Spanglish." All laughed.

I came home to the message that Esmeralda would be in Court Thirteen again the next morning. I laughed that I missed possibly being present on her jury pool by one day. I went to Court Thirteen in the morning and standing outside in the hallway with my Juror badge I imagined that people might look and wonder why I was there.

I met with Margaret and Sister Gertrudes and entered when the court doors opened. The same bustle as always. Attorney calling out names of people to approach the bar. A group of prisoners inside the white cage off to the side.

I could only stay a bit because I had to report to my Court at 9:00. I did not see Esmeralda but was told later that the appearance was just another procedure and her date was still on line for the first days of October.

Entering the second day of jury selection all are in there place again. A couple of jurors are excused almost immediately, and I am called to take a seat. Again, language seems to be an issue, and the Judge makes a clarification from what he said yesterday. The jurors were not to disregard the testimony in the first language of those speaking but were only to weigh in if the juror believed that somehow the translation was off. We are now told that it would be expected that we write our concern on paper and hand it to the bailiff if we hear a difference between the testimony in Spanish and the translation in English.

One by one the two attorneys ask the jurors how they would feel if X was a factor.

The jurors are given a paper to consider before being questioned.

"Ventura County Superior Court

Jury Panel Questionnaire

Eight Questions

1.   Have you or any of your close friends or relatives had any connection with the court system or law enforcement?

2.   Have you or any of your close friends or relatives ever been a victim of a crime?

3.   Have you or any of your close friends or relatives ever been arrested for any crime more serious than a minor traffic offense, or otherwise, had some distressing contact with law enforcement or the court system?

4.   Have you ever been a witness to a crime being committed or a witness in any courtroom proceeding?

5.   Do you belong to any group or organization, which takes a definite legal position on issues that may be involved here?

6.   Is there any reason why you would be reluctant to render a verdict?

7.   Do you have anything on your mind that would make it difficult for you to be fair to both sides in this case, including any strong feelings about the particular crime with which the defendant charged?

8.   Is there any reason why you should not be a juror in this case?"

I am eventually called to fill in the seat of an excused possible juror. I wait my turn to be interviewed. I have a few items that I want to mention from the list I still have in my hand.

The five new potential jurors are asked if we know or recognize any of the persons in the court. I raise my hand.

The judge asks, "Who do you know."

"I recognize the defense attorney."

"Where do you know him from?"

"I have been in Court Thirteen a few times, and I'm sure that I have seen him. Maybe in other places also. He has a face one remembers."

A laugh comes out in the court room.

"But you don't know him personally?"

"No."

"Can you be impartial?"

"Yes."

They start with the process of questioning the new potential jurors.

My turn comes up. "Denis O'Leary. I have lived in Ventura County for twenty years. I am a teacher and elected School Board Trustee for the Oxnard School District. Married, three sons ages 18, 19 and 24." I know what to say from the poster asking these questions taped to the white board.

The prosecuting attorney, a short man, Anglo in his mid-fifties, well-groomed asks if I can be impartial.

"Yes, I believe so."

"Do you have any items from the list that we should know about?"

"Yes, one, two, four and five," I say as I am looking down at the marks I made on the paper.

"Tell us about number one."

"I belong to a few organizations that are involved in civil rights. I have met attorneys on many occasions. I even once helped investigate wrong doing in the District Attorney's office for the League of United Latin American Citizens together with the NAACP." The court staff seem to all have a big grin on their face when I say this.

"Who do you know?"

"No relatives, but I have had interaction with the DA, Jack Stanton, Paul Manter, Oxnard Police Chief Handen and several officers. Probably the only person I have known well over many years is Public Defender Felipe Sesto."

The judge seems interested. "Well, you seem to know some people from all sides. Will any of this stop you from being fair?"

"No."

"What groups are you associated with?"

"The League of United Latin American Citizens, and the ACLU."

"And what do you do in these groups?"

"I was the District Director of LULAC at one time. I would be called to investigate concerns of civil rights."

"Would you be able to be fair and consider all the evidence presented before you make a decision?"

"Yes, I try to find out what the truth is."

"Tell us about number four."

I look at my paper in hand. "I am a possible witness in a murder trial that might be coming soon."

"Did you witness the murder?"

"No, I was first contacted by the Sheriff's Department to help locate the person and later by the Mexican Consulate to help."

I can tell that the judge is at the edge of his seat. "What is the person's name?"

"Would it be appropriate to say the name in this court?"

He pauses for a moment. "Yes, you can say it."

"Alba Flores Zapata."

"Oh yes. I know that case."

The defense attorney comes up. "So you say I'm ugly."

I sit up a bit thinking, what do I say now. There is laughter in the courtroom.

"No. You have a face that you can remember."

"What were you doing in Court 13?"

"I've been there a few times. I even went there today for a bit to see a person I have been advocating for."

"Can you be fair?"

"Yes, I believe so."

The attorney turns to walk back to his bench. "That will be all."

"By the way," I say. He turns. "I am fluent in Spanish."

"You are?"

"*No tengo la cara para hablar español.*" I say in a low voice. There is some laughter again.

"What did you say?"

"I don't have the face to be speaking Spanish?"

"Are you fluent?"

"I am a bilingual teacher and am on Spanish radio quite a lot."

The judge steps into the conversation.

"Do you understand the guidelines I spoke about?"

"Yes. I only have one concern."

"What's that?"

"I would hope that if a translation is off that, it would be addressed somewhat fast." "Yes, I agree," he says.

The attorneys and judge now turn their attention to the last new person to be questioned from this group.

The attorneys follow by taking turns in dismissing jurors. I am immediately asked to sit in seat number one. They drop off. And then the prosecuting attorney calls my name.

I walk out wondering if this guy on trial has had some of the same issues as Alba and Esmeralda in the court system. By appearance, he could have been very well indigenous.

I go to the double doors to leave, and the bailiff extends his hand. My reaction is to shake his hand and think, "Do I know you?" He looks at me.

"We have that case up on the docket. It will be coming soon."

"Thank you," I say.

"See you then."

Interesting. Out of the strangest places we may find out what is happening. Later in the evening I call Margaret to pass on the word.

28. Drop dead date

October 8, 2015, comes and passes. The "Drop Dead Date" was not a guarantee. I call Margaret and text her every few days.

"Any news?"

"No. I think they are still preparing for the trial."

"I hope they are in negotiations." I would say back in the texts.

My experience is that movement almost always comes at the very last minute.

Margaret visits Esmeralda in mid-October. Sister Gertrudes accompanies Margaret, but Esmeralda seems to have the same response as always. She is waiting and saying that she wants to be with her mother in Southern Mexico.

We haven't heard anything about the date for Alba's court date.

October 22, 2015, is another date for trial. Margaret is in Court Thirteen again with Sister Gertrudes and Sister Teresa. I am to go from work after school was out at 3:30 if I get the word.

The day before I have a School Board Meeting and this is more tiring than most. I seem to be on the losing side in talking about building more classrooms to bring down the number of students in each school classroom. My fellow trustees seem to think that extra classrooms would mean extra students in already overcrowded schools.

I have my moment in the board meeting though: A parent wanted to read a statement, but she started her statement by saying that she meant no disrespect to the Superintendent, Marisol Cruz-Ortega, the Board President took this as a negative and started to argue with the parent openly.

"No disrespect is intended to the Superintendent Lozano…"

The Board President reacted that this was a sign that the Superintendent was to be disrespected. They argue for most of the three minutes given to the public speakers. The digital timer counting down as they go back and forth. At the end, the bell sounds and a red light flashes on the podium. Time is up. I ask that time be given back to the parent.

"Her time has run out." The Board President seems not to want to hear what was to be said. The parent turns around and walks away, but a few minutes later she passes out a copy of her letter, written in Spanish to myself and the other four trustees.

Reading the paper while in the meeting I find it benign and somewhat well written in parts. Some two hours later I see that the parent is still in the board room.

Most parents will have left well before the closing of the meeting. I have a plan, but it won't make my fellow trustee and board president happy.

The trustees took a moment to speak for themselves at the end of the meeting. I usually mention what school related things I have done in the last two weeks and ask for the same list of items

I wish the board to address, these it ignored for at least three years since a new majority block won seats on the board.

"I would like to yield my time to Mrs. Juliana Amparo," I announce.

"You can't do that. She can come back in two weeks." Cruz-Ortega tells me.

"Then, I will read her letter." Silence.

Before I read her letter in Spanish I announce, "Even though I disagree with some parts of what Mrs. Amparo writes, she has a right that it be said to the board."

I start: "*Estaba la calaca sentada junto al Sr. Lozano, cuando de repente empezó hablar y dijo en este Distrito todo está en paz por que las quejas ya las podemos ignorar y a las escuelas ya las podemos controlar pues a los maestros y padres a nuestras juntas los dejamos de invitar, aunque a su escuela se le venga hoy a celebrar y a sus estudiantes los vengamos hoy a usar para personficar algo que no es realidad los estudiantes con sonrisas inocentes vienen a recordar del por que ustedes estan ahora sentados donde estan. Porque tambien son padres y algun dia tambin estaran en mi lugar y la calaca esto podrá contemplar.*"

Silence followed from the Trustees. Silence from the Board President. Applause from the handful of parents in the back of the room.

I guess I won't be Board President again when the board selects the post in a month and a half. Well, I've learned that I must take some blows to the ego to defend the rights of others.

Thursday, October 22, 2015: I am told again by Margaret that once again the court case for Esmeralda is up. I am pretty busy today in that I am tired from the meeting last night and that I have been invited to the Mexican Consulate to be on a scholarship

175

committee to allocate funds to applying organizations to provide English language and academic classes to the Spanish and Mixteco speaking communities from Oxnard to Santa María.

I have been involuntarily transferred to teach fifth grade at Rio Plaza Elementary school in the same Rio School District. Though it was an 'involuntary' transfer, I consider the change as a possible positive change. I had increasingly become a target at the junior high I had worked. The principal, a few teachers and a parent from hell had thrown words at me and didn't seem to mind that I be beaten up. The two cases I had been working on, protests outside the local Walmart and a vote against having a police substation in César Chávez Elementary School in Oxnard seemed to be too much for these people.

My new principal told me that I have a reputation.

"Just what is my reputation?" I ask.

"It doesn't matter."

And my 2015-16 school year begins.

I am able to have the school counselor come to my classroom and take my fifth graders for the shortened day. I can make it to the other side of town and site on the Mexican Consulate Scholarship Committee. Sitting on the small committee is an Assistant Superintendent from the Rio School District. In itself, I am thrilled that the school principal is willing to see the benefit to the community and to education to allow me to leave the classroom. This has not happened in the Rio School District unless they had direct control of the situation.

I forget about the court date for Esmeralda and instead of checking in with a text to Margaret at my 10:15 recess for the kids, I write around 3:00. Nothing happened. Another delay. I am disappointed, but not surprised. Just another endless delay. I call Margaret in the evening and tell her of my hope that a negotiation is going on.

"What happened to the October 8th drop dead date?" I asked.

"I don't know. Let's hope you are right."

We both have been exhausted a long time ago in hoping that this thing would come to an end and to go further, to expect some positive outcome.

29. Innocent

Friday, October 23, 2015: I start class at 8:00 in the morning to have one of my co-fifth grade teachers come to my door with a line of students behind him. Mrs. Figueroa is sick today, and we could not get a substitute teacher. Mr. Bradbury asks if I could take half of her class, he will take the other half.

"Sure." I have no choice.

He counts off, "One, two, three, four..." until fifteen students come in my room. A few can take empty seats, and I send about nine or ten to go to their classroom and bring their chairs to my room.

I am busy. Lesson plans change on the fly, and I am much more vigilant. Forty-five students! The day works out pretty good. I am busy, but the kids seem not to mind the school work. Time goes by, and I had forgotten that Margaret is to report in again.

My cell phone buzzes in my shirt pocket. I am reading and discussing the Hopi Indians in the early Southwest. I finish and look at my cell phone as the kids are writing an answer to a couple of questions at the end of the chapter.

Margaret's text reads, "Her lawyer tells me it may be dismissed. Or she could be summarily deported. Let's keep in touch."

I write back at 11:44. "Any word?"

Margaret writes at 12:33. "Yes. Sent you a text. 6 p.m. tonight."

I call at 12:35 after letting my students go to the lunch line.

"Margaret, what happened?"

"They dropped the charges!"

"What?"

"They dropped the charges. She should be released after 6:00!"

"I can't believe it! Where is she now?"

"She is at the Court House now. They will take her back to the prison at 6:00 to gather her things and she is free to go."

"I want to be there."

"Sure. Me too. I am trying to find out when and where she will be released. Esmeralda called me twice from the jail," Margaret tells me. "The machine asked me to dial 0 if I wanted to accept the call. I did, and it hung up on me twice!"

"Figures. Please keep me up to what is happening."

I am showing my overflowing classroom of students a video of the Pueblo Indians of New Mexico. I have to say, I am not one to cry, but my eyes have been tearing since I heard the news of Esmeralda's pending release.

I step outside the classroom door which looks out

to a grassy area, chain-link fence and residential street beyond. I have tears streaming down my checks for about thirty seconds. A smile on my face, I am recalling the three years that I have known this woman and how I stepped far away from my comfort zone to advocate for first Alba and soon after Esmeralda. I compose myself and turn towards the door. "Good," I think to myself, "the students didn't notice."

At the end of the school day, I get on the phone again to get an update, if any from Margaret. The Gonzalezes husband and wife have been contacted to pick up Esmeralda, but it sounds like a friend of theirs will be the actual person to pick her up at the prison.

This is getting confusing. I had never heard of the Gonzalezes. Questions at the prison were always limited due to the microphone we all knew connected to the telephones. Also, apparently the Gonzalezes and others were intimidated to approach the prison because of their legal status.

I remember having been told when I first made contact with Esmeralda that she had no visitors in the year that she had been in jail before Alba brought me into contact with these issues. It was apparently right, but that she did have friends and acquaintances that rooted for her from a distance. Today she would be free to join the community that lives in the shadows and were unable to make contact while she awaited trial.

On the way home I pass within a block from the Mexican Consulate in Oxnard. At the last second, on the way home I decide to go straight instead of turning left. I need to ask if there are any details that I or we need to be prepared for before we make this transfer from accused child killer to innocent, free person.

Luckily, Attorney Silvia Nieves is in, but also finishing up with another person. I am led to the second floor and greeted and asked to wait just a short time.

We sit down in Nieves's office.

"Esmeralda has had her charges dropped?"

"All the charges?" She doesn't receive news like this often.

"Yes, she is being released today."

"That's great. Where is she now?"

"The best I know; she is still in the Courthouse. She will be transferred to the jail at six to collect her belongings. If it were me, I would be ready to leave the courthouse at once."

"Me too."

I pause for a moment. "I'm here to ask if there is anything else that I need to know about before it happens today."

I am being a pessimist again. Victories, a clear recognizable victory doesn't come along too often.

She looks at me for a moment. "We need to make sure that ICE isn't outside the door to arrest her again and have her deported."

"I thought that we were a sanctuary county."

I knew that there had to be something! Sometimes it's good to be a pessimist. Sanctuary was a big issue in recent months. A man apparently shot and killed a young woman at random while walking on the pier in San Francisco just months ago. The shooter was an undocumented man from Mexico who had been arrested several times before. The news came out just in time for the Republican Presidential candidates to highlight the problems with immigration.

"No. Let me make some calls."

Mrs. Nieves gets on the phone. I'm listening to her side of the conversation and can only guess what the other side was saying.

She tells me after she hangs up one call that she is concerned that ICE will be waiting. She says that she had another situation very similar once. The same arresting officer from the Oxnard Police Department she says arrested a Beatriz Camacho Mares for shacking her baby. The baby was alive and unharmed. The police construed a confession was according to Mrs. Nieves.

Beatriz stayed in jail for a year and a half before the charges were finally dropped.

"Immigration was waiting for her outside the prison. They arrested her and held her for deportation." The attorney tells me as she calls another person.

"Did Esmeralda have a prior," I ask.

She takes the phone from her ear and looks my way, Beatriz was stopped once before for entering the country with someone else's identification. She makes another call and mentions Esmeralda's name again.

"No priors." She hangs up. "Her husband was arrested once and served time."

Nieves dials another number. While she is on hold, three children come in and exchange a kiss on both checks.

Grandchildren? I don't ask.

"Yes, this is Silvia Nieves, Consul for the Mexican Consulate. We would like to know if Esmeralda Martínez will be detained after she is being released today from jail." She waits for an answer.

"Yes, she had charges dropped today in Court."

Then she surprises me. "I will wait for her and take her under protection if I have too." She looks my way.

I wish I could hear what came next. Nieves thanks the person and hangs up.

"They don't want to touch her. She's OK. After four years in prison and having the charges dropped for her son's death, it would look bad."

It would look bad. Mother of an eleven-month old loses her baby; husband takes off the same morning, mother is charged with murder, stays in jail just one month short of four years without a trial, has charges dropped and is arrested as she leaves the jail. Not good P.R.

I ask the attorney, "It's my understanding that if Esmeralda had been found guilty, she could seek reparations, but now that the charges were dropped she won't have the chance to see any money come her way. Is that true?"

"I believe so. She is free."

"Free rent for forty-seven months."

"Yup."

On my way out, another person hands Nieves a paper and she shows me it with a small black and white photo about two by three inches. "Do you recognize him?" she asks.

I look for a few moments.

"I think so."

"Where do you know him from?"

"I think from MICOP."

"This is Esmeralda's husband."

Getting into my car out in front of the two story Consulate, flags of the two countries waving between me and the street I get another call.

"She has been picked up." Margaret.

"By ICE?"

"No. By a friend of the Gonzalezes. She is on her way to their house."

"OK. Then I will go home and find out what is happening. She's safe, right?"

"I think so."

I somewhat expect that I, we will see Esmeralda this night,

but soon we both decide in conversations on the phone that she is more than likely taking a long, hot shower and sleeping on a good mattress.

I know that Esmeralda will want to see her "Grandma, " but I mention that I understand that I may not be a priority. In a way, this is why I asked Margaret to see the two ladies in prison: They would be able to interact and relate much better with a female than a somewhat overweight, balding white man. It is what it is.

Margaret calls me one last time that evening. "Apparently we are not seeing Esmeralda tonight." I reflected.

"No, I'm sure that she is exhausted."

"I can imagine that she is more interested now in a very long shower and sleeping on a real mattress."

"I'm sure that Esmeralda will be fine from here on."

We also talk about how this must be one of the worse nights for Alba since she was first arrested just one month short of three years ago. We agree that we will get together at 2:15 the next day, Saturday to go up to the Todd Road Jail to visit Alba. We want to go early in case her family is expecting to visit. The Zapata family has taken up most of the visit times away from Margaret since they took control of Alba's defense with hiring Mr. Tim Ruby.

I spend the rest of the evening reflecting on the victory we experienced with Esmeralda's release. It was hard to believe. It should have come years ago. She probably shouldn't have been arrested in the first place!

I think of all the 'Good Christian' friends and acquaintances that had given me the evil eye over the time knowing of Esmeralda and Alba, how many had to express their horror that somehow I was in favor of child killing. Now, we know that one of the two will be forgotten once again. Innocence meant being able to go into the shadows once again. Being forgotten and not sending any ripples out into the pond that would not attract any attention from anybody.

The Ventura County Star newspaper came out with an article about what had happened. What caught my eye was that the prosecution seemed to have found a way to try to save face. Mentioned in the article was that in the motion to drop the charges, prosecutors said critical evidence needed to conclusively determine the cause of death was destroyed during surgery to save the boy's life. This could have been very true, but I believe that it was to save professional face in the release of Esmeralda. I wonder how many days she stayed in jail until this one point was agreed. Well, she is out. Charges are dropped, and Esmeralda could now decide where to take her life.

Saturday morning went by fast. Family and few phone calls. I half expected to hear that Esmeralda might be expecting Margaret and I to see her. Close to two o'clock Margaret calls and says that she will be by soon.

"I talked to the Gómez couple, and Esmeralda is running around with some girlfriends today," Margaret tells me.

"Good. I didn't know that she had girlfriends." I dryly come back. "Nobody came to visit her in jail except us."

"They probably couldn't come to the prison."

"I wonder if Alba will be willing to see us. This will be the first time that I will try to see her since Tim Ruby told me to stay away."

I found myself walking down the long hallway once again.

Margaret and I talk about how unnatural and unrealistic this long hallway with no windows and only a few shut doors is. Margaret mentions that the distance was getting longer for her body to take.

"I am only now feeling that I can take walking a hundred yards, or whatever this is without any pain."

Margaret looks at me kind of funny. "It has been almost a year now that I had to get through with my cancer."

I had a tumor removed from my right kidney the December before. I timed the surgery for Christmas break from school. Though I should have taken my doctor's advice, I returned to work just two weeks after the five-hour surgery.

Truth be said, my wife saved my life. Unexpectantly she had showed up at the doctor's office the day I was to hear the news. We sat as the doctor explained that the tumor was cancerous, but not to worry because I had two or three years to take care of it.

A five-hour surgery to do a biopsy, or a five-hour surgery to take the tumor out, I looked at Viviana, and we both said, "Take it out now." At the same time.

Shortly after coming too after the surgery the doctor came and told me that it was cancer. He also apologized to me saying that the tumor was very rare and that I didn't have years, but weeks or months.

Lucky and happy to be alive, I was still groaning these months later of the aches and pains from the surgery. "Oh yeah. I forgot that you went through that."

"Viviana has told me to stop complaining about the pain. She says that she gave birth three times. How can I come back against that?"

Margaret laughs, "You can't!"

We wait about ten minutes in front of the windows. A few other people are also waiting for their family members to open one of the doors in the small booths on the other side of the glass visiting sections.

"There she is," Margaret tells me while I am looking the other way.

"¡*Abuelita*!"

Margaret and Alba talk for quite a long time. General things, no specifics. Margaret by far does most of the talking and Alba seems happy to listen to her voice.

Alba doesn't seem phased by having spent the night alone. She seems to like the quiet. Who knows, maybe Esmeralda was a snorer!

I hear Margaret explain that I brought her because her car had broken down. Later Margaret tells me that the question was why I was here.

I am given the phone, and besides 'hello' and a few pleasantries and a smile, Alba didn't want to say much to me. I have taken it for granted that Tim Ruby has told her that I am the Boogie Man. So be it. I don't have much to say and ask if she wants to speak with Margaret again.

"Please, can I speak with my Grandma again?"

I stand and let Margaret continue their conversation. It was the best decision I made to ask Margaret to connect with the ladies back when I was the first person who came to visit either one of them.

I helped translate a few things for Margaret when she had a hard time thinking of the words in Spanish and a couple of times

Margaret just held up the phone to let me say the whole phrase that she was trying to get out.

We probably were given more time than normal to talk with Alba, but at a point, both heard a signal on the phone that their time was coming to an end. Smiles and good byes. Margaret and Alba both put their hands on the glass. I nodded, and Alba smiled at me and turned to the door behind her to leave.

Sunday morning comes with an invitation. The Nuns call Margaret saying that they wanted to bake a cake for Esmeralda. Could I come by mid-day to pick it up? It sounds like a good excuse for us to visit Esmeralda. I am asked to call Sister Teresa and get the details. When I do, I find that the cake has been postponed, but we are invited to have lunch at the convent.

We get a call while we are a couple of blocks away from the convent. Sister Teresa is asking if we are on our way. She said that the ladies keep a strict schedule for all activities. She explains that it is the best way to run the daily activities with a large group of Nuns.

When we arrive, we are given a quick tour of the very clean and new two story convent on the way to the dining area. Entering, the cafeteria style area we are taken to the left to the service line. The large area had at least a dozen dining table; each table can sit four persons. About 30 elderly ladies are in the room. None had on their habits, but I still have flashbacks of being a teen and going to Catholic school.

All greet us and sit at a table with Sisters Dolores and Sister Gertrudes along with a younger lady who is also visiting Sister Gertrudes.

Sister Teresa goes to the speaker's podium at the front

of the room. She introduces Margaret and myself as the two missionaries who helped Esmeralda. She reminded everyone that Esmeralda had been in jail for four years after losing her son and was now free with the charges dropped. The Nuns applauded us, and as we were at the table, several came to the table to thank us individually and say that they had prayed for Esmeralda, Alba and ourselves.

Father Joseph introduces himself, and one Sister in particular comes and thanks us for our work. Shorter than the average, she had a face that said, nun. I am also told that this Sister had only recently retired after forty-five years and that she spent most of those years in the prison system of Bangladesh! I want to come back some day and listen to her story.

We are thanked for our visit after eating and the Nuns seem to all be gone as we were in conversation. They had a schedule, and though the gathering is very rewarding, the Sisters have things to do.

I mention to a couple of the Sisters how much I appreciated that they prayed for Esmeralda and Alba and how much their support meant to me.

"You wouldn't believe the dirty stares and terrible things I got from many good Christians," I told them.

"Yes, we understand." The Sisters smile and seem to have the twinkle in their eyes as to say that they know exactly the attitude I am talking about.

"No, I am not in favor of baby killing." I continued as in answering the bigots who through verbal gaps throughout the three years.

Margaret mentions to them how I refused to say that I

delivered ministry to the ladies. I explain that I try to separate myself from a religious purpose while trying to help.

Sister Teresa laughs and explains that we all are doing God's work, including me.

This is a great recognition and celebration with the Nuns. I feel great for the rest of the day. Too bad I wasn't able to convince my sons in joining us. Viviana was at work this weekend, but I got to tell her about the experience in the evening after she got home.

Margaret writes a letter to the Ventura County Star that gives kudos to the Ventura County Public Defender's Office, and gratitude to Deputy Public Defender Kevin Taylor that later gets published.

30. Alba

Monday, October 26, 2015.

I am in my classroom. A couple of teachers had mentioned in the morning that they had seen the article in the paper. "Is that the woman you had been helping?"

"Yup. She's free now. Innocent."

It was a good feeling, but I don't want to share the experience or my feelings where it will hit the ears of my students. This is well over their heads, and by the time the information gets home, I will have helped an ax killer get free. We have school work to do.

At 5:31 in the evening at home I get a text from a friend. "Jury being selected in dead newborn case."

It had a link to an internet article from the Ventura County Star.

It has happened! Finally, Alba will now go to trial!

I am not in the inner circle for Alba's case. In fact, I have heard several times to go away. I have questioned my involvement many times, and as the case has changed several times, I now want the best for Alba. I want justice. I never claimed to know how this case will come out, or how it should come out. Justice at this moment is seeing that her attorney gives the best defense possible. The bottom line is that I don't want another baby to die and another woman to be lost because of the terrible influences they confront.

I can already claim some victory. In the article that had come out reminds the public of the death, but it also said "Community activists who have supported Zapata over the years said she had been sexually assaulted in Mexico and was pregnant when she fled to the United States. She has family in Oxnard."

Excellent! We got our word out. First of all, the case wasn't lost to only being reported after the fact as most cases are. Also, we can get our word out to the public that Alba is in some form a victim.

It had been two years since Margaret, and I had spoken to her attorney, Tim Ruby. He was not interested in defending her at the time with anything other than a language defense. Now, the public and he had been openly and widely told that she had been raped. Hopefully, we have pushed Mr. Ruby to earn his community service as well as his $10,000.

Jury selection takes two days. The result is a jury of twelve and three alternates. Ten women and five men. Most appear to be over forty, some over sixty years of age. One Latina woman, one Latino man who is an alternate, one woman who appears to be of Indian heritage and the others Anglo. Not necessarily the peers of Alba or her lost son, but I remember again about the crabs in the bucket: perhaps her peers would bring her down.

The jury is told not to read the newspaper or search for information on the case. I always wonder how much this happens. I guess it depends on the person. The jurors are sent home around noon on the second day of jury selection. The trial will start at 9:00 the next morning, Wednesday.

I have always expected that I didn't know everything involved in the case. I was given more information over time than the public, but I know that I wasn't privy to all the information. There were times when I was at the prison that I wanted to ask Alba herself, why did you do it? What happened? It wasn't my place.

I was asked to get involved by people with different interests. I agreed to get involved out of curiosity as well as trying to be a Good Samaritan, an advocate.

I guess I know that I will never please everybody. In life, in marriage, in family and as an elected official, I know that not everyone will agree or understand motives. As an elected official I have been surprised that I don't get the support of some good friends at the time of elections. Oh well. My wife was not a citizen the first time I ran for School Board, but we joked that once she became a citizen that I would have to work for her vote. Now, I am working for my principles. For the baby. For the culture and my vision of justice.

Even when I was asked to search for the mother of the baby found in the strawberry field I had people somehow thinking that I was in favor of killing babies.

Justice, I guess is off at a distance. Other people's problem to take care. Other people in other places need to take care of these things. Satisfaction is at the sofa watching the evening news. Thirty seconds and another report before the commercial distracts again.

I have always said that I believed that Alba was a victim. She also did a great offense and is guilty of that offense. I am trying not to make excuses, but those who think that an accusation means guilt, then they forgot that our country is based on law, not opinion.

Everyone likes a winner, and everyone wants to be on the side of the winner. Calling for a fair trial for a woman who killed her baby son, does not look like a winner.

The case of Esmeralda Martinez was different. I always believed her to be innocent. I hope she was. She was allowed to go free. The injustice is that she had to wait one month short of four years to be allowed to be innocent.

I wish her well.

The echo of the few good Christians who repeated time and again, "Who is going to speak for the baby?" Well, I hope that we can prevent future tragedies because of these two lost babies.

Wednesday, October 28, 2015

People of the State of California v. Alba Zapata

Alba Flores Zapata, twenty-three now has waited three years for what she always believed to be a positive moment, at this moment to set her free. Dressed in blue jeans and a dark T-shirt, sitting quietly between her attorney, Timothy Ruby and an interpreter to her right. Alba has a pair of white headphones covering her ears. The woman who is interpreting speaks quietly into a small hand held box that has a black cord that runs from the box, down towards the floor and then up to Alba's headphones.

Tim Ruby, sitting to Alba's left is wearing a light blue shirt, bolo tie, dark blue pants, a large Jack Daniels brass belt buckle, light blue jacket and cowboy boots. He is a tall man, elderly, very hunched back; head pointed down when he stands.

Judge Simpson gives the ground rules to the jurors. The jurors are only to use the evidence that is presented them in the court. No outside sources can be considered. The jury is to wait for all the evidence from both sides before they make their minds up.

194

The jurors are to disregard the translators. No sharing of thoughts or information with spouses, family, friends, and reporters.

The defendant is assumed innocent, and it is the job of the prosecution to the jurors that she is guilty.

I have always wondered if jurors as a whole honor the innocent until proven guilty pledge. Listening to jurors often trying to get out of jury duty often pop off that they think the person looks guilty. I have seen jury candidates talk about the immigration issues of how the person shouldn't be here or how they are appalled that the person doesn't speak English. Again, on this last point, I would always want to use my first language if I was facing charges in a court than relying on a second or third language even if I was fluent in the language of the court.

The courtroom is set with Judge Simpson's bench in one corner, California State seal on the wall behind him. To his right, the witness-stand, looking at this moment as an empty penalty box in a hockey match. Behind the witness-stand, on the wall is a white board with two wooden doors that can be closed over the white board. To the right of this, another corner of the room and the jury box fills the next wall up to a desk where a Bailiff sits with computer and further down the wall the division on the room with the bar separating the court with the public benches lined in two columns facing directly towards the witness stand.

The attorneys' tables are in front of the bar, facing the court. A podium separates the two sides. Defense to the right as seen by the public, prosecution to the left of the podium. Behind the prosecuting attorneys is a wire file table. Blue binders and files fill the two levels. Alba, the translators, and attorneys are facing the judge and court.

The people of the State.

This Wednesday is the day. I am going to work. I have no idea how long the case will take. I am a teacher. I must be with my students. I must gain my wages to pay the bills for my family. Advocacy in my case doesn't do that.

Margaret, Sean Justice, and my son David go to the first day of the trial. Sean Justice was hoping that he can talk his editor into allowing him to write an article about the trial. He had already reported on the case more and better than anyone else. David, my son had just turned 20 a month ago. He is going to Ventura Community College and hopes to transfer to a four-year university in the next school year. Besides wanting to be an attorney, he is taking a class with a Prosecuting Attorney as his teacher. One of the assignments is to sit in a trial for at least three hours and write about the experience. What an opportunity. Just the same, I had to convince him not to wait closer to the due date. Typical. At twenty, I would have done the same.

Also, apparently in the room is a reporter from the Ventura County Star. Victory! Marisa Fernández sends out her first report on the paper's website mid-day. She later updates the article. Tim Ruby has to feel that he is being watched now! We can do nothing to advocate at this moment. We can now have the eyes of the community on the trial!

Senior Deputy District Attorney Michelle Snyder presents her opening statement in Zapata's jury trial. The case is laid out before the jurors.

Snyder describes the first encounter of the baby in the La Esperanza strawberry field. She describes the search for the mother and the first encounters with Alba. There were several lies told by Alba at the beginning. The prosecution told of how the truth started to come out and that Alba did not help herself as the lies turned to truths or possibly different lies.

Margaret sits with a small notepad on the public side of the bar behind Alba. She will become the anchor fixture in the court. On the other side of the walk way that divides the two sections of public pews, towards the back wall near the electric outlet is Marisa Fernández, reporter for the Ventura County Star. Friend Sean Justice sits with Margaret several of the days of the trial, hoping to get the nod from his editor from the free weekly VCReporter. I can make it only after the school day is over, and I can get to the courthouse. Arriving at roughly 3:30 I am happy to see that I see what I later find out is the climax of the presentations of the day. Not sure that it is planned this way, but the hour at the end of each of the days I am told seem to be the most exciting.

The story comes out. There always have been questions that I wanted to know the answers.

The prosecution delivers their opening statement. The baby was found in the El Canto strawberry field between Oxnard and Camarillo, California on May 21, 2012. The autopsy showed that the baby was born full term and alive. The search for the mother culminated in November 2012.

Attorney Michelle Snyder speaks of the first encounters with Alba Flores Zapata. The lies that are first told to lead investigator Sheriff Luis Silva. Alba did not know about the baby. She had never been pregnant, and her name was Rosa Martinez.

The DNA results came in; it was a match. The blood was a match. Rosa Martinez is Alba Flores Zapata, and Alba is the mother of the child.

"On May 21, 2012, Alba Flores Zapata murdered Baby

John Doe willfully and with malice."

Prosecuting Attorney Michelle Snyder:

May 21, 2012, 9:30 in the morning. El Canto farm. Central Avenue between Santa Ana Blvd. and Simon Street.

César Olivas is in charge of rows of strawberries. He notices that one of the water lines was leaking. César went to investigate by a dirt road next to the first row on the side of the highway. He noticed there was a water pressure issue. First row of strawberries had a bed of flowers to attract the good insects. César walked down the row in the ditch. Moving flowers aside and as he's walking down and notices something in the thick brush. He becomes startled as he notices that there is a baby doll. One hundred and fifty feet from the highway. César observes a deceased male baby. The baby was concealed in a ditch. The baby was cold to the touch and the skin was leathery. Paramedics confirmed with the fire captain that the baby was confirmed dead for a couple of hours. Baby was very well concealed.

One hundred and fifty-feet away from Central Avenue.

César states that the gate by the road isn't securely locked as he states that "realistically" you can get in if you want to.

DNA swabs were taken and a pool of blood presumably from the mother was found on the scene.

An autopsy was later performed. The baby was full term. Organs were fully developed. Piece of lungs in water demonstrated that there were bubbles in the lungs. This is a physical proof that the baby was alive at birth.

No milk or colostrum was found in the baby's stomach.

Cause of death: environmental exposure following delivery.

Night temperatures were below a livable temperature,

baby suffered from dehydration and exhaustion due to the baby instinctively crying. Detective Luis Silva investigated the case.

The baby was very well concealed according to the prosecution. It was a Monday when César noticed the baby. No workers were on the site Sunday. Suspected the farmworkers may have been the culprit. So Detective Luis Silva requests a DNA sample from the fieldworkers.

Detective Silva is bilingual, speaks English and Spanish.

DNA was a match with Cecilia Flores Zapata as a close relative of biological mother. Cecilia was discovered to have a match with some of the alleles of the baby. It wasn't a direct match but closely similar. Scientifically a close relative to the mother of the baby.

Surveillance began at 1326 Arbol Street in Oxnard. Cecilia had no prior information on the baby. Detectives set up surveillance at the house and discovered the likely defendant, Alba Flores Zapata. Picture taken of Alba gleefully playing with nephews are flashed onto a white screen on the wall opposite of the jurors. Alba was employed in the past at the very same farm. El Canto field.

Defendant had worked at El Canto from January 2012 to May 15, 2012. Other family members have been employed at these fields as well.

Defendant was arrested due to substantial evidence from Detective Silva. A warrant had been signed by a judge to collect a DNA swab from Alba.

During the booking process, defendant said she had not been pregnant nor given birth in the last year. The jury is told that the DNA results showed that the defendant is the biological mother.

Further interviews of the defendant were given on November 30, 2012 by Detective Luis Silva. Alba said that she arrived in the United States from Mexico in January 2012. Alba was spoken to in Spanish at this as well as all further interviews. She crossed the border through the mountains with man she didn't know. She told Sheriff Silva that her coyote ditched her. She sought help from others who were crossing over to the United States as well.

When confronted by the detective, Alba was denying any connection with the case. Detective Silva states he had evidence that she was the mother.

The test is regarded as being 100% and without error. It was claimed that no one knew of the baby in the family. Alba agreed she did not make any preparations for the baby. Defendant said once she reached the United States she was pregnant. She told the detective that she had contacted the biological father and he refused to help her or the baby.

When Alba was having labor contractions, she was working in the fields on Sunday. She had no method of contacting an ambulance and no cell phone on her. When confronted, why she didn't ask for help from the other fieldworkers, she simply said that she didn't know them.

Detective Silva kept asking questions regarding the reason she didn't take care of the baby. She told the detective that she walked to Oxnard from the farm which is eight miles. Detective Silva told her that is very unlikely and she later confesses that she called her sister Citlali, who also works in the same field, asking her to come and pick her up.

Detective Silva confronted her in regards to the cell phone, telling her that she just told him that she didn't have a cell phone. And since now she did have a cell phone, why didn't she ask her sister to care for the baby's transportation?

The fieldworkers arrive in the morning and are gone by afternoon. No workers work on Sunday, which Alba claimed was the date of the birth.

Alba refused to tell anyone about the baby.

Then the prosecution asks to put into evidence a video! On the large white screen, the baby is alive! This video would later come back to the screen in the court.

For now, we know that a breathing baby is grasping in the air. The left hand has a blade of grass clinging to the palm. The cat like cries of a new born baby and a hand enters the frame to touch the baby. The mother's hand!

Two photographs proceeding the video. The video was discovered on the cell phone recorded by Alba after a warrant was made on the cellphone's contents. The angle of the video demonstrated that Alba moved the baby's leg, possibly to show that the baby was a boy.

A question asked by the detective was how she got to the location. First she stated that some unknown worker had given her a ride. When further questioned these workers were her sister and brother-in-law who worked at the field along with her.

When she contacted Citlali in order to get a ride the reason was due to a headache. Detective Silva asked what's her reason for making a recording of the baby? Did she keep them as a memory of the baby?

I can guess that Alba could see the baby. He was real and she out of adrenaline and exhaustion took out her cell phone and made the video. Would any other woman have done the same? No psychological analysis was given to Alba. A weakness in her defense or an oversight from our legal system. Counseling or a psychologist would I'm sure have been made available to anyone of wealth or acceptable race. Alba was not afforded mental health.

The photos screenshots taken were suspicious to the detective and he further investigated. Silva believed the pictures were meant to send to the father with emphasis on the genitals to demonstrate that it was a boy. Detective Silva asked who she was trying to send the photos to.

Prosecuting Attorney Michelle Snyder: "We seek first degree murder charges in the death of Baby John Doe. The actions were willful, deliberate and premeditated."

Snyder went on to point out that the baby suffered from a harsh, short span of life.

Snyder: "Jurors, I hope you will be compelled to find beyond a reasonable doubt of the verdict that she willfully deserves. We will present enough evidence to prove beyond an unreasonable doubt that she was the culprit."

In the first sign to us that Tim Ruby is not going to be aggressive, he defers his opening statements until the prosecution has rested.

The jurors leave the courtroom and the judge speaks.

Court's Exhibit 1. The PowerPoint will be reserved as evidence in the case. Defense Attorney Tim Ruby disputes that the ending made by the prosecution was in an argumentative state and not justifiable for an opinion statement.

Judge Simpson believes that the last comment made by the prosecutor was of an argumentative state and will be stricken from the record.

Prosecuting Attorney Michelle Snyder: "If Tim Ruby would give an objection next time I could have made a change in the statement to make it not seem as an argument."

Judge Simpson: "I believe the statement wouldn't have been necessary and would be fixed when the jurors came back to the bench."

10:53 am: Ventura County Sheriff calls for the jurors who have been waiting in the public entrance hallway.

A podium is placed between the tables of the prosecutors and defendant.

Judge Simpson makes a remark on his feeling of aromas. Apparently at least one juror was using perfume. Someone complained. No perfumes will be allowed. Judge Simpson then rules that the comments made to the jurors were argumentative and will be stricken.

Prosecution calls its first witness. Deputy Sheriff Simon Moyano was the first to arrive upon the scene. Moyano has been with the Ventura County Sheriff's Department six months before the event. His formal education was at USC, and the Sheriff's Academy in 2000. He had served as a Custody Deputy, Court Bailiff, and patrol. After this he was assigned to headquarters. Headquarters station patrol, unincorporated zones of the cities of Oxnard and Ventura.

Moyano came to the crime scene in full uniform in a black and white vehicle. He describes the strawberry farm. He was the first Deputy to arrive. He is certified as a Spanish speaker.

Paramedics arrive on the scene.

Prosecutor pulls up an image of the field labeled as Exhibit 1A. The baby is difficult to see in the first photo.

Exhibit 3A is an image showing the baby and trampled flower berm.

Starting the first cross examination, Tim Ruby asks at what time did Deputy Moyano arrive at the fields.

Moyano recalls that the fieldworkers were present. He doesn't recall what day of the week it was. By the time he arrived the workers were already working the day shift.

The officer doesn't believe that the baby had been moved.

Ditch is one foot to two feet wide according to the Deputy. No wild animals were around at the time he arrived. There was no evidence of coyotes, dogs, or birds. Farm workers were at center of the field. No birds of prey, owls, crows, no hawks.

No bites were noticed on the baby.

Michelle Snyder: "Objection, speculation, personal knowledge."

Judge Simpson: "Sustained."

I am somewhat surprised that there were not animals around. Interestingly, there is no mention of pesticides or chemicals used in the field. These could be an answer to why there are not birds or animals. It could also be a contributing factor into the baby's death.

The Deputy described his arrival. He did not need to go through a metal gate or bar. The division is composed of black plastic fabric.

Tim Ruby: "Were there any strawberries present by the baby?"

Simon Moyano: "Yes."

Michelle Snyder summons Patrick Guzman as a witness. A paramedic for four years, he responded to the call to the field. Guzman has emergency room experience for five years before going to paramedic's school for one year. He studied at Ventura Community College. He is State and County licensed.

Exhibit 3B is introduced. Close up of diseased baby projected on large screen.

The umbilical cord is still attached. The baby has dark, long hair.

Guzman did touch the baby to check if joints were locked up. Baby wasn't limp, and had muscle tone. The fists were clinched, and legs crossed, he explained that these are not signs that the baby was alive.

Paramedic Guzman doesn't recall any insects around the baby. The baby was cold to the touch.

Snyder: Are you familiar with the Safely Surrendered Baby Law?"

Guzman: "Yes. The mother could release the baby to the hospital within 72 hours of birth."

He did not make an observation of the temperature on the ground. The baby was dried out. He did not move the baby.

During the investigation at the sight of the death, the field workers continued to pick strawberries on the other side of the field.

Snyder: "Is the Safely Surrendered Baby Law source available to the public?"

Guzman: "I believe that signs are posted at fire stations and hospitals."

Snyder: "Do you know if there are any public service announcements about the Safely Surrendered Baby Law?"

Guzman: "I don't know if there are any public service announcements."

Tim Ruby: "Objection." Judge.

Simpson: "Overruled." Lunch until 1:30.

César Olivas takes the stand. Ortiz is a supervisor at La Esperanza Farm, and Cristiano Portillo called him right after calling the Sheriff's Department. Ortiz was a ten-minute drive from the field at the time of the phone call.

Judge Simpson asks Tim Ruby to use a microphone to speak. His voice is low, and while looking towards the ground, his projection is terrible.

Dirt is moved around towards the foot of the baby. Some marks in the mud are made by the hands and movement of the baby.

Baby is laying within a row, face up.

El Canto fields is 130 acres in all, divided up into twelve blocked sections of strawberry fields.

The section where the baby is found had last cut on Thursday, May 17th.

Tim Ruby, even with the microphone in hand is very soft spoken and some of the jurors lean forward to hear his words better.

Prosecutor Snyder draws out a time line of the investigation with Sheriff Luis Silva.

July 27, 2012, the DNA results of Baby John Doe are available.

August 22, 2012, a close match with Cecilia Flores Zapata is made.

November 19, 2012, Alba Flores Zapata is arrested with the charge of false documentation.

The blood on the site is tested and comes as identical to Alba's blood.

No cross examination by Tim Ruby.

Alba had a LG CU720 "Shine" cell phone 805-415-XXXX. The cell phone was analyzed in December 2012.

The results of the analyst are that the cell phone had two sent text messages, one received text message, and one draft text message. 331 text messages had been deleted, and along with a call, the log was later extracted.

People's exhibit 17 is the video of living child from the cell phone was shown to the court. Alba's hand can be seen on the left side of the screen. Her hand reaches over and lifts the baby's leg as to show that the baby is a boy. The child moves his arms, and a blade of grass could be seen in the baby's left hand. The child made new born baby sounds.

The baby has long dark hair. The umbilical cord is over one shoulder.

Alba, sitting with her face turned towards the table

does not appear to look at the screen. She makes no motions while the video was being shown.

The 42-second-long video was taken on May 18, 2012, at 5:14 pm according to the phone. This is three days before the baby had been found!

I had never imagined that the baby had gone undiscovered for three days. This is an impossibility that apparently happened.

No people, no animals had noticed? The real, live baby cried out. He was a breathing and crying baby. A cry that any parent would recognize as a new born. Nobody heard? Nobody sew the baby? Alba did, she walked away. I can't believe that the cries faded off not at night time, but in the day, evening and possibly into the night. The mother did not return; the shadows of people did not come to the aid of the infant! More questions. What are the answers? What is the truth? What happened?

The screen shots or photographs from the video were taken from the video. One was taken on July 23 and the other on July 24, 2012.

There were fifteen contact phone numbers on the phone.

Court will reconvene on Monday at 9:00 am.

I leave with Margaret and Sean Justice. I talk them into meeting at Presto Pasta Restaurant, a few blocks from the County Court Building. David comes with me, and Margaret arrives before us. What a conversation to listen to if you are a customer at the Italian eatery!

The three of us are astonished that the baby was born three days before any of us had imagined.

Sitting at a table, the food comes to us. We are in deep conversation, trying also to keep our voices down.

I was very critical of Tim Ruby. "If I were Tim Ruby, I would ask Alba to ball crying while the video or photos are shown."

Margaret looked at me somewhat surprised. "She is in shock. The jurors can see that."

"No. The jurors will only see that the accused showed no remorse. Her crying is the best and maybe the only thing she can do to make her point that she might be a victim of any degree."

At home, I share the day's events with wife and sons. Viviana takes it for face value as she sees it, "She's guilty."

Friday, May 18, 2012, afternoon. The fieldworkers had been in the Sombra strawberry field since sun up. It is just after noon. The workers had had their lunch break, some going to the food wagon that shows up between the two company's fields and others grab the lunch bag they had brought in the morning. The workers start work again. Picking up their wheel chart and box the workers go in their directions of work. Alba walks to her post and continues. Alba, dressed in blue jeans, and several layers topped off with a sweatshirt had been fighting a headache most of the day, but now she is feeling cramps.

Alba looks around and spots a section of field across Central Avenue that is empty of workers. She walks to the wagon to drop off her twenty pounds of strawberries, turns and walks away with an empty box. Walking towards the section she had been at, she drops the box and walks towards Central Avenue. Pain stops her, and she grasps her belly and groans. Cars pass. Workers are starting to leave the field. She lets them pass and crosses the road between two fields, two separate strawberry companies.

She enters the field towards the corner; a chain stretched across the dirt road to the side of the field. Alba walks forward on the dirt road some 150 feet.

The invisible figure sits. The invisible figure stands. The invisible figure, Alba paces. Alba is in plain sight, yet the cars and trucks that pass do not see her, they do not think of noticing, she blends into the scenery. The field workers do not look up. They do not look ahead. They do not see the invisible woman. The woman who is going to be a mother. Alba.

Pain, she is going into labor.

Stepping over a high waste hedge of California poppies, Alba is giving birth! She cannot walk one step more. Blacking out, she lowers her pants and drops to the ground.

Alba opens her eyes. The sun is to the west, still a couple of hours to darkness. She slowly sits up. To her feet is blood, a baby, and afterbirth. Alba moves to her knees. Looking at the baby, she stumbles. She reaches out and lifts herself up, pulling her pants up, she stumbles again to look at the baby at her feet.

The baby doesn't seem to be moving. Alba realizes that the umbilical cord is wrapped around its neck. She reaches and lifts the baby's head and with the other hand removes the umbilical cord from around the child. The baby moves its arms and starts to cry.

She holds the baby. It's a boy, long hair and grasping in the air with his fingers. Alba takes the baby into her arms and holds the baby. She is still weak and is still on the boarder of passing out again. She lifts her sweatshirt and layers of blouses up, exposing a breast, she holds the baby towards a nipple. The baby is crying and doesn't take to the nipple. Alba places the baby down and rolls back closing her eyes once again.

Coming too once again, Alba looks at the baby in the row between the strawberries. She gets to her knees and whispers a prayer for the baby. She reaches for her cell phone and pushes a button to take a picture. The baby has a grass blade in the palm of his hand. Alba reaches down and rolls the baby partially, allowing the baby to show that it is a boy. She looks at the baby, looks up and turns towards the road. A car! Alba stands and waves her arms at a second car driving. Nothing.

210

Who looks at a fieldworker in the field? Alba would later claim that a police car also passed by. One hundred and fifty feet away from the road, to the side of a strawberry field, the five-foot-tall woman is standing in the foot-deep row, waving her arms. An invisible person who up to now lived in a shadow world. Wanting to be invisible.

Alba stands up. She looks at the baby, turns and steps over the hedge, out of the row. She walks to the road and calls her sister on the cell phone. She doesn't see another car. She doesn't see people. It is still light out, the sun setting this summer day at 7:53 pm.

I had been wrong. All had expected that the baby had been born in the darkness of night. A line of questions I had wanted to ask Alba while at the window in the Todd Road Jail. A window was between us. The phone was surly being recorded. I was not investigating the case; I was advocating for justice. Whatever that would be.

In the opening statement from the prosecution, the lies Alba gave were mentioned. Attorney Snyder showed the jurors the 42 second video tape from Alba's cell phone. Instead of hitting the photo button, she had taken a video. The jurors watched silently, not blinking. The talk about a baby was now real. The baby boy was real! No explanation for the video was given. The accused had taken a video of the baby she had given birth to and later, silently walked away.

Snyder showed photos of the strawberry field and showed photos of the baby taken by the Sheriff's Investigators when the baby was discovered. Blotted and blue, the infant looked little like the live baby of the video. The prosecuting attorney closed her opening statement saying that a woman accused of the 2012 death of her newborn child willfully abandoned the baby to die in a strawberry field.

Tim Ruby, attorney for Alba, stands facing the judge and states that he wants to not give his opening statement until after the prosecution rests their case.

I spoke to my son, David about this the night before and he didn't seem too interested in going to the first day of court. He still has two months before the assignment is due. Typical, I tell him that he surely would wait for the last moment and not do it. Surprisingly, he agrees and not only goes to the courtroom but is still there when I arrive at 3:30.

I walk down to the end of the second floor hallway at the County Court Building. A window side facing out to the central area between the two County buildings. I come to Courtroom 27 at the end of the hall. My heart is racing as I slowly open the door to walk into the court. I sit next to David who is still writing notes.

Attorney Snyder is questioning Cristiano Portillo, a supervisor of the El Canto strawberry field. Poster photographs of the field are being shown. The foreman says that he doesn't know Alba, but does know a couple of other members of the Zapata family.

Portillo was called by César Olivas while on the way to the field. Ortiz also had called 911 to report that he had found the baby. Portillo would arrive about ten minutes after the call, seeing the first Sheriff Officers arriving at the sight.

The El Canto farm of 130 acres is divided up in twelve blocks. Portillo tells how the fields are broken up in four parts and the strawberries of one section is picked every four days. This section, where the baby was found had been picked on Thursday, the day before Alba had given birth.

Tim Ruby is asked if he would like to cross examine Mr. Portillo. "Yes." Mr. Ruby is very slow in standing up from his chair. He walks past the prosecutors. It is difficult to watch Mr. Ruby. He seems much older than the two years since the first time I had seen him. His cheeks are sunken, and there seems to be little meat on the bones of his fingers. He dressed in dark blue slakes, brown cowboy boots pointing from his feet and a tweed suit jacket that follows his very hunched back. Mr. Ruby slowly goes to the center of the courtroom between the judge, jurors and attorneys and shuffles through the poster board photos that are propped up at a table in from of the Court Reporter's desk.

Ruby pulls out a poster board and sets it up on a flimsy tripod already standing but empty. Ruby asks questions that confirm the four day picking cycle that the prosecution had just asked. Ruby than picks the poster from the tripod and takes it to the witness. "Can you place an X on the photo where the baby was found?"

Cristiano Portillo takes a marker and places a small X to one side. Snyder objects because the poster hadn't yet been placed into evidence for the case. The two attorneys go to the bench to speak with Judge Simpson. A simple thing, but I can see this may be a signal to the lack of preparation from Mr. Ruby. Yes, it is a simple action, mark an X on the poster where the baby was found. On the other hand, the evidence is the State's to present, not for the defense to deface.

The poster is admitted with the mark and now as Ruby continues to ask about the size and layout of the field, the witness,

Cristiano Portillo turns again with his marker and draws out the rectangles of the strawberry field with another X at the spot of interest. He placed this on the white board which was behind him which later caused some concern in that it could be used as evidence as well. The judge mentioned that the marking pen was a permanent marker. Smiles were on everyone's face at that second. Judge Simpson says that the two sides could take a cell phone photo of the drawing if they wish. Mr. Ruby responds that he doesn't know how to use his cell phone. Boy, I remember that! A couple of jurors chuckled quietly at Ruby's seemingly joke, but I know that it was a very accurate and true statement.

We are told that the case will resume the following day. The jury is excused, and the attorney's asked to speak off the record with the judge. Shortly after the judge tells us that the case is over for the day. Alba stands up and turns towards the opposite wall passing behind the attorneys' desks. A sheriff accompanies her with hands behind her back, but no hand cuffs. She looks towards us for a moment but with no expression. Entering the open door, I can see that she sits at a bench still with hands behind her back.

The door closes. At this moment I see Tim Ruby getting up from his chair and giving a pretty dirty look at Margaret, David and I who were sitting just behind him. The case had begun.

Monday, November 2, 2015

Detective Luis Silva is once again at the stand. Details from the questioning are voiced out for all to hear.

Some answers.

We are told how Alba tried to open the baby's eyes, but the infant would close them.

Alba told Silva in the interrogation that the baby looked just like the father of the child.

214

Alba said that she didn't know how to support the baby. The first excuse or explanation may have been what was going through the mother's mind at the time. For that matter, even being prepared to welcome a baby into life, I'm not sure if any mother or father knows how to support a baby. We do it, despite every fear we may have.

Alba is weeping openly today during the detective's testimony. The jurors are given a break after a time as Alba is crying. They leave the courtroom for fifteen minutes while she is given a chance to compose herself. A box of Kleenex tissues to dry her face is given. Alba doesn't get up, and she is quiet again after a moment.

On the record, the judge asks if Alba would like a glass of water, or if she would like to finish for the day.

Alba takes a few seconds to answer, always looking at the table says in a low voice that she wants to continue.

Court resumes and the jurors, no expressions on their faces enter the room and take their seats again.

Alba told the Sheriff that she had not given a name to the baby. Eternally known now as Baby John Doe. The muffled sobbing can be heard throughout the day in the courtroom.

Judge Simpson asks the attorneys to meet with him in the back hallway. The two sides of the table follow the judge through a paneled door to the back of the jury stand. A bailiff announces that he still has some Halloween candy if anyone is interested. A nice thought, but no one takes his offer. A few of the jurors stand and chat. Alba stays seated and is quietly looking at the space of empty table and her hands to her front.

When Judge Simpson and the attorneys enter, the testimony resumes.

Detective Luis Silva answers questions as the attorneys are reviewing the questions and answers Alba gave him shortly after being arrested from the texts they hold open. All including the jurors have a stapled copy of the interaction, in the peanut gallery I can only listen and wait for the next question.

Margaret asks the bailiff if we may have a copy. She is politely told that the transcripts will only be made public when the trial has ended.

Luis Silva reads from the script: "You didn't make any plans to have the baby?"

Silva reads Alba's answer: "I wanted to have the baby. They would; he would laugh at me."

We also found out that the name of the father of the baby is Saul. No mention that Saúl had raped her.

I am sure that this has been agreed to upon with her attorney. The family is paying for her defense, be it $10,000 is nothing for a defense attorney in a murder trial. Rape was brought up by Sheriff Silva back when she had been first picked up, and later the attorney at the Mexican Consulate also brought up rape. The last was more specific in that Alba was asked to sign a document which would have started the legal investigation in Mexico. Alba declined to do so.

The Consulate's attorney would then tell me that Alba has up to ten years to sign the complaint. Depending on how the trial goes, this may be an ace up Alba's sleeve. In the case that she is found guilty, I couldn't say if she would want to continue protecting her family, protecting her rapist!

Tuesday, November 3, 2015

Another day. All are in their places again. Sheriff Silva has his papers in hand again and is asked to read from a certain page and certain line. The jurors and judge flip to the page.

Luis Silva reads from the papers in his hand: "You didn't make any plans? You didn't go to the doctor? You didn't go anywhere?"

Alba had told Silva that she called the father of the baby in March of 2012 who said that she was on her own.

Alba said that she had no money because she spent it to come to the United States.

She didn't want to talk with her family.

The baby's father didn't want to help, and she still wanted the baby.

She didn't tell anybody.

Recordings are played of the interrogation with the original Spanish while the jurors read from the translated transcripts.

Michelle Snyder: "Strike line twelve on page fifty nine."

The people rest on Tuesday at 3:40 pm.

Tim Ruby wants to speak to his client more. He announces that he may have two or three more witnesses.

The defense is given two days to put their case together.

Thursday, November 5, 2015

Several California Lutheran University students are observing the case today.

Tim Ruby shows the DA a half page paper and paragraphs on what he will say.

The judge announces that juror #6 (Indian woman) is absent due to family death. The alternates' names are placed in a cup and drawn at random. From the three alternates, the clerk picks one of the two Anglo men. The Latino juror is still an alternate.

Tim Ruby starts off by saying that he wants to speak to the judge prosecution attorney in the hallway behind the chambers.

Alba is wearing the same now wrinkled teal sweatshirt she has been wearing the whole case. Alba is sitting quietly, not moving.

9:30 Tim Ruby returns with the judge and Prosecutor Michelle Snyder from the hallway.

Everyone stands, facing the jurors as they walk in from the hallway. Tim Ruby is facing the opposite direction.

Judge Simpson announces a break for the day. The court will be in session again on Monday, November 9 at 9:00 am.

It seems that Tim Ruby has asked for and been granted the weekend to bring his defense together.

Judge Simpson: "We are very much ahead of schedule." He explains to the jurors, "We are contemplating matters of law that may not be apparent to the jury."

I get word at school not to come to the court. Margaret tells me that she heard that Tim Ruby may ask for a delay in the trial.

Monday, November 9 Jury enters at 9:12.

Tim Ruby starts off the day by talking about Alba's living conditions. He tells the jurors that she "Lived alone." Wearing baggy clothing so nobody would notice the pregnancy.

Judge Simpson: "I don't see how her living conditions are relevant."

Tim Ruby tries to explain that even though Alba lived with six people, her work schedule and solitary living conditions means that the family didn't notice her pregnancy.

Michelle Snyder: "We aren't contesting that the family didn't know since when she came over, she was six months pregnant." The prosecution goes on to say that living circumstances doesn't justify murder.

Tim Ruby follows that he believes that the court is suppressing testimony.

Judge Simpson decides that he is willing to entertain Alba's living conditions in the case and that they may affect intent.

Tim Ruby very clearly and with a note of victory or perhaps renewed energy raises is voice. "I will be calling Alba Flores Zapata, Detective Luis Silva, and two others to testify."

Tim Ruby calls Alba's oldest sister, María Guadalupe Zapata to the witness stand.

Ruby explained that María Guadalupe will tell the jury that on May 18, 2012, she was working on three acres. María Guadalupe saw her sister across the street around 3:30 she did not see her sister after that and finished her work.

Alba lives in a non-connected structure at the back yard of her sister's house. The sister said that Alba would stay in her room when not working.

The family home doesn't have a TV, radio, computer or newspaper delivery.

Citlali, sister to Alba, has a special needs child at Elm Elementary School, he starts school at 5:00 am. She makes the 30 minute walk each way twice a day.

Tim Ruby leads the jury through the life of Alba. She comes from a simple town with no cars. "Rudimentary medical care." She went to school up to the fifth grade. Distances are measured not in miles but in how long it takes to walk somewhere.

Tim Ruby: "Alba had a sexual affair with a young man.

Alba obtained a prescription from a girlfriend to have her period return. It didn't work."

Alba later picked strawberries in Ventura County for juice. She crossed the field to portable toilets. She had a headache, gave birth and fainted. When she awoke, she saw the baby with the umbilical cord wrapped around his neck. Fearing he was chocking she removed the umbilical cord and held the baby, put him down and passed out again.

When she awoke, the baby was moving, and she prayed to Jesus because he sent her this baby and took photos with her cell phone. Since everyone was gone when Alba awoke the second time she began to hail passing cars. A passing police car passed by as Alba waved at it. When no one pulled over, she called her sister.

Recess is called.

The defense version is introduced. I am taken that Alba will claim that she tried to wave down passing cars and even a police car. The field worker who separated the workforce to walk across a road, who gave birth wasn't noticed by her own family, her fellow workers of the shadows. Cars and even a police car could have seen her. They could have noticed the woman waving her arms, but if they had would they stop?

The assistant to Prosecutor Snyder took a moment in the break to talk with a person in the public section about the case. "The funny thing is that patrol cars don't go by there."

"It's hard to keep a straight face..." she tells the gentleman.

... "If a police car passed it would have stopped."

"I don't know why the judge entertains this." The jurors enter.

Alba stands up and walks towards the witness stand. Her

Mixteco translator follows her and sits at a chair next to her in the box.

I hope that Alba had practiced and prepared for this. Tim Ruby may have worked much harder on this than I had envisioned. Taking the stand could be the best or worst move they could make. Truth, in Alba's words, can be the deciding factor in the case. The jurors now have a chance to see from the same mother what had happened and what Alba was thinking at the time.

Tim Ruby: "When and where were you born?" There is a pause after each question as the translator speaks to Alba and she responds. The translator then speaks into the microphone.

Alba: "August 10, 1992. I was born in Oaxaca, Mexico."

Tim Ruby: "Describe the area where you were born."

Alba: "A small town, very poor, no electricity, no running water."

Alba explains that she needs to get water from a well, chop wood. There are no roads. She lived with her father and mother. At the age of nine, she went with her father to go work. Alba is one of twelve children in the Cruz Zapata family. Seven females, five males.

When Alba lived in the wilderness, she slept under a tarp that was covered with wood.

When Alba came to the United States, she left her father and two siblings who were still at home in the countryside. Her mother stayed behind in their house. Her other siblings had already made the journey to the United States.

In her early years, Alba's school was a 30-minute walk away. Her father took her so she could learn. Alba would go to school from 8:00 in the morning to 2:00 in the afternoon. She stopped after the fifth grade.

Alba would cook, do chores, and take care of animals. Her father would sell the animals to buy Alba shoes, clothes and food.

No stores, no medical clinics were close to here village.

Other than in the school, no Spanish was spoken in the town.

Alba said that she came to the United States because there was no one to support her once her father died. She was nineteen.

Mother was sick and wanted to send money to help.

Tim Ruby: "Did you have a sexual relationship with a man before leaving?"

Michelle Snyder: "Objection 352."

Michelle Snyder, Judge Simpson and Tim Ruby step into the back hallway.

Alba still seated in the witness stand, looking down the whole time and has not made eye contact with the jury.

The three come in from the back door. Tim Ruby talks with Alba and the translator in whispers and the witness box.

Tim Ruby confirms aloud that Alba was pregnant before leaving to the United States.

Jury enters.

Tim Ruby: "How did you get to the United States?"

Alba: "I walked about a week in the wilderness. Then I arrived at Cecilia's home."

Alba said that she arrived to the house in Oxnard in January 2012. Alba worked at El Canto fields for four months. She began working at the new field for about a week before giving birth.

She was one of about twenty pickers working at this field at the time.

Tim Ruby: "Were you ever asked if you were pregnant?"

Alba: "No one asked me."

Tim Ruby: "Who were you living with on May 18, 2012?"

Alba: "My sister and a couple who was renting." Cecilia would take Alba to work.

Alba's room was built onto the back of the house. She had no furniture, four walls and a door leading to the backyard, no windows.

Alba said that she would cook for herself and eat by herself.

Alba would go to bed after she finished cleaning the main house and mopping the floor.

She would leave her room fully dressed to go to work. She claimed that there was no reason that anyone would ask if she was pregnant.

Tim Ruby: "Did you ever seek any medical help?"

Alba: "No, I didn't know where to go."

Alba made no effort to find a doctor or a hospital. She was afraid that ICE would find out about her and her family.

Alba: "When I was sick in Oaxaca, I would stay at home and drink a tea."

She paid about $200 a week to her sister for the rent of the room. She paid for her food and necessities.

Alba sent money home to her mother when she could. $100 to $150 at a time.

Tim Ruby: "What did you do when you didn't feel well? Take medicine?"

Alba: "A friend of mine gave me a medicine and said, 'drink this, and you will get your monthly back.'" Alba told Saul that she was pregnant. His response was to see how she should deal with it.

Tim Ruby: "Beginning in March to May, did you have any illness that made you think you were pregnant?"

Alba: "I don't understand the question."

Fourteen college students enter the courtroom. The spectator section is almost full.

Alba explains that she was having problems with her periods when she was very young. Over time, she didn't seek any advice or talk to anyone about her medical problem.

Alba would go with Cecilia at 6:00 in the morning to the field. She wouldn't leave anything in the car.

Alba took her lunch and cell phone but kept them inside her back pack.

Tim Ruby: "Did you feel any pain while you were picking?"

Alba: "No. Around 3:40 I started feeling funny. I started having a headache."

Alba said that she told her sister that she wanted to go home. Cecilia asked her to wait an hour.

Alba: "But then I started having pain."

Tim Ruby: "Did you ever figure out a date of delivery?"

Alba: "Didn't know when." (Repeated this multiple times.)

Tim Ruby: "Did the question ever cross your mind?"

Alba: "No."

Alba explains that the baby wasn't crying or moving.

She started getting tunnel vision and fainted.

Alba came to and started waving at cars passing by. She couldn't think clear or remember if she had a cell phone with her.

The court goes on break.

Michelle Snyder wants to release Alba's work record to the

public.

Tim Ruby: I want to read them and discuss them.

Alba is excused from questioning for the day. She walks to the seat next to her attorney.

The jury enters.

Citlali is called in from the hallway and is escorted by the Bailiff to the stand. The Mixteco translator is at her side.

Tim Ruby: "Do you recall when you received a call to pick Alba up?"

Citlali: "No. I don't recall."

Tim Ruby questions about son's school activity.

Citlali: "No. I don't recall."

It is said that she is required to pick her son up Monday thru Friday at 5:00 pm.

Tim Ruby: Did you ever receive a call from your sister to pick her up from work?"

Citlali: "No. I don't remember. I don't remember when I got the call."

Tim Ruby: "Do you recall looking around the field and noticing that Alba was gone?"

Citlali: "I can't say because I was working by myself and she wasn't with me."

Citlali has four children. Two are American citizens because they were born in the United States. All four children, from the United States as well as Mexico, were born in hospitals.

All the other relatives that she still keeps in contact with all had their children born in hospitals.

Citlali saw Alba about three times a week.

Citlali clams to speak just a little Spanish.

Tim Ruby asks about the phone conversation: "Alba called and said that she had a headache and asked to be picked up."

Citlali: "I don't remember."

Michelle Snyder: "How old are you?"

Citlali: "I don't know."

Michelle Snyder: "You don't know how old you are?"

Citlali: "No."

Michelle Snyder: "Do you know your birthdate?"

Citlali: "No."

Michelle Snyder: "Do you have more brothers and sisters?"

Citlali: "Yes."

Michelle Snyder: "How many brothers and sisters do you have?"

Citlali: "I don't remember because I came several years ago."

Michelle Snyder: "Are you the oldest?"

Citlali: "No. I have an older sister."

Michelle Snyder: "Is Alba the youngest?"

Citlali: "No. There is one sister that is younger."

Citlali did not know the age of her four young children. This conversation went on for a while as well.

Michelle Snyder: "How did Alba look when you went together?"

Citlali: "She looked normal. OK."

Michelle Snyder: "Was she carrying a baby?"

Citlali: "No."

Michelle Snyder: "Was it a busy road?"

Citlali: "I don't remember."

Michelle Snyder: "She wasn't crying?"

Citlali: "No."

Michelle Snyder: "Did she have blood on her?"

Citlali: "No. We did not know she had a baby. We didn't know that she was pregnant."

Michelle Snyder: "Was she by herself?"

Citlali: "Yes."

Michelle Snyder: "Were other workers there?"

Citlali: "I do not remember."

Michelle Snyder: "Did your husband offer to stop and get medicine for her headache."

Citlali: "No."

There were four people in the car. (Citlali, husband, son, and Alba.)

Citlali claims that she cannot speak Spanish at all.

Michelle Snyder: "When you called Alba in jail, did you speak Spanish?"

Judge Simpson interrupts and calls a recess.

Citlali has to go home to breast feed her baby.

An audio tape is later played. Both Citlali and Alba are both speaking fluent Spanish.

I arrive at the court. Dominick, my eldest son, hands me his note book.

Tim Ruby: "When you were in Oaxaca, how did you get to the hospital?"

Citlali: "We went by car."

Tim Ruby: "Did you own a car?"

Citlali: "No. We went by the road and waited for someone to take us."

Citlali's third and fourth child were born in Ventura

Community Hospital.

Michelle Snyder: "How were your children paid for?"

Citlali: "MediCal."

Michelle Snyder: "Do you pay for their education."

Citlali: "No."

Michelle Snyder: "Do you pay for their meals at school?"

Citlali: "No."

Michelle Snyder: "When did you first know that she had a baby?"

Citlali: "No one ever told me."

Michelle Snyder: "Now you know that she had a baby?"

Citlali: "I did not know."

Michelle Snyder: "You know now that Alba had a baby?"

Citlali: "No."

Michelle Snyder: "Alba had a baby. That is why we are here in court. You do know that Alba had a baby?"

Citlali: "I was told when the men took her."

Michelle Snyder: "Was that when the police told you?"

Citlali: "Yes, when she was arrested."

Michelle Snyder: "Did Alba ever tell you about the baby?"

Citlali: "No. She never did."

Michelle Snyder: "Did you have any clothes or crib for your baby?"

Citlali: "Yes."

Michelle Snyder: "Alba never asked you to barrow anything?"

Citlali: "No."

Michelle Snyder: "Did you know anything from the news about the baby found in the field?"

Citlali: "No."

Tim Ruby: "When you brought Alba back, did your sister talk?"

Citlali: "We did not talk. That's the way we are."

Tim Ruby: "Did you know that Alba was pregnant?"

Citlali: "She did not show."

Citlali is excused and allowed to leave the courtroom. Passing the attorneys on the prosecution side, Margaret invited Citlali to have a seat, and she sat just behind us. As the second sister, María Guadalupe was called into the court the bailiff came to Citlali and asked her to leave the courtroom. She got up and passed her sister coming in.

Later I was told by my wife Viviana and son Dominick that they had a conversation with Citlali outside the courtroom in Spanish. It was pleasantries, but it was in perfect Spanish.

María Guadalupe stood in front of the jurors, facing Judge Simpson to be sworn in. The translator at her side said that she did agree. Both took a seat in the witness box.

Michelle Snyder: "Mrs. Zapata, while Alba lived in your house, did she have her room?"

María Guadalupe: "Yes."

Michelle Snyder: "Is there any furniture in that room?"

María Guadalupe: "No. She didn't have anything."

Michelle Snyder: "Where did she sleep?"

María Guadalupe: "A small mattress."

Michelle Snyder: "With blankets?"

María Guadalupe: "Yes. She had a mattress and blankets?"

Michelle Snyder: "What about clothes?"

María Guadalupe: "Yes, she had very little."

Michelle Snyder: "Who else lived in the house? Your husband?"

María Guadalupe: "Yes."

Michelle Snyder: "Children?"

María Guadalupe: "Yes. Two and a new born."

Michelle Snyder: "Was Alba's room in the main house?"

María Guadalupe: "No."

Alba ate in the living room and cooked in the kitchen. Alba could use the bathroom. Alba would sometimes eat in her room.

Michelle Snyder: "Did you notice that she was pregnant?"

María Guadalupe: "No. She never told me. I wasn't aware of it."

Michelle Snyder: "When did you find out?"

María Guadalupe: "When they came. That's when I found out."

Michelle Snyder: "When the police came?"

María Guadalupe: "I don't know what they alled them."

Michelle Snyder: "Alba would talk with your two children?"

María Guadalupe: "Yes."

María Guadalupe: "I don't remember the name of the ranch. Strawberries. We would go in the same car. When we got to work, we didn't see her."

Michelle Snyder: "Was it that day?"

María Guadalupe: "I don't remember."

"When we arrived she just got there."

"She didn't say anything."

"She ate that evening."

Michelle Snyder: "How many days a week did you work?"

María Guadalupe: "Six days a week."

María Guadalupe: "When work was good, we would just work. I don't remember."

"The box would weigh over 20 pounds."

"Yes. Alba was working."

Michelle Snyder: "When did Alba come home?"

María Guadalupe: "5:00 or 5:30. I don't remember."

Michelle Snyder: "Who brought her home?"

María Guadalupe: "I did not see who. When I noticed she was already inside the door."

Michelle Snyder: "Did you have your babies in the hospital?"

María Guadalupe: "Yes. I had a doctor. Las Islas."

Michelle Snyder: "How did you pay?"

María Guadalupe: "Medical."

Michelle Snyder: "Did you ever tell her that you would take the baby?"

María Guadalupe: "Yes. When the people took her, that's when I found out."

Tim Ruby: "Was that on a payday?"

María Guadalupe: "I don't remember."

Tim Ruby: "Where did you look for her?"

María Guadalupe: "I looked. I didn't see her."

"We were about thirty people. We left."

No heat in the house. She wears the same clothes.

María Guadalupe has been in the United States since 2012.

Alba arrived later.

Twelve-year-old son was born in the United States.

Michelle Snyder: "Were there still workers in La Esperanza?"

María Guadalupe: "I don't remember."

Court is called for the day.

Tuesday, November 10, 2015

Alba is reminded that she is still under oath. She takes a seat in the witness stand, translator at her side.

Tim Ruby: "Did you have a cell phone in your back pack?"

Alba: "Yes I did."

Tim Ruby: "Did you have lunch?"

Alba: "Yes, after we had break."

Alba says the break was around 3:20 for ten minutes. She says that she is not sure of the time, but says that it's usually the break time.

Alba says that she felt fine from the start of work to her break.

After the break, she started picking strawberries again.

She claims to start having a headache between 3:00 and 3:50 pm. She left the field and went towards the area where the cars were parked.

The jury exits for a break.

Judge Simpson asks Tim Ruby if he wants to talk about anything. Ruby says "yes" turns and looks at Dominick sitting behind him. Ruby tells the judge, "Let's step outside."

Jurors enter.

Tim Ruby: "When you got a headache, where were you?"

Alba: "A different field." (Separate from where she was working.)

After turning in her tools to the supervisor, she went to

the other field.

Alba: "I was going to go home. I told her I have a headache and will be going home."

Alba asked the sister if we are going home. María Guadalupe said to wait one more hour.

At this point there is a break and upon coming back we find that Juror 9 is excused due to an illness. The new juror is picked at random, again by using paper in a cup. It is the Anglo alternative. The Latino alternate is still on the end of the jury box.

Tim Ruby: "Before you crossed the road, did you stop at María Guadalupe's car?"

Alba: "Yes. I went there and stayed there for a few minutes."

Alba told María Guadalupe that she had a headache and started bleeding.

Eight college students and their teacher enter the public section.

Tim Ruby: "Could you get into the car?"

Alba: "No. I didn't have the keys."

After Alba was waiting by the car, she felt like she needed to use the restroom and crossed the street to the other field because there were porta potties set up to the side.

There was a locked gate that she was able to jump the mesh fence. This fence was more to keep the dust down than to keep people out.

Alba crossed into the neighboring strawberry field where she had worked in the past.

Tim Ruby: "What did you feel?"

Alba: "The feeling grew stronger, more intense. I started feeling dizzy, really dizzy. Then I fainted."

Before fainting between the rows in the field, Alba pulled her pants down.

She told the court that she gave birth while she was passed out.

Tim Ruby: "Was there any place where you were working at that you could use a restroom?"

Alba: "No there wasn't."

When Alba awoke after she fainted she "felt something heavy around me, and I saw it was already there." Between the birth and prayers, the baby looked fine she said, the baby had his eyes shut.

Alba collapsed after fainting again. She came to a second time and was very dizzy and had a hard time seeing.

Alba was trying to rationalize what was happening, then she knelt down and started praying and thanking God.

Alba started asking God to bless her and protect her also to "thank him for the baby he had sent me."

Tim Ruby: "After the prayer, what did you do?"

After the prayer, she thought it was dead because it was not moving. She noticed that the umbilical cord was wrapped around the baby's neck and moved it. There was an immediate reaction from the baby who was lying face up between the strawberry rows.

Alba: "It had the cord tangled around its neck. I untangled it, and it started moving. Then I held it."

Alba: "The baby felt warm." She went on to describe how she placed the baby down where he was born before starting to wave at cars.

Alba: "I saw cars passing by, and I stood up and started waving at cars for help."

She waved at cars and claimed to have even seen a police car go by without stopping. She then called her sister on her cell phone.

Had a car stopped, the evening news would have celebrated the miracle baby that was born in the strawberry field. The news would have ended on the note that the baby and mother were fine.

While everyone likes a good warm fuzzy story about a baby being born in an unusual place, some would have soon taken up the cause of political anchor babies and the evils of illegal immigration. The proclaimers of patriotism would sorrowfully lose tax moneys. The Presidential races were on the horizon in mid-2012 would possibly have made the story a national debate. The God given child, alive would have been an anchor baby, with full American citizenship rights.

A car did not stop. Help did not save the baby.

Three more people enter the courtroom.

Alba put the baby down "because it was sleeping again."

Alba admits to hiding the baby when she put it down.

The translator becomes confused about a wording of the question asked her. The question is re-stated. Court Reporter: "Did you want to hide the baby?" After placing the baby down, Alba called Citlali.

Alba "The baby looked fine, and I left it there."

Alba: "I left the baby when Citlali came." "I was on the road."

The new mother did not think about what she was going to do with the baby when Citlali came.

Tim Ruby: "Did you consider the baby would be safe when

you left it?"

Alba: "Yes, it was warm there, and there were flowers there… to protect it from the wind."

Tim Ruby: "Have you ever slept outdoors?"

Alba: "Yes, we had a tarp roof and would sleep on the ground in the mountains."

Tim Ruby: "Why didn't you move the baby to another place?"

Alba: "Because it was warm there."

Alba: "I thought someone would pass by that day or the next day and take the baby."

Court Reporter: "Did you consider the possibility that it would not protect the child?"

Alba: "That is what was going to protect the baby."

When she called Citlali, Alba told her that she would be on the road between the two fields near the porta potties. The baby was lying, set in some 40 yards into the field.

When the car arrived, Alba opened the door and got in. No one asked her questions why she was there or why she was there after all the workers had gone home.

Tim Ruby: "What do you think would happen when someone saw the baby?"

Alba: "They were going to take it."

Tim Ruby: "Did you intend just to have the baby and never see it again?"

Alba: "Yes, I would have seen it. They were going to find it, take it and raise it."

Alba: "In time if I could take care of the baby I would take it back."

236

Tim Ruby: "If you stayed home with the baby for a few days and went back to work, would someone be able to take care of the baby?"

Alba: "No."

Tim Ruby: "If you stayed home did you have any savings you'd rely on?"

Alba: "No."

Tim Ruby: "Was there anything you could have done that would allow you to keep the baby and have you or someone in your family to take care of it?"

Alba: "No, because they have their own families."

Tim Ruby: "Did you ever think of leaving the child, running away and doing nothing about it."

Alba: "No."

Alba went back to work in the strawberry field the next day. People were working.

"They were already there taking strawberries where I left the baby."

"That's what I thought since I heard someone left the baby."

Tim Ruby: "Did you go back to where you left the baby?"

Alba: "No, because everyone was working."

Lunch is called, the jury and staff leave the court.

Alba is escorted off to a room to the side.

Judge Simpson telling jurors that if anyone bugs them in the hallway to tell a bailiff and the person will be ejected and arrested. Apparently, one or a few jurors were spooked outside in the courtroom's hallway. The closed space and milling about may have let a juror listen to the comments of Margaret, Sean Justice or my son Dominick. There were also several university students attending the court, and they may have taken advantage to talk amongst themselves. In any case, this was the first of several statements from the judge over his concern of the jurors' anonymity and what they might hear.

Tim Ruby: "What made you positive that someone would find the child?"

Alba: "I thought they might go there the following day to work there."

Tim Ruby: "Did you believe the cord was harming the child?"

Alba: "Yes."

Once the cord was removed, the baby started moving and making sounds.

Alba: "The baby moved for a bit and stopped."

Alba then moved its leg, and both legs started moving.

Alba: "Then I started recording the baby. I took a video."

Alba: "I knew someone would find him, then at some point I would have the baby back."

Tim Ruby: "Did you give detectives permission to search your cell phone?"

Alba: "Yes."

Tim Ruby: "Having in mind that you were going to give birth. Did you intend to hide the fact that you had a baby?"

Alba: "No."

Tim Ruby: "Did you walk away because you did not know what you would do?"

Alba: "Yes."

238

Recess 2:30

Jurors enter the courtroom from the door the attorney had retreated to with the judge to discuss matters out of earshot of the court. The jury is concerned about possible influence or reprisal from the public. The case may only now have become a serious matter for the men and women of the jury. They are now exposing their opinions in a deeply emotional and moral realm. The jurors would make law, judgement and religious beliefs without guidance from trusted friends or family. It seems as a spectator that reality had set in.

Michelle Snyder starts by using the word "ditch" instead of row or field row. She is also establishing that the baby was alive.

Michelle Snyder is for the first time, in this case, being very aggressive and asking rapid fire questions of Alba. The translations and understanding seem to make the fast pace slow down at each step.

Alba says that she tried to breast feed the baby.

Michelle Snyder: Why hadn't you mentioned that before?"

Alba: "I tried to feed him, but he didn't take it."

Michelle Snyder: "So you left him and didn't feed him?"

Alba: "No."

Michelle Snyder: "You left him naked?"

Alba: "I had no clothes."

Michelle Snyder: "You had a shirt."

Alba: "It's a work shirt."

Michelle Snyder: "You had a sweatshirt."

Alba: "Yes."

Michelle Snyder: "You do know that it gets cold at night?"

Alba: "It doesn't get cold here."

Michelle Snyder: "Here in Oxnard, you sleep indoors and not outdoors, correct?"

Alba: "Yes."

Michelle Snyder: "You know that it gets cold here in Oxnard because you wear a sweatshirt, correct?"

Alba: "No."

Michelle Snyder: "Did you dry the baby off or was he still wet?"

Alba: "He was dry."

Michelle Snyder: "You have seven sisters in Mexico. What are their names?"

Alba lists the names.

Michelle Snyder names three of the sister's names and asks if they are still in Mexico.

Alba: "They all live in Oaxaca."

Michelle Snyder: "Why did you say you left your mother alone?"

Alba: "They are all living their own lives and not living with the mother. Two brothers are still in Oaxaca."

Michelle Snyder: "You took care of animals and their needs in Mexico?"

Alba: "Yes."

Michelle Snyder is making the point that the father and mother raised twelve children with little money or resources.

Michelle Snyder: "Do you speak Spanish and Mixteco?"

Alba: "Some Spanish."

Alba's father only speaks Mixteco and Alba only speaks Mixteco to the family.

Michelle Snyder: "Don't you speak Spanish to your sisters?"

Alba: "Sometimes they have to speak Spanish to their kids."

Michelle Snyder is establishing that Alba and at least her two sisters do speak Spanish.

Michelle Snyder: "How did you get from Oaxaca to Oxnard?"

Alba: "I came with my brother in law."

Michelle Snyder: "How did you get to the US-Mexico border?"

Alba: "I don't understand."

Michelle Snyder repeats the question.

Alba: "I don't understand."

Michelle Snyder: "Who invited you to Oxnard?"

Alba: "No one."

Michelle Snyder: How did you decide to go to Oxnard?"

Alba: "No one told me."

Michelle Snyder: "How did you and Ruben arrive?"

Alba: "We left then came here."

Alba admits that she came by car. She spent three days traveling by car. She slept in the streets. After three days they walked into the wilderness.

Alba admits that she lied to the police about getting lost in the desert when crossing over. She was never lost or left alone.

Alba admits that she had her cell phone for a while and knows how to take photos and videos.

Recess

Jurors enter.

Michelle Snyder: "You were pregnant when you came with

Ruben?"

Alba: "Yes."

Michelle Snyder: "When you got to Oxnard you lived with Cecilia?"

Alba: "Yes."

Cecilia's husband is named Claudio.

Brother of Alba is Kabil.

Michelle Snyder: "Who taught you to work at the strawberry fields?"

Alba: "The boss."

Cecilia got Alba the papers to get a job.

Cecilia and Claudio would get them back and forth in the car to work.

In the process of questioning, it became apparent that Alba did not know her left from her right.

Photo of a birthday cake for one of the children is shown on the large screen. The stove in the background of the photo has aluminum foil wrapped on the hood, back and stove burner sections. I can't say why but it stands out.

"Sa" means "yes" in Mixteco.

Michelle Snyder: "You didn't tell your three sisters that you were pregnant, right?"

Alba: "No."

Michelle Snyder: "Why?"

Alba: "They had their own families, so I didn't tell them."

Michelle Snyder: "You did not want to tell them?"

Alba: "I just didn't tell them."

Michelle Snyder: "Who paid for you to come here?"

Alba: "Myself. I worked, and that's how I paid for the trip."

242

Michelle Snyder: "Who paid for the things on the way of the trip?"

Alba: "I paid when I arrived."

Michelle Snyder: "Who did you pay?"

Alba: "Another person. I did not know them."

Alba: "They were here in Oxnard. I worked to pay. three thousand dollars."

Michelle Snyder: "Did that include the paperwork to work?"

Alba: "No."

Michelle Snyder: "Did your sisters pay for their trips?"

Alba: "I don't know."

Michelle Snyder: "Did you do anything to plan for the baby?"

Alba: "I do not understand."

Michelle Snyder: "Did you do anything to prepare for the baby?"

Alba: "No."

Michelle Snyder: "Why not?"

Alba: "I just didn't."

Michelle Snyder: "How were you able to hide it?"

Alba: "I did not show."

Judge Simpson calls a close for the day. Tim Ruby did not know that tomorrow was a federal holiday, Veteran's Day. Court will be back in session on Thursday at 9:00 in the morning.

Thursday, November 12, 2015 9:14 in the morning.

For the first time since the trial has started, Alba is wearing different clothes today. A blue sweatshirt.

Michelle Snyder asks Alba why the cell phone was in her back pack. She asks why she didn't leave it on the ground.

Alba pays forty dollars a month for the cell phone.

Michelle Snyder asks if she presented an ID when applying for work at El Canto. "Did you know that they were false?"

Alba: "I did not know."

Courtroom has four people in the public section.

Michelle Snyder: "You wear handkerchiefs?"

Alba: "Yes, two of them."

Michelle Snyder: "Why?"

Alba: "I don't know?"

I can say that the sun, the dust, and the pesticides are a good reason for the workers to cover their faces. They use handkerchiefs for generations. The uniform might be unknown to the new fieldworker like Alba, but the veterans know very well why they use them.

Bailiff is talking to Tim Ruby. I am unsure if it is related to the case. Bailiff is talking on the radio and phone.

Tim Ruby walks over to the bailiff's desk while the DA is questioning Alba.

Alba doesn't work past 6:00 in the evening. DA is asking if Alba knows what happens to the field at night.

Michelle Snyder: "Are there porta potties there?"

Alba: "Yeah."

Michelle Snyder: "How much do you get paid per box?"

Alba: "I don't know."

Michelle Snyder: "How did they pay you?"

Alba: "A check every week."

Alba is saying that she makes two-hundred dollars per

week, sometimes three-hundred dollars per week. She would go to a store in Hueneme to cash the check.

Michelle Snyder: "Are you related to the father of the baby, Saul?"

Alba: "No." Alba wanted Saul to come to Oxnard.

She is unsure where he is now.

I remember that someone in the Mexican Consulate

told me that the father of the child was the brother of a brother-in-law. This would be considered a close relation in Latin America.

Michelle Snyder: "Did you ask about adoption?"

Alba: "No."

Michelle Snyder: "Did you ever try to get an abortion?"

Alba: "No."

I'm sure that Alba didn't consider the special herbs and tea to bring back her period an abortion.

Michelle Snyder: "Why did you say that you had no brothers or sisters in Mexico?"

Alba: "Because I didn't understand the question."

Michelle Snyder: "When you were pregnant, you didn't want to keep the baby?"

Alba: "No."

Michelle Snyder: "Why didn't you keep it?"

Alba: "There is a difference between wanting to keep it and being able to keep it."

Michelle Snyder: "Why didn't you ask your sister where the hospital was?"

Alba: "They have their own lives."

Michelle Snyder: "When did you decide not to keep the

baby?"

Alba: "I didn't."

Michelle Snyder establishes that Alba has knowledge to the date and day of the week she gave birth.

Michelle Snyder: "Why did you tell the police you didn't have a cell phone?"

Alba: "Because at that point I didn't remember."

Michelle Snyder: "Did you think that you could have called for an ambulance on your cell phone to help you with the baby?"

Alba: "I didn't know what an ambulance is."

Michelle Snyder: "Did you say this to Detective Silva?"

Alba is saying she did, but she didn't know what an ambulance was because she didn't know how to pronounce it correctly.

Michelle Snyder: "Did you tell detective Silva that you would call the police if you had a cell phone?"

Alba: "Yes, but I didn't even know the number."

Michelle Snyder is asking Alba why she lied to police saying that she didn't know her coworkers.

Alba: "Because I didn't want to get them in trouble."

Note: One juror chair is empty, upper row, first chair next to the bailiff's desk.

Michelle Snyder: "Why did you cross the street?"

Alba: "To use the porta potties."

Michelle Snyder: "Didn't you say that there were porta potties where you work?"

Alba: "Yes, but they were far away from where I was."

Alba says that they were next to where they were picking.

Michelle Snyder: "Why did you go into a locked fenced off area?"

Alba: "Because it was closer to me."

Note: A Sheriff entered the courtroom and is sitting in the public section. Now there are three in the room. It appears that they expect a seventy-year-old woman, a teacher, and a homeless journalist to be disruptive. On the other hand, I always expected Margaret to be the disruptive type.

Michelle Snyder shows Alba photos to establish where she had the baby.

Michelle Snyder is asking if it isn't going to the bathroom in the field against the rules.

Alba: "I don't know."

Michelle Snyder is showing photos of the scene and asking if Alba can see the baby on any of the photos.

Alba can only see the laser pointer on the picture.

Recess until 10:45.

Tim Ruby tells the judge that he has to go down to Court 13. Ruby is talking to bailiff clarifying what room he is in since he will be handling two more cases today.

Courtroom doors open at 10:58.

Jurors enter at 11:00.

Twelve jurors are present. Extra seat?

Michelle Snyder asking if Alba expected where she would deliver the baby.

Alba said she would have it at home, but she didn't know how.

Alba: "To go to the bathroom."

Alba took off her shoes (seen in the video) says she pulled down her pants, but not off.

Michelle Snyder is asking why Alba said to Detective Silva

that she left the baby in the field because you thought the baby was dead.

Michelle Snyder: "Didn't you lie to Detective Silva saying you didn't know how the baby was?"

Alba: "I was really scared. I was scared that I would get hit by Detective Silva."

Michelle Snyder: "When did you decide to video record him?"

Alba: "Spur of the moment."

Alba is saying she picked the baby up and held him because she loved him. But she put him back on the ground.

Alba was scared she would get kicked out of the house if she took him. Alba starts crying softly.

Michelle Snyder: "You said you planned on keeping the baby. What were you going to tell them?"

Alba: "I don't know." Alba says that she was scared of her family.

Alba got hit when she was growing up.

The Bailiff passes tissue to Alba. She starts crying uncontrollably. Tim Ruby asks for a break. Recess until 1:40.

When we came back, it was the prosecution's turn to question Alba.

Michelle Snyder: "Did you try to wave down cars next to the baby or next to the road?"

Alba: "Next to the baby."

Michelle Snyder: "Time between calling Citlali and being picked up?"

Alba: "I don't know."

Michelle Snyder: "If someone had stopped, you would have had them take it?"

Alba: "Yes."

Michelle Snyder: "Did you mention the baby to Citlali after she picked you up?"

Alba: "No."

Michelle Snyder: "When you left the baby, did you think the baby would be cold?"

Alba: "I left him where it was warm."

Michelle Snyder: "Is 48 degrees cold?"

Alba: "I don't know what that is."

Michelle Snyder: "Have you ever spent the night in the field?"

Alba: "No."

Michelle Snyder: "How did you know that a coyote would not come at night and get the baby?"

Alba: "God was going to watch over him."

Michelle Snyder: "Why didn't you have God watch over him and you?"

Alba: "I do not understand."

Michelle Snyder: "You could have taken the baby and protected him."

Alba: "I don't understand. I was scared."

Michelle Snyder: "Clothing?"

Alba: "He was protected."

Michelle Snyder: "Did you take care of baby lambs?"

Alba: "Yes."

Michelle Snyder: "Did you protect them?"

Alba: "I was mainly concerned that one would get lost. If

they got lost, I would go the next day to find them.

Sometimes I would find them; sometimes I wouldn't.

Michelle Snyder: "Why would you not want to lose a lamb?"

Alba: "Sometimes I can find them, and sometimes I'm not."

Alba went to work the day, Saturday after she gave birth to the same field across from where she left the baby. Alba did not see the baby because she was at work.

She did not look.

Michelle Snyder: "Did you tell anyone about the baby?
Alba: "No."

Michelle Snyder: "Were there people working in the field?"
Alba: "I don't remember."

Michelle Snyder: "Did you tell anyone about the baby?"
Alba: "No."

Michelle Snyder: "Did you bring a lunch?"

Alba: "No. I was fasting. It was a sacrifice to God. I assumed that someone had found the baby. I assumed that someone had found him by then."

Cecilia, Reynato, and their son Francisco work in El Canto.

Michelle Snyder: "Why did you tell Detective Silva that you walked home that day?"

Alba: "Because they asked me too many questions."

Michelle Snyder: "Was it a lie?"

Alba: "Yes. At first, I did, and then I started telling them the truth."

Alba slept at her house in her room Friday and Saturday.

No work on Sunday. Alba stayed home.

Michelle Snyder: "Did you see any police on Monday?"

Alba: "No."

Michelle Snyder: "Did you hear on the radio a week later that a baby had been found?"

Alba: "No. It was a lie."

Michelle Snyder: You tried to send Saul that video?"

Alba: "Yes, but I wasn't able to."

Michelle Snyder: "The picture?"

Alba: "Yes, but I was not able to."

Michelle Snyder: "How did you know that the video did not go through?"

Alba: "It was not sent. He told me. He asked me to send it to him."

Michelle Snyder: "How did you know that there was a video?"

Alba: "We talked. I do not understand. He did not talk to me about the video. He said the picture and not the video. He was trying to send it, but it was never sent." Michelle Snyder: "Did you ever know that the baby was found until you were arrested?"

Alba: "No."

Sean Justice jumps out of his seat in the row in front of me. His arm is pointing at Tim Ruby seated at the defendant's table. "He's asleep!"

The court looks at Sean Justice, and the bailiffs jump half way from their seats. I look at Ruby and am shaking my head at the same time. I'm afraid that the judge will throw David out.

No. Tim Ruby seems to have startled himself awake, and Judge Simpson and bailiffs both let the court resume. Sean whispers to me that Ruby has nodded off several times today. Apparently, it was not something that they were going to even speak to Sean about. Thank God. Now, maybe Tim Ruby will be shamed enough to stay awake.

The court is adjourned for the day.

31. Friday the Thirteenth

Friday, November 13, 2015 10:18 in the morning.

Note: Bailiff mentioned the "attorney isn't here yet" and he saw him "running downstairs for a case he forgot about yesterday."

The jurors enter at 10:33.

Michelle Snyder mentioned someone named Lorenzo.

Plays audio recording of Alba talking to Lorenzo. (Exhibit 50)

Michelle Snyder is talking about text messages.

Asks Alba to read a message. (She reads it to herself.)

Alba refers to Lorenzo multiple times as "my love."

Alba tells Lorenzo not to call and that she will call him.

Note: Alba and Lorenzo seem to be in a relationship.

Alba is telling Lorenzo to be careful with the police.

Alba says that she isn't the only one who uses the cell phone. She had loan it out to her friends.

The prosecution mentioned that Alba called Lorenzo and used a *67 code to keep the phone number anonymous.

Michelle Snyder: "Do you know what *67 is?"

Alba: "No."

Alba also texted Saul.

Alba doesn't recall most text to him. She says that she can't read a text message in Spanish.

The messages show that Saul is marrying someone else and Alba is upset.

Michelle Snyder mentions that Alba's three sisters visited

her multiple times in the Todd Road jail.

Michelle Snyder: "Did you leave the farm because police kept coming back?"

Alba says she changed employer to a blackberry farm after the baby had been found because she didn't have a ride otherwise. She switched with her sister Magdalena.

Michelle Snyder: "Yesterday you said that you didn't have Facebook."

Note: It appears that Alba does have a Facebook page though she says she didn't make it.

Break for lunch. Back at 1:30.

The defense desk has a box of tissues and a pair of sun glasses placed on top of it now.

Tim Ruby objects about the transcript of the recorded call.

Judge asks why. Tim Ruby seems confused. The judge asks if he has had a chance to read it. Tim Ruby says he hasn't. The judge tells Tim Ruby to discuss it with him at 1:30.

Michelle Snyder is arguing that Alba's credibility is suspect and that they should play the ten-minute tape. She is trying to show the jurors that Alba is categorically lying when she is backed into a corner.

The judge thanks Tim Ruby for having a "good eye on the objection." (Doors were locked but seemed to be the irrelevance of the Alba – Lorenzo relationship.

The jurors enter the courtroom from the back.

Judge Simpson reminds Alba that she is "still under oath, that means you have to tell the truth."

Michelle Snyder plays the phone conversation from the

Todd road Jail between Alba and Lorenzo. Alba does speak Spanish very well in the phone recording.

Lorenzo plays Mexican music on the phone, so they can talk in secret. Alba acknowledges that she understood him when the song was turned off.

Alba admits that Lorenzo is a boyfriend.

Clarifies that they had no physical or romantic relationship.

Michelle Snyder asks why she would call him.

Alba said she called her family too.

Michelle Snyder: "You say you never called him before."

Alba: "No."

DA: "How did you call him from jail?"

Alba: "I remembered it."

Actually, I now believe that this is why the jail allowed Margaret to give Alba and Esperanza cash for things such as making phone calls. A reality check on how all our conversations are listened to when we are speaking with the ladies. The legal system never rests. Too bad that Mr. Ruby hadn't informed his client about this.

Note: Michelle Snyder says that Lorenzo is married.

Michelle Snyder: "If you wanted the baby to be found, why didn't you put him where a bunch of people were?"

Alba: "As I told you before, all the people were gone."

Michelle Snyder has no more questions.

This is a point that I believe that Tim Ruby could have or should have stopped. Had he closed this dialog, the prosecution would be unable to continue unraveling Alba's story. He got up to continue the questioning.

Surly he will clarify a point that will sway the negative thought in the jurors' minds.

Tim Ruby: "Do you know what is meant by the word vocabulary?"

Alba: "I do not."

Tim Ruby: "Mixteco is an oral language, not a written one."

Alba: "Yes."

Tim Ruby: "Who took you out of school?"

Alba: "My parents didn't want me to continue."

Tim Ruby: "Were there times in school where you didn't understand what the teacher was saying?"

Alba: "No."

Tim Ruby is making a point that there are words in Spanish that do not translate. Also the amount of words that Alba understands decreased over time.

Tim Ruby clarified that while Alba was being interviewed by Detective Silva if there were words that she did not understand because she was interviewed in Spanish without a Mixteco translator.

Here it comes! Ruby told me two years earlier that he would use the Mixteco language as a defense. He seemed to throw everything else he could out in the court, letting Alba speak and speak and speak without objections or any noticed preparation. Now he would say that his client was innocent because she spoke Mixteco. And yes, it was made obvious that she was also very fluent in Spanish.

Tim Ruby: Those times you asked me to repeat or that you didn't understand because you have "a lesser vocabulary than ever."

Alba: "Yes."

Tim Ruby: "Towards the end of the interview did you tell the detective that the facts were truthful?"

Alba: "Yes."

Tim Ruby: "And weren't some of those lies?"

Alba: "Yes."

Tim Ruby: "Was that because you were trying to protect your family?"

Alba: "Yes."

Alba in now saying that Detective Silva was talking too fast and she didn't understand everything. Ruby also lead her to say that she was trying to protect her family.

Tim Ruby: "Did you start crying at the interview?"

Alba: "Yes."

Tim Ruby: "Did he slow down to let you catch your breath?"

Alba: "No."

Tim Ruby: "Did you before December 5, allow Detective Silva to search your phone?"

Alba: "Yes, but he said he was looking for something important."

Tim Ruby is now saying that Alba lived to what amounts to a wooden crate. She was in an extension room that only door opened to the back yard of the house. No window, only a lightbulb hanging from the middle of the room. A small mattress lying on the floor. Boxes for the few pieces of clothing that Alba had. No radio, no communication of any kind. She did have her cell phone that she used as an alarm clock.

The court takes a 15-minute break.

Alba is back in court with her hair braided in a bun now.

The jurors enter and take their seats.

Tim Ruby: "What was the very first thing you did when you realized that you gave birth?"

Alba: "I prayed and then I started waving at cars for help."

Tim Ruby: "How many cars passed by?"

Alba: "Maybe two or three times."

Tim Ruby: "Why did you call your sister?"

Alba: "To come and pick me up."

Tim Ruby: "Why not pick up the baby and wait for your sister?"

Alba: "I was afraid of my sister."

Alba said that she was confused: dizzy and couldn't think straight.

Tim Ruby ends questions.

I held my breath. Tim Ruby had gone over old information to the jurors. I'm not sure that I saw the point.

Will the prosecutor now continue to oppose Alba? Yes.

Michelle Snyder: "If you knew you weren't going to keep the baby, why didn't you make arrangements?"

Alba: "I was scared. I intended on keeping it."

Alba said that she did not know what the baby would need.

Michelle Snyder: "You did not know it would take nine months?" She looks at the defendant and then at the jurors.

Alba: "I did not know."

Michelle Snyder: "Did you do anything to help the baby?"

Alba: "I don't understand."

Michelle Snyder: "Do you know what help means?"

Alba: "I don't understand the word."

Michelle Snyder: "You prayed to God that someone would find him. Why didn't you pray to get to let you take him home?"

Alba: "I was scared."

Michelle Snyder: "Why didn't you take him to a church?"

Alba: "I didn't know where that is."

Michelle Snyder: "But you knew where the cell phone store was."

Alba: "Yes. Sometimes my family would take me there."

Michelle Snyder: "You thought that the family would turn their backs on you?"

Alba: "Yes."

Michelle Snyder: "So you stood up and walked away from the baby in the strawberry field?"

Alba: "Yes."

Judge Simpson: "Further direct Mr. Ruby?"

No! Please don't! The last questions did not help Alba in the least. Her defense did not help. The prosecutor's questions were more direct, they sharpened the reasons for finding her guilty. I look at Margaret and slightly shake my head. Margaret opened her mouth. We both hoped that Ruby would drop it here!

Tim Ruby asks: "About getting a family member accepting you and the baby in home, would that include additional expenses?"

Tim Ruby asks questions while sitting down, microphone in hand. He seems to be hunched over looking at the table top as he speaks. Even with the microphone, he is hard to hear. He is holding the microphone too far from his mouth.

Alba: "Yes."

Tim Ruby: "Babysitting?"

Alba: "Yes."

Tim Ruby: "Transportation?"

Alba: "Yes."

Tim Ruby: "Did you think any of your family members would do that?"

Alba: "I don't know."

Tim Ruby: "Is it true that you and your sister wouldn't speak with each other?"

Alba: "I don't understand."

Court is recessed until Monday at 9:30 in the morning.

Monday, November 16, 2015

As the court is getting prepared we could hear Judge Simpson tell Tim Ruby, "Well you have been at this longer than me."

Who knows what the context was. Interesting.

Michelle Snyder is reviewing newly edited transcripts that Tim Ruby presented her.

Detective Silva is in the room. There is a total of four people in the public section.

Tim Ruby is talking to an aid. She is reminding him of his other cases.

Judge rubs his cheek. He had dental surgery yesterday and mentions that the Novocain is wearing off and with a chuckle says that he will get grumpy today. Margaret looks over to Dominick and tells him, "Oh, oh. He's going to be mean today."

Jurors enter at 10:05.

Tim Ruby is calling Alba to the stand again.

Not again! It was brilliant to have her testify. Then after she spoke, I can't say why Ruby wants her to continue. Maybe he wants to show us that he is working on his case.

I hope it is helping, but I think he is only digging the hole deeper.

Tim Ruby asks about a conversation with Lorenzo.

Tim Ruby: "Why were you crying?"

Alba: "I was very sad for my child. I wish someone could have found him. He could have had a good life."

Alba: "I thought if someone could have found him he could have had a better life than with me."

Well done. This should have been said a few days earlier. Now, it appears that the prosecution will rebut.

Michelle Snyder is asked about specifics of the conversation on phone with Lorenzo.

Michelle Snyder: "Is this the first phone conversation you had with Lorenzo?"

Alba: "Yes."

Alba is saying that a friend programmed and texted Lorenzo using her phone.

Michelle Snyder: "And you talked the entire conversation in Spanish."

Alba: "Yes."

Michelle Snyder: "Not in Mixteco."

Alba: "No."

Saul and Lorenzo share the same last name. Alba is unsure if they are related.

Michelle Snyder: "Is Lorenzo related to your brother in law?"

Alba: "I don't know."

Michelle Snyder: "Is Lorenzo from your village."

Alba: "I don't know."

Michelle Snyder: "Is Saul?"

Alba: "Yes."

Note: Alba is saying that Lorenzo does not know about the baby.

Alba argues that the transcript is wrong.

Michelle Snyder: "So you can read Spanish?"

Alba: "Yes."

Michelle Snyder: "How about English?"

Alba: "No."

Alba is saying that the word "presiosa" (beautiful) is supposed to be "tristesa" (sadness).

Michelle Snyder: "How do you remember what you said?"

Alba: "Because it's said here."

Michelle Snyder is asking why Alba said: "They are trying to get me out."

Alba says that she was talking about something else, (not bail). But she can't remember.

Michelle Snyder: "Lorenzo said, 'What did they tell you yesterday?' and you said, 'I can't tell you.' What can't you tell him?"

Alba: "I don't know."

Michelle Snyder: So after listening to the conversation and transcript, can you still say he isn't just a friend?"

Alba: "If you read the Bible it says love your neighbor."

Michelle Snyder: "Have you been to church before?"

Alba: "Yes, a few times." She doesn't remember where or the name of the church.

Michelle Snyder: "There was an unsent message that says, 'Yo cuento contigo.'" ('I'm counting on you.")

Alba doesn't know what the message is. She doesn't know the words.

Multiple messages on Sunday in the morning.

Alba says that her friend borrowed her cell phone that day.

Michelle Snyder is talking about a message calling someone 'mi amor.' (My love.)

Alba: "Why do you want to know?"

Michelle Snyder: "Do you know the name of the person?"

Alba: "I do not remember." Break for ten minutes.

Jurors enter.

Michelle Snyder: "Did Lorenzo live in the same house as Citlali?"

Alba: "No."

Michelle Snyder: "Where did he live?"

Alba: "I don't know."

Snyder pauses, turns her head towards the judge and lets him know that she has no further questions. True to form, Tim Ruby stands up.

Tim Ruby: "Why did you call Lorenzo?"

Alba: "Because he is my friend."

Tim Ruby: "Did you know your call would be recorded?"

Alba: "I did not know."

Michelle Snyder: "You said you were sad about what happened to the baby. Did you know what happened?"

Alba: "Detective Silva told me."

Michelle Snyder: "But this call happened before talking to Detective Silva."

Michelle Snyder: "Were you crying because you missed

Lorenzo?"

Alba: "No."

Note: Alba had borrowed someone else's phone card to call Lorenzo. I can only guess that the phone card belonged to her cell mate, Esmeralda. The prosecutor points out that she did have her own card.

Alba: "From the outside, you can't see my pain, but I felt it on the inside."

Alba said that she hadn't heard the announcements about the baby.

Lunch is called until 1:30.

Note: Tim Ruby seems to be standing slightly straighter today.

Tim Ruby is waiting for a "computer person" to turn on a computer and play an audio file.

1:50 pm: The court is in session, and they are on record without the jurors being present.

Tim Ruby enters "Defense A" into evidence. 94 pages.

Jurors enter.

Judge: "Portions of the transcript have been deleted." (To jury.)

Tim Ruby plays the audio from an interview for the court to hear. He pauses the tape at the end of each line for the jurors to keep up with the English written translation.

The judge stops the tape and asks to see council in the hallway.

2:25: The Judge and attorneys return to the courtroom.

Tim Ruby talking to Detective Silva.

The second interview date between Alba and Detective Silva was December 5, 2012.

With an unnatural pause between questions because of computer problems, Tim Ruby walks Detective Luis Silva through the transcript. Line by line, Detective Silva explains his reasoning for questions he asked Alba when she was first arrested.

All are seated, Tim Ruby is bent over the papers at his desk.

Silence as Luis Silva goes through several pages, reading in silence. The jurors each have a copy of the pages.

Ruby: "On page forty-three, lines one to eleven, on line twelve you say that is when you thought about that."

Detective Silva: "I asked if that's when she decided to video tape."

Ruby: "She said yes, at that moment I thought of having him and decided to record him."

Detective Silva: "Yes."

Ruby reads from the manuscript: "How many times have you watch it? I always watch it. Do you watch it daily? Twice a day, or…" Ruby pauses, "I always cry."

Detective Silva: "Yes."

Recorder: "I'm sorry to interrupt again. I'm having a hard time hearing him."

Judge Simpson: "Speak up Mr. Ruby."

The recorder is given a copy of the transcript to aid her.

Alba from December 5, 2012, transcript: "Now I feel bad not having him."

Pages 48 to 55.

Tim Ruby, Silva, and Snyder are all quiet. It seems that they are waiting quietly for someone to finish reading.

Tim Ruby: "Page 98. On line 12. On that day instead

of leaving the baby did you think what you could have done?

Alba: I would have had him."

Tim Ruby: "You said that the baby was born more or less after Twelve."

Alba was picked up about two hours after calling her sister.

I don't know why trucks and cars couldn't see you.

Alba held the baby while she waited.

As the cars went by, I waved but the cars went by fast.

Alba: "I was scared that they were going to scold me."

Tim Ruby: "Line 10 on page 52. She wasn't sure if they were going to scold her or support her."

32. FaceBook and the Experts

Tuesday, November 17, 2015: 4:00 in the morning. I wake up too early. It's cold, and I go to the kitchen table to not wake anyone if at all possible. My thoughts will not allow me to sleep until I vent them. I turn on my computer and go to Facebook. I write:

"Alba's attorney has allowed her defense to spin out of control. Calling Alba to the stand, he has allowed her to argue that she was scorned by the father of the baby. Alba's amorous phone call to another lover from jail was presented. Alba has claimed not to have shared the news of her pregnancy with anyone away from the father of the baby. She has claimed that she was fearful of being scorned by her family and kicked out of her Oxnard home. And it goes on."

I go back to bed and at 5:45 the alarm goes off. The start of the day. Off to work, leaving at 7:00.

Hours later in the courtroom, Defense Attorney Tim Ruby is now reviewing with the Investigating Officer, line by line her interrogation after being arrested. This appears not to be winning any friends amongst the jurors.

Ruby, "What does it mean when she says 'Ah hah'?"

Sheriff Silva: "Yes."

Attorney Tim Ruby is difficult to hear and slow. He seems to be going through the motions. The questions seem to be basic and monotonous on purpose. The one thing he has missed is bringing in expert testimony on the Mixteco community.

I know of two UCLA professors who amongst other things could testify that many Mixteco women go to the forests with their husband and midwife to give birth. Also that in the case of an unwanted pregnancy, (incest and rape are not uncommon), the woman may go alone into the forest, leave their babies and return 24 hours later. If the child is still alive, it is believed by many that God meant them to take care of the infant.

The trial of first degree murder against Alba seems to be winding down.

Coming into Courtroom Twenty-seven I see Sheriff Luis Silva at the stand answering questions from Tim Ruby and in turn Michelle Snyder. They go back and forth a bit. Ruby objects to several questions, but only one is sustained. Ruby is asked if he has any further questions. "No."

It seems to be over. Silence for a few moments. The judge asks if the witness can be excused. Officer Silva stands up and walks across the court, passing next to the prosecutor and places the large white binder into the cart already holding several large black binders.

Judge Simpson asks if there will be any further witnesses. Tim Ruby says something not quite auditable into the desk. Judge Simpson asks him to repeat it. "I may have one or two more witness," Ruby repeats. "I may have one or two witnesses, but I won't know until late tonight or tomorrow."

Judge Simpson sits up and is visibly disturbed. Ruby had said that Sheriff Silva would be the last witness.

The three days of testimony was slow and tedious.

"Are they ready? Do you want to call your witness tomorrow morning?"

"I won't know until late tonight or late tomorrow," Ruby responds.

"I want the attorneys to join with me in the hallway." Simpson snaps.

The judge is not happy. I look over to Margaret at the other side of the public section. Sean Justice is two seats next to her and is writing the notes down in a reporter's pad. Margaret is smiling and nods to me.

The attorneys, judge and court reporter walk out through a back door to the room. All are quiet, and I get up to walk over to Margaret.

"He's going to call someone else," she tells me.

"I think he is going to call an expert witness."

I come back. "Did you read what I wrote in Facebook in the morning?"

"No, I didn't get to it yet. What did you write?"

"I suggested that he get the two experts from UCLA.

I think he read my Facebook post!"

I went to the other side of the isle again and sat down, looking at the clock. I need to leave early today. A few minutes later I get up to leave. As I open the courtroom glass door to leave, the judge and attorneys walk in from the door they left on the back side of the courtroom. I stand at the door and step in again.

The bailiff who sits at the back asks me to take a seat. Judge Simpson sits down at the bench as the attorney take their positions. This whole time Alba has sat silent, but at this moment she looks back for a couple of seconds to look in my direction. There is no expression on her face.

"There has been a new development, and I will give Mr. Ruby until tomorrow to contact other witnesses. Mrs. Snyder, do you have anything further?"

"Yes, Your Honor, I would like to call Jacqueline Jiménez as an expert witness."

"Is she here?"

"Yes, Your Honor. She is in the hall." The aide to the prosecutor gets up and leaves the courtroom to come back with a woman about thirty seconds later.

"Are there any objections Mr. Ruby?"

"Yes. I want to know if she is qualified as an expert."

"In the meantime, I will dismiss the jury," Judge Simpson announces. "We will start tomorrow at 10:30. Please do not discuss the case amongst yourselves or anyone else. If someone harasses you in the building or on the grounds, contact me, and I will take care of it."

The jurors leave out the back door. In the past, the judge had also mentioned to watch anyone taking pictures and that if this happened, he would have the person arrested. I guess that this wasn't on the judge's mind today.

I left the courtroom as the prosecuting attorney had started asking where Jiménez was employed and if she was fluent in Spanish.

"Thirteen years at the District Attorney's Office." Yes, she was fluent in Spanish. I left to meet my sons.

Did Mr. Ruby read my Facebook post? I could only hope

so. I called later to Margaret to cover our bases. She wanted to contact Dr. Yadira Irarrázaval at UCLA.

Margaret would later leave a message on her cell phone.

"I can only hope that Ruby is thinking of who I am thinking of. I wonder if, by any chance, he saw my Facebook post from the morning."

"I hope so."

"Maybe he is going to contact MICOP," I mention. The organization could also bring several "experts," and they are local. I finish, "This might be our Perry Mason moment."

"It might be."

I repeat, "We need the jury to know that it has been known that a woman sometimes deliver an unwanted baby alone and come back after a day to see if God wants them to take care of the baby. It probably won't make her innocent, but it can sure put everything into context. It's probably the only thing Ruby can bring up to help."

Margaret tells me that when she and Sean Justice left, they took the elevator. Before the door closed, Tim Ruby rushed inside. Even though it was only one floor, she said that he looked very nervous being alone with them.

"Good."

Wednesday, November 18, 2015 10:40 in the morning.

Tim Ruby is calling a Filiberto Sevilla as a cultural expert on Friday.

Michelle Snyder is telling Judge Simpson that culture is not an issue on the question on trial.

Michelle Snyder points out that while going over the transcripts, she has noticed that Tim Ruby has asked more verbally complex questions than she has. Alba can answer Tim Ruby's questions and not the prosecutions'.

Michelle Snyder says that multiple native Spanish speakers have said that Alba speaks it very well and that Alba willingly chose to have a Mixteco translator even though a Spanish interpreter would facilitate communication.

Michelle Snyder adds that the jurors have been instructed to ignore issues of race, income or occupation.

Judge Simpson: "I am denying the testimony from a cultural expert this late in the trial." Jurors enter.

Tim Ruby rests.

Michelle Snyder calls Jacqueline Jiménez. (Investigative assistant in the DA's office.)

She is born in Mexico. Fluent in Spanish.

She arrived in the United States six years ago. Jacqueline Jiménez is being called to translate text messages from Spanish to English.

Jacqueline Jiménez: "JK is 'just kidding'. Q is que."

Jacqueline Jiménez is saying that short hand text messages are the same in English and Spanish.

Michelle Snyder is asking if Jacqueline Jiménez translated the messages accurately and fairly.

Jacqueline Jiménez: "Yes."

Alba was sending text messages asking for Radio Union requesting a song and sending a message to be read aloud. (Romantic leaning.)

Alba sent another song request with a love message to Saul saying she will go back to him soon.

Alba is sent text messages to Saul in Spanish.

Michelle Snyder to Jacqueline Jiménez: "Do you think she is fluent in Spanish?"

Jacqueline Jiménez: "Yes."

Michelle Snyder asks if the words could be in any way interpreted as only being friendly in nature.

Jacqueline Jiménez: "No, that type of language would only be used boyfriend and girlfriend or husband and wife."

Michelle Snyder clarifies if Jacqueline Jiménez has seen or heard anything in the texts that would imply that Alba didn't know Spanish.

Jacqueline Jiménez: "No."

Jacqueline Jiménez is saying that due to the speed that she speaks, Alba speaks Spanish fluently.

Tim Ruby asks for a cross examination. Then before he gets started, Ruby asks for lunch. This is granted and the jurors are allowed to exit the courtroom.

Without the jurors in attendance, Tim Ruby complains to the prosecutor that he has never seen the texts messages.

Michelle Snyder says, "Tim, I have given you everything, and you never bring any of it."

Michelle Snyder brings up that she wants to play the interview video so the jurors can see through body language if Alba was scared, forced or did not understand the context of the questions of the interrogation.

Tim Ruby brings up that Alba is perceived to be guilty because the video will show she is in jail at the time. He continues to say that the jurors should know the content of the case, not the circumstances that his client finds herself.

Michelle Snyder replied that it wouldn't make a difference

since Alba is dressed plainly and not in jail blues in the video. Actually, I have never seen Alba in orange she continues.

Tim Ruby is now showing more energy than ever in his argument. He openly questions the prosecutor's opinion of him.

Michelle Snyder says she isn't accusing Tim Ruby of being unethical.

Michelle Snyder says the video through nonverbal cues proves intent, knowledge, and reaction.

Michelle Snyder: Alba said on November 30th to detective Silva that she heard the news about the baby dying. She later said that she first heard about it when Detective Silva told her.

Judge Simpson to Michelle Snyder: I will watch the video over lunch hour and look for the nonverbal cues to see if it's relevant.

Michelle Snyder: "It's not the whole thing. It's thirty-five minutes.

Judge Simpson: "No. It will be less than five minutes."

A young lawyer comes into the court, passes the bar and is whispers to Tim Ruby seeking advice for another attempted murder case.

Guy shoots in Police Officer's direction in an open field to scare them off, and they charge him with attempted murder. Simi Valley.

Michelle Snyder: Alba was describing or gesturing specifically at the events while talking.

Judge Simpson plays video in open court to see if it's admissible.

Tim Ruby objects and asks judge to see it in chambers.

Judge: "No, I will see it right here."

Judge Simpson will only allow pages one to seven to be played. This is the first moments of being accused of the death of the baby.

Tim Ruby and Michelle Snyder approach the bench.

It sounds like Tim Ruby wants a delay due to a back surgery or a doctor's appointment.

Judge Simpson shouts very loudly: "What? Are you going to Vegas?"

Judge Simpson to Tim Ruby: "Let's go back to the back and talk. I need to say something to you."

Even though the general courtroom rule has been to not look at cell phones, two court staffers are texting frantically. It appears to be non-business or perhaps in reaction to what is happening because they both seem to be giggling.

The jury enters at 2:20.

The judge allowed only about 30 seconds to a minute from the video to be shown. The quality and angle are not the best of quality and one can only guess what the impression is on the individual jurors. Alba did not jump up and go into convulsions, nor did she show calm casual conversation. She was answering questions in what I preserved as a 'What do I say now?' fashion. I am not on the jury.

32. Verdict

On Monday, November 23, 2015, I left with my wife, Viviana in the morning to go to the Ventura County Courthouse. I as a teacher have the week off because this Thursday being Thanksgiving. I know that it may be a waiting game and even though I know that the jury is deliberating, it may take a couple of days.

We arrive at the Courthouse around 9:00 in the morning. It seems that there are a lot of people around. This seems to be the hour that those lucky enough to have Jury Duty are to present themselves. We go through the metal detectors and take the elevator to go to the second floor. At the end of the hallway, there are many people waiting outside Court 26 and 27. At the door, I see a paper taped to the door. It has some names on it.

I ask a nearby bailiff, "Do you know where the announcement of a verdict will be for the State versus Zapata case?"

The older bailiff seems to be waiting too. "I don't know. The cases on the list are in line to use the courtroom today."

I smile and tell him, "My goal is to not get anyone upset for being in the wrong place. Do you know where I can find out?"

"Go downstairs to the Information desk. They have a list of all the cases."

We go down the hallway, and I call Margaret who is now in front of Courtroom 27. I ask where she is and turn to see her walking towards us with the people standing all around the different courtrooms on the floor.

At the Information desk, I ask if the Zapata case will report their verdict when it comes. Typical answer, I am asked to look at the list. While flipping through the pages to the Z's, the Bailiff asks, "Is that the baby in the field case?"

"Yes."

You can probably get better information in the Traffic and Court Administration Office. We then find out that we should check into them again later.

Instead, we decide to go home. I tell Margaret that I will call up Tracy Lahr with the local TV news. Margaret leaves to go home, while Viviana and I go to the County Government building in the same grounds.

I tell Viviana that since we are here, I want to see if I can speak with someone in Supervisor John Zaragoza's office. He isn't there, but I sit down with his Chief of Staff Jim Cotton.

It's been a while that I have seen Jim or for that matter, gone by John Zaragoza's office. We sit down. The reason I am here is to plant a seed. The connection with Esmeralda and Alba was that they both were arrested for the deaths of their babies. But the connection goes beyond their losses, or their being imprisoned. They both came in the shadows and lived in the shadows. Information was missing. They both missed out on information that could have led to services and options that could have saved and changed lives.

Bill thanked me for working on behalf of the ladies. I haven't gone out of my way to advertise what we were doing. But this is why we were here.

"We are waiting for a verdict." I look Jim Cotton in the eye. "The verdict isn't going to help the next mother or child."

"What are you up to?"

"I want to get information out to the newest immigrants."

"I'm listening."

"The best way to reach our target audience is through the radio. I want to put on Public Service Announcements over the Spanish and Mixteco radio stations every hour. Twenty or thirty seconds."

The idea is received well. In following days, it is considered a good idea by others as well. Now the implementation will take some time and work not on only my part, but hopefully of others who can give their time and talent.

Later in the day, I see that Marisa Fernández has written on the Ventura County Star website. Alba is found to be guilty of first degree murder.

I can't believe that she got first degree! The jurors must have thought that this was all premeditated. I call up Margaret who was still hoping that Alba would be not only found innocent but that as Esmeralda was would be set free later in the day.

"I can't believe it," Margaret tells me on the phone. "First degree murder? What is she looking at?"

"Twenty-five years to life."

"No. Is there anything that we can do?"

"I don't know. The judge will give the sentence on January 7th. I think that we can address the judge during the sentencing. I will look into it." I tell her.

"Tim Ruby was a terrible attorney. He didn't help her out at all." Margaret tells me almost out of breath.

"I know. We tried, we did what we could do. We couldn't force Alba to drop him. We didn't know if we were going in the right direction at the time or not." I pause. "It looks like we were right."

We agree to call if we hear anything else or have any other thoughts. It is a time to reflect and to prepare. A few minutes later Margaret calls me again.

"I have Marisa Fernández on the line. She wants to talk with us. Can you hold? We are going to have a three-way conversation."

What a great idea. I would rather have a conversation alongside Margaret rather than give my statement separately. I expected a guilty verdict, of lesser charges but Margaret I know truly expected with her heart that Alba would be found innocent.

I could now hear Marisa's voice. "Hi. I wanted to talk to the both of you because you were the closest to the case."

"Thank you. What a great idea to do it in a conference call." I say.

"You know that Alba was found guilty of first degree murder. What do you think?"

I deferred to Margaret to begin. Ladies first.

We talk about the case and how we were disappointed with the verdict. We speak about our deep dissatisfaction of the defense that Tim Ruby had given. True to form, much of our words about Ruby never made it to print.

"Woman who left baby in field guilty of murder" made print in the Ventura County Star on November 23, 2015.

The feeling after the verdict is somber. Alba is guilty. A baby died.

The verdict, in my opinion, is harsh. First degree murder

in my understanding shows premeditation. I can't say that I saw any planning to kill the child. Perhaps the fact that no planning happened was the premeditation.

Friends scorned me when I would bring up the fact that the jury was eleven Anglos and one Latina. "Race had nothing to do with it!"

I'm not sure. Would the verdict had been different had the jury been eleven Latinos and one Anglo? She had been found guilty of first degree murder! Couldn't have been worse with a minority jury. May not have been better.

Had the mother been a 19-year-old American citizen, Anglo, blond haired, blue eyed? The report of a mother leaving her child during the past Christmas season in a nativity scene in New York brought a hint of delight that the child was just like the baby Jesus. The baby was found in time, alive. The Anglo mother was found shortly after the news broke. Psychological help. So close to having the baby die of exposure in the winter New York night, so far away from first degree murder.

I have a state conference with the California School Boards Association usually the first week of December. This year it is in San Diego. Amongst classes and talking with colleagues in the halls of the convention center, I also have the chance to meet many of the attorneys who specialize in education law. They come to the conference to meet with Trustees and administrators from other districts along with inviting the ones they represent out to dinner.

The handful that I have contact know also followed the cases of the two ladies. They were congratulatory for the freedom of Esmeralda Martinez. More than once I was told, "That never happens." The verdict of the jury for Alba seemed puzzling to the friends, but they seemed very pleased that I have been involved.

I was told that the judge could indeed reduce the verdict! I passed this news on to Margaret by cell phone as soon as I could.

"We still have time to solicit Judge Simpson!" I told of how the judge could reduce the verdict and even the sentence.

Margaret would write a letter right away. She also hopes that Alba would be let free with the three and a half years that she has already been in jail as time served.

"I don't think that we will be that lucky." I will also write, but I can't imagine that the 25 years to life mandate will be reduced anywhere under ten years.

On another front, I do have broad interest in helping with what I am now calling "Project Golondrina." Golondrina is "swallow" in Spanish. The birds often appear in the warm months in California and fly low over the rows of crops and fieldworkers while feeding on insects. The swallows will travel south as far as Argentina and Chile in the winter months.

I have a friend writing a music score for the background of the radio public service announcements. I want the community tips to be recognized, even though they are on different radio stations.

I finally make the phone call to Sheriff Luis Silva. Now that we had finally finished with the trial, he and I are to have a sit down for lunch. I tell him that I have two projects that I want to tell him about. He seems happy that I wanted to sit down with him and we agree to meet just after Christmas.

The post-verdict also brought a surprise: a family member of Alba contacts me through my Facebook account.

"Hi." A screen shot of me holding a photo of Alba at the press conference. "Is this you?"

I answer, "Yes."

They send me a copy of the article that Michael Justice wrote. A black line is drawn under one paragraph. "She's guilty and would serve life anyway."

"Did the LAWYER say that?"

I write back, "Yes."

"I'm a close relative to her family. I just saw this today."

"I'm sorry to say; it's probably too late for much action now. Alba stayed with Tim Ruby, and he did a terrible job. She has now been found guilty of first degree murder.

The only hope at the moment is to write to the judge and ask that the charges be lessened. She is now looking at 25 years to life in jail.

I tried to help her. Her family and Tim Ruby insisted that he take her defense.

"How are you related to her?"

"Yes, I'm aware of that, but we never knew my family was scared to speak up since their immigrants. We are family."

"Alba protected the family the best she could. Yes, I understand the fear. She trusted the wrong person."

"Yes. We all did."

"Alba did not help herself in the process. She lied several times to police and then changed her story. It made her look very bad in court. Her attorney, Tim Ruby did not help."

"Yes. We read about that."

"Do you live in the Oxnard area? Would you be interested in sitting down for coffee or tea to discuss Alba's case and what can still be done to help?" I ask.

"Yes. And when and where?"

"How about Wednesday the 23rd? Starbucks at Plaza Park. What time would you be available?"

Unfortunately, the meeting never came to be. I am not sure how it would have turned out, and it appears that the relative may have had more reservations than me. I haven't heard from the family member again.

I did, however, have lunch with Sheriff Luis Silva on December 23rd. We met at Anaba Restaurant on Victoria Ave. and Wooley Ave.

We both had been looking forward to having the sit down. The case over, I felt that we could now talk about what we had lived through.

"Thank you for coming. I am glad that we can finally meet."

"Oh, we could have met before."

"Well, it's more comfortable now."

We spoke of our frustration with the case in general. Nobody, absolutely nobody wants to see a baby die. Nobody wants to put a mother in jail.

"I gave Alba every chance to let her tell me that somehow she helped the baby. It never came." Officer Silva orders fish and I am an udon soup for the cold day.

"Do you think she really didn't tell anybody about her pregnancy?"

"No, they knew. Someone knew."

We both talked about how our families had changed in the three years since we first spoke about finding the mother of the child in the strawberry fields.

"I always wanted to ask you, why did you contact me?"

Silva looks at me, his plate and around the restaurant for a moment.

"I don't remember."

Not the answer I had been waiting for.

"You were on the internet or something, I'm sure."

"Did you call others?"

"No."

I was wrong on this account as well. I'm glad that he had made that call, but it also brought negativity into my life as well. I guess I can say that I learned a lot. I never thought that I could actively help, or try to help someone in a real life, life or death action like I had been through.

Silva looks up at me. "Do you think that she understood enough Spanish to understand what was happening to her and how to defend herself?"

"I think so. She spoke a simple Spanish, and I'm sure that the technical stuff was hard, but she understood. How did you come about thinking that she could answer your questions in Spanish?"

"We had her answer questions. We also asked if she could look for words written in Spanish. She found them in no time. Then we asked her to find a paragraph. She pointed at it and then read the words back."

"I still think that she was right to use Mixteco in the court."

"Really? You don't think it affected her?" Silva asks.

"Possibly. But if I were on trial for murder, I would want to know what is going on in my first language, not my second."

"By the way," I ask. "Should I be afraid of Alba's family?

Are they the Mexican mafia or something like that?"

"No. You don't have to worry. They are simple folk. They are trying to survive."

Thank God! I was afraid that my wife's concerns when I first got started in this case may still come true. I remember that she was afraid for the safety of the family. I preserved that we were OK, but this is the opportunity to ask.

I tell Luis Silva about my plan to get Project Golondrina started and asked if the Sheriff's Department might be able to support the project.

"I know that there must some law or item that you guys want to get out to the public at any given time."

"Oh yes. Could you put out that we need information on a given case?"

"I haven't thought of that. The mission will be laws, services, and responsibilities. I would think that asking for someone to go forward to help the police would be a responsibility. We need to let people know that they won't be deported for being a victim. You know that too many crimes are committed that are never reported."

"That's always an issue. We don't deport people for being a witness or a victim."

Silva tells me that he will pass the word on and see if others would be interested in helping.

33. Safe Surrender Baby Law

I have still been asked how the ladies are who we have tried to help. When I say that Alba has been found guilty, they seem to remember having heard the news report on that. I tell them about the possibility of the judge lessening the charge or the time to be in jail. Most the people who ask then tell me that they hope that the three and a half years already in jail will be looked upon as time served. I don't expect such a sweeping change from the decision of the jury.

Early in the morning on January 29th, I turn on the TV while I am getting ready to go to work. Rushing around and making a large glass of ice tea I hear from the other room the new anchor talking about the Safely Surrendered Baby Law. I hadn't heard them talk about Alba. I go to the living room, tea in hand.

I rewind the news to the beginning of the report. KEYT channel three anchor Stacy Sakai announces, "Welcome back. Well, a young mother in Santa María is charged with killing her baby, but the young woman had a choice. News channel three's Vickie Gwinn has the story."

"A fifteen-year-old girl could face time behind bars for allegedly killing her newborn baby. The State passed the Safely Surrendered Baby Law in 2001." The new article described the law and reporter Gwynn spoke to a Santa Barbara County Fire Captain Dave Zaniboni.

Later in the day, while leaving work, I hear the radio report.

Fifteen-year-old mother is being charged with murder of her new born baby.

The headline is what people remember. The headline is what people know. In a few bold words, opinions become valid. Details are not important. There are headlines every day. If the general public reads the article, it doesn't add much information beyond the bold title words. The headline sells newspapers and the public, split into conservatives and liberals see the headline through their frame.

We also want to have the news fast. It is a competition to get the news out, and in some social circles, you are ahead if you have the pulse of the news. Unfortunately, events are often complicated. The first reaction does not tell what happened; it tells what satisfies the news cycle of the moment.

This morning's local news doesn't add much to the information. A sixty-second feed from a fire station, "tragedy" used to describe what happened. The concrete that is opinion is set well before the viewer, the public knows what happened, what may have happened. An evil person left a new born innocent child to die.

A life is lifeless. A baby. A newborn. Yes, a mother has to be involved. The devil of a mother who left her newborn drop from her body and walked or perhaps ran away, leaving the infant to die.

This was a fifteen-year-old mother. A child herself.

What is her story?

Alba was nineteen when she gave birth. Four years older. It makes a difference to some, and yet the background lives are unknown. The background story is unknown.

The father of the child? Was he involved in the death of the baby?

I call Ventura County Supervisor John Zaragoza that afternoon. I tell him about Project Golondrina. I tell him about the public service announcements I want to get on the radio. I also tell him about the fifteen-year-old in Santa María. He calls me back an hour later. I will be speaking with the CPO of Ventura County next Monday.

I call Margaret to ask if she had heard of the news about the fifteen-year-old. She hadn't.

Margaret had been out to visit Alba once a week and tells me that she has been trying to prepare Alba in that a state prison will be very different than the jail that she has been held.

The end of our involvement with Alba may end a month from now with the sentencing and her transfer to a state prison. The Golondrina Project perhaps is the positive outcome that we can feel good about. Perhaps this book may bring positive results to others.

Alba will have to defend herself and her record. She will be in a general population of prisoners. I believe that a woman who killed her newborn child in a woman's prison will be very low if not on the bottom of the totem pole.

Margaret talks about appeals and appealing the case, but at best this will take several years. I question if Alba will survive the prison system.

Texting reporter Marisa Fernández on Thursday, February 25, I find out that the sentencing had been delayed once again. Now set from March 15. She told me that Prosecutor Michelle Snyder was unavailable because she was in another court.

I call Margret who reminded me that the sentencing is now on the Ides of March.

I tell Margret that Marisa Fernández is interested in interviewing Alba in jail. I doubt that Alba will be willing.

I also get a call from Estrella with the CRLA asking if she can pass on my name and phone number to a university professor from UNAM. He is apparently interested in the Alba case and has taken up Mexico's indigenous human rights with the Mexican federal government.

I get four calls with no messages from Mexico while watching a movie in a local theater with my family. Not able to talk with him yet.

On Friday I get a call in the day and can tell him that I am interested in talking with him and he says that he can call me at 9:00 in the evening.

I get the call at 9:00 sharp from Juan Pablo Esquivia. He knows about the Alba case and has been stymied on his end because of confidentiality laws in Mexico. Alba would have to sign off on allowing information to be made public. He is surprised when I say that it was Alba and her

family who have dragged the case on and impeded in her own case.

I call Margaret to let her know of the conversation.

She is very interested.

We decide to visit Alba today, Saturday, February 27 at 3:00.

I will stand out of sight of Alba until waved over by Margaret. Alba may not want to speak to me.

I call Margaret, Saturday morning to tell her about my conversation with Juan Pablo Esquivia the evening before. She seems very interested in that others are aware of the case.

Margaret asks me what we can do now. The sentence is only two weeks away, and that is after having it delayed twice.

I come up with three points.

Our objective is to ask if Alba is interested in interviewing with Marisa Fernández. This would not have been a good thing to do before the verdict, but we both agree that she doesn't have much to lose now. I would like to get Alba to sign the document to have the investigation of Saul in Mexico through the Consulate. This would set an independent investigation into action. The problem again is that the word rape was never mentioned in the court proceedings, and if it was claimed now, I'm sure that it would be scoffed upon. Also, a signature allowing the UNAM professor Juan Pablo Esquivia access to government records could open up other parallel lines of investigation.

The optimist, Margaret still asks if Alba could be freed without going to prison. I don't think this can ever happen, but we can work on shortening her sentence in prison.

Alba should grant an interview with Marisa Fernández with the Ventura County Star newspaper. The big break needs to be that she will make a break from her testimony and admit that she had been raped. It will not be believed by the vast majority, but it would open a closed door.

We decide to go to the Todd Road Jail and speak to Alba on Saturday at the 3:00 visiting hour. We want early to be because even though her family hasn't visited her since the verdict, we don't want to be pushed out of the spot.

Margaret and I decide that I will stay in the waiting room while Margaret asks if Alba is willing to talk with me. Then we realize that if Margaret leaves the booth to look for me, the guards will surely call an end to the visit. I will now stay off to the side in the visiting section. Margaret will turn and call for me if Alba agrees.

I stand there, out of sight, but the conversation touches on the three points very fast. No. Now, Margaret goes into the normal conversation. I never am called to the side to be in view, and Margaret never mentions that I am only feet away. Alba is frightened but she in on cruise control.

Past the twelfth hour. March 21, 2016

I am standing in middle of a strawberry field. I had been invited by a friend who is with the California Strawberry Association to tour the site along with a County Supervisor, and representatives to the different school districts in the area. We met in a barn in middle of the field and now are walking down the rows to listen to our guide and come closer to the workers picking the fruit.

My cell phone rings and I see that it is Jessie Licea.

I smile and hit the button.

"I'm standing in the middle of a strawberry field at this very moment." I ask Jessie. "Did you know that I was out here?"

Jessie Licea is a friend. He is also the local representative to the United Farm Workers. I hadn't heard from him for some time.

"What are you doing out there?"

"I am taking a tour."

"Who are you with?"

"Roger Nelson. We have a group from the Strawberry Commission and locals. It's been interesting."

"Good. Say hi to Roger for me."

I chuckle because I would have thought that there may have been some animosity between the two. Roger Nelson had already surprised me in that he remembered me from 1999 when I was working with a UFW contract, and Murray was the manager of Coastal Berry Strawberries in Oxnard. I played a minor roll, but apparently after seventeen years was remembered. It's all good.

I ask, "What's up?"

"We can talk later, but I called to let you know that Alba Zapata's family came over to ask if there was anything that we could do to get their sister out of jail."

"Really? It is past the twelfth hour! They want help now?"

"That's why I am calling. Can I trust them? Is there anything we can do?"

I look out over the twenty field workers bent over picking strawberries with both hands moving in a blur. "They have done everything wrong in the whole process. They have been misled and have obstructed Alba throughout the process. If you ask me, a couple of them should probably be in jail too."

"That's why you are the first person I am calling. Is there any grounds that we can look at an appeal?"

"Sure there is. But if Tim Ruby is still representing her all bets are off."

"They said that he lied to them. They want to let him go."

"We only have sixty days from the sentencing to file an appeal. I don't know if it will be possible."

Jessie offers to put together a group of people to sit down in a few days. "Monday, March 28 at Noon. At the UFW office. Can you make it?"

"Yes, I'm on Easter break starting Monday. I will be there."

March 28, 2016

Viviana enters the United Farm Workers office with me a bit before noon. We are the first to come for the meeting. The office looks like it had fifteen, sixteen years ago when I seemed to have worked in the place. While walls, posters and photos pined in odd places around the main room. Cubbyhole offices to the side, all filled with stacks of paper, and two long white plastic tables pushed together in the center of the main room with plastic folding chairs set around it.

Jessie greets us and we take advantage to talk about our kids who were now all growing up now. Jessie's youngest is now a senior in high school and two daughters are in universities. We all share the fear and expense of seeing our kids going to college. Roman and we agree that it would be worth it in the end.

Soon the others of the meeting arrived. Dr. Víctor Yañez from UCLA, Maritza Marquez, Editor of El Tequio Magazine, Inta Angeles from MICOP, Margaret and perhaps most important: Alba's two sisters, their husbands one teenager and four year old arrive.

Handshakes and introductions seem pleasant, but the meeting is to be one of the most important discussions about the death a baby and trial of Alba to date.

We introduced ourselves mainly to the Zapata family. I introduce myself as a teacher and Viviana as my wife. The Zapata's know Margaret somewhat by encounters and by her reputation of being Alba's "Grandma."

The Zapata's introduce themselves in a shy low voice. Citlali, Margarita, and Bruno. María Guadalupe has an 18-month old child who soon after we sit at the table is at her breast.

Dr. Víctor Yañez seems to head the meeting and introduces why we are together. He asks if anyone can give a brief history of the case. I raise my hand.

I try the best I can to highlight how the rollercoaster of an investigation and criminal case developed I cite my points that I think can be used in an appeal.

The DNA was taken from over one-hundred fieldworkers. Knowing that regionally, over half are usually undocumented, I bring up the question that I believe most if not all the workers didn't know that they had the right to say, 'no thank you.'

The university professors are interested in the cultural background that could explain the mindset of Alba throughout the events that created this crisis. The court did not want to consider any cultural norms that may have influenced Alba and what she did. In part, we agreed that this was because it was not brought up from the beginning. The attorney must be removed. He is the person who would be involved in the appeal if nothing else changed. The attorney must be removed from representing Alba.

Her family say across from me at the gathering. They were quiet, almost shy and apologetic. They claimed a few times during the discussion that they didn't know what was being done. They put their trust into the attorney. They felt that Alba would be released and forgiven for her actions.

At the conclusion of the meeting, I was asked to go to the Court and ask if Tim Ruby had pulled papers to appeal the case. I was also to find out when the transcripts would be made available and how much they may cost.

The sisters were asked to talk to Alba to ask that she agree to drop Tim Ruby. We were to also look into other organizations that might be interested in taking on this case.

May 16, 2016

I haven't heard much for the last month. I know that Alba is in Chowchilla and that because of the change of location she is now some three-hundred miles away. Also because of the change, she is not allowed visitors for the first ninety days.

She must be allowed to speak with a legal representative, but in this moment that person is still Tim Ruby. We want to get her the documents to sign allowing her to change over her legal representative to the California Appeals Project. To make the issue more complicated, we have been asked to also find a translator in Mixteco to accompany the person who is delivering the papers to be signed.

Had she still been in the Todd Road Jail I know we could have gotten this done?

Today is day sixty. In talks with the attorney with the California Appeals Project, they had said that they had spoken to Tim Ruby. I guess out of professional curtesy, it corresponded. Ruby had said that he planned on filing the appeal.

I expect that Ruby would want this thing to go away. He did not expect that Alba would have the support from anyone who could do anything about his actions or her case. I was told that ninety-nine percent of the time an appeal is filed within the first ten days. Now we are at the end at day sixty.

The attorney also told me that if Ruby did not file, that they would have more on Tim Ruby concerning malfeasance than before. There must be another line that we can take. The legal system must allow an appeal at day sixty-one, but I can't say what would be involved.

I send out a text to Margaret, Dr. Yanez of UCLA, Odilia, Jessie Licea of the UFW and Tom of the CRLA who had given unofficial advice.

"From what I calculate, today is day sixty for Alba Flores Zapata to have her case appealed.

Any word? What is our status?

Denis O'Leary"

I am in my classroom. It is lunch, and the kids are in the playground. I have failed to stand up and save the day. I had excuses before: The legal investigation, the court, a Geneva Convention violation, Alba's family and Alba herself. The obstacles came and went, and I a teacher and advocate rode the rollercoaster while looking at the case and learning about this emotional third rail of a legal case, and a dead baby.

Day sixty. It is over.

I read a response.

"Denis, I was under the impression you and JESSIE

were working on that. I have been pretty clear from day one that I can only pass information on to those who are helping Alba. I cannot orchestrate what needs to be done. I have no idea if a declaration was signed requesting new counsel. I have no idea if it was filed with the court. I have no idea if an appeal was filed."

Tom

"I earlier texted you the above link to an organization that ran a battered women's project and has a pool of attorneys who have taken on battered women cases. Did anyone contact them?"

Tom

"I am happy to help to the extent I can, but I have not been contacted for some time and really do not know what steps have been taken."

Tom

"I remember having been told by the California Appeals Project that they had contacted Tim Ruby. He had told them that he would file the appeal. I was then told that if he didn't follow through, they would have a better argument against Tim Ruby's representation.

I am NOT accusing anyone of anything. I don't want to be accused either.

I have for close to four years on this case told people that I am not an attorney. I expect that others know better about the process than me.

Do we know where we are at now? Do we know where we can or should go from here?"

Denis

"The appeal was filed by the current attorney."

Jessie

"I'm blanking on his name."

Jessie

"Tim Ruby"

Margaret

"Yes, that's him. Thanks Margaret."

Jessie

"He's a snake. Be careful!"

Margaret

"Yup. But it was his duty to file the appeal. Still moving forward with Alba's declaration for new counsel."

Jessie

"Yes."

Margaret

"Thanks, the all the Saints and God all mighty. This is great news."

Denis

"Hallelujah!"

Margaret

"It's all very good news, but a long and very difficult struggle awaits. Contacting the organization, I linked to earlier might prove very helpful."

Tom

"Tom, do you have a contact there?"

Jessie

"Not yet, but they were highly recommended. I will follow up and get a name."

Tom

Apparently, we have bridged the gap of not appealing and appealing the case. It was Tim Ruby who filed the papers. I can't imagine what is on his mind, knowing that the appeal will call his representation into question. He filed at the end of the sixty days.

I can breathe again. Who knows where this is going to go. I can't say how long the appeal will go on. And I can't say what the outcome will be.

I do have my own outcome that I want to see happen. Something that will take work, but I think I can control the outcome.

Project Golondrina

It is time. I have talked about Project Golondrina with others and tried to anticipate the questions to come and the obstacles.

It always seems to come down to money. I want to pay the two Spanish language stations and one Mixteco station for airing the 30 second spots. I believe that I will get the funds, but I must show my vision to the people with the money. I have had a good reception with County Supervisor John Zaragoza and his staff. I even have spoken to the person in charge of communications with the county. All had good responses, but I need to show the product before I can go on.

Viviana and I talk about how many words fit into thirty seconds. The topics are many; the categories are three: Laws, responsibilities, and services.

We want to help inform the newest immigrant communities know that they are not alone and this is not a lawless wilderness. We also want the community to know that they have people who can help.

Viviana and I text out a script to each other, fifty-seven words.

"*No le pegues porque la quieres. El abuso doméstico destruye la pareja y la familia. Hay donde ir en nuestra comunidad para obtener ayuda, consejos y también refugio. No le van a arrestar por ser víctima. Si le pega, no sufra más. Llama a la policía local o a 911. Esto fue un consejo del Proyecto Golondrina.*"

(Don't hit the person you love. Domestic abuse destroys the couple and family. There is a place to go in our community to look for help, advice and even refuge.

You will not be arrested for being a victim. If you are hit, don't suffer more. Call the local police or 911.

This is advice from Project Golondrina.)

I record Viviana reading the message on a voice memo program on my cell phone. 27 seconds! Perfect. Over the next two days we write and record several other spots. Some are in Viviana's voice, some I read. Messages for men and messages for women.

Some subjects will be listened to with more attention coming from a woman's voice, some will be better coming from my voice.

Later, we will have these translated into Mixteco and possibly other indigenous languages. I will place this on a web site still to be put together. I want to pay the stations for the spots, but with the internet I hope that many other stations will decide to air the messages.

"Mujer, si estás esperando un bebé, recuerda de alimentarte bien, descansar lo suficiente, ir a control médico para controlar que todo este normal en el embarazo y recuerda de no consumir drogas, fumar o beber alcohol todo eso también afecta a tu bebé dentro de ti.

Esto fue un consejo del Proyecto Golondrina."

(Woman, if you are expecting a baby, remember

to eat well, rest, go to the doctor to see that everything is normal with your pregnancy. And remember not to use drugs, smoke or drink alcohol because if you do this, your baby will too.

This is advice from Project Golondrina.)

"No es de hombre golpear a su mujer ni a sus hijos sino de amarla, protegerla y ayudarla con la crianza y educación de sus hijos. Hombre es el que ama a su familia y vela por ellos.

Esto fue un consejo del Proyecto Golondrina."

(It's not manly to hit your wife or children, but to love them, protect her and help her raise and educate you children. A man loves his family and provides for them.

This is advice from Project Golondrina.)

"Padres, es el deber de todos de educar a sus hijos y ayudarles con

sus deberes escolares. En el hogar busquen un lugar tranquilo y pongan un horario para sus estudios y asegúrense que vayan siempre a la escuela con las materias listas.

Esto fue un consejo del Proyecto Golondrina."

(Parents, the duty of all is to educate our children and help them with their needs in school. At home, look for a quiet place they can study at and make a schedule to study. And make sure they always go to school with the materials they need.

This is advice from Project Golondrina.)

"Si tienes una emergencia y no sabes dónde ir, no hablas el idioma y no tienes papeles, no te preocupes llama al 911 ellos te ayudarán, ellos hablan español, no te arrestarán y no te deportaran. 911 policía, ambulancia y bomberos.

Esto fue un consejo del Proyecto Golondrina."

(If you have an emergency and you don't know where to go, you don't speak the language and you don't have papers, don't worry. Call 911. They speak Spanish. They won't arrest you and they won't deport you. 911, police, ambulance and fire fighters.

This is advice from Project Golondrina.)

"Mujer, si fuiste forzada a tener relación sexual con un extraño o con un miembro de familia, eso es violación. No lo ocultes, denúncialo a la policía inmediatamente. Recuerda tú eres una víctima. No importa tu estatus migratorio. Busca ayuda para que eso no vuelva a ocurrirte, denuncia al culpable y estarás ayudando a otras mujeres víctimas como tú.

Esto fue un consejo del Proyecto Golondrina."

(Woman, if you have been forced to have sexual relations with a stranger or a member of your family, this is rape. Don't fall, report it to the police immediately. Remember you are a victim. Your immigration status doesn't matter. Look for help so this doesn't occur again.

Report the rapist and you will be helping other female victims as yourself.

This is advice from Project Golondrina.)

"Mujer, si estás esperando un bebé recuerda de ir al doctor. Si tú no deseas a tu bebé una opción es entregarlo en forma segura sin peligro de enjuiciamiento a los tres días de su nacimiento, siempre y cuando no haya dano físico en la criatura al cuartel de bomberos o a hospitales de acuerdo a la ley de California.

Esto fue un consejo del Proyecto Golondrina."

(Woman, if you are expecting a baby, remember to go to a doctor. If you don't wish to have the baby, one option is to give the child in a safe way without the danger of judgement within 3 days of birth, always when there is no physical injury on the child to a fire station or a hospital under the law in California.

This is advice from Project Golondrina.)

November 2016

The Mexican Consulate has a new Consul General. Election day came. I won re-election against a retired teacher who had the teachers' union endorsement. I spent election night with my family, first at the United Farm Workers office on A Street and later at Anaba's Sushi Restaurant. In the parking lot between the two sites, my son, David calls from the University of California, Irvine. The first vote count is on the Ventura County Elections Office website. I am 411 votes ahead. We sit down to a good victory dinner. As we are laughing and enjoying the moment, we are also looking at our cell phones. Donald Trump will be our next President of the United States of America.

The Consulate calls me to ask if I can attend a scholarship presentation. I accept since I was a panel member in awarding the funds. During the evening the Consul General and several others ask me about Project Golondrina. My recent excuse has been that I wanted to wait until after the election. Campaigning takes a lot of time and energy. I didn't want Project Golondrina to become a political campaign item.

No one used the fact that I had advocated for two women accused of killing their babies. I didn't want to use it and was happy to see that no one else saw fit to attack me with it. I will be on the Oxnard School District Board of Trustees until 2020.

I can't say until when Donald Trump will be President, 2020 or 2024. America seems to have snapped. Trump started his official venture into a presidential campaign with a very clear attack on "Mexicans." Perhaps this is what caught the attention of many of his faithful. Walls and chants of 'send them back' may be an indicator of where his administration will go.

Alba did enter the United States of America without permission. I don't believe that she pushed and unemployed American welfare recipient out of the way to get her job, but had she stayed in her village in Mexico, I can't say that the baby would be alive today or not. I don't believe that Alba will be a threat to anyone else in her life from this point forward. If released today, she may be the victim in Mexico of her own environment. American tax dollars will be spent for many years, and the lesson will fall of the angry Christians instead of the pregnant immigrant who may someday find themselves in a similar situation as this 19-year-old had on that May day in 2012.

I understand that Esmeralda is still in the Oxnard area. She has never contacted Margaret nor myself after having her charges dropped. She is in the shadows, and I understand picking strawberries.

The young girl in Santa María has been found guilty. I only know what I heard on the news. No details, only the headline. She killed her newborn baby. What is her story? I don't know.

Alba is in Chowchilla, California serving twenty-five years to life. We await a retrial.

California's Safely Surrendered Baby Law

The Safely Surrendered Baby Law responds to the increasing number of newborn infant deaths due to abandonment in unsafe locations. First created in January 2001, the Safely Surrendered Baby Law was signed permanently into state law in January 2006. The law's intent is to save lives of newborn infants at risk of abandonment by encouraging parents or persons with lawful custody to safely surrender the infant within 72 hours of birth, with no questions asked.

From January 1, 2001, to December 31, 2015, 770 newborns have been surrendered in California, and 84 newborns were surrendered during the 2015 calendar year. This is compared with 169 infants abandoned since 2001, five of which occurred in the 2015 calendar year. Available data indicates a generally decreasing trend of abandonments since enactment of the SSB

Law, from 25 cases in 2002 to five or less cases per year since 2010, representing a decrease of at least 80%. The CDSS continues to identify abandonment cases from various sources and will continue to report updates to this trend.

SAFELY SURRENDERED BABY LAW FAST FACTS

Background The Safely Surrendered Baby Law (SSB) was implemented on January 1, 2001, with the intent to prevent harm and possible death to newborns. The Law The SSB law (California Health and Safety Code, section 1255.7) provides a safe alternative for the surrender of a newborn baby in specified circumstances. Under the SSB law, a parent or person with lawful custody can safely surrender a baby confidentially, and without fear of prosecution, within 72 hours of birth. The SSB law requires the baby be taken to a public or private hospital, designated fire station or other safe surrender site, as determined by the local County Board of Supervisors. No questions will be asked and California Penal Code Section 271.5 protects surrendering individuals from prosecution of abandonment. The process at the time of surrender, a bracelet is placed on the baby for identification purposes and a matching bracelet provided to the parent or lawful guardian, in case the baby is reclaimed. A parent or person with lawful custody has up to 14 days from the time of surrender to reclaim their baby. A medical questionnaire must be offered, however it is a voluntary document and can be declined. The questionnaire is offered solely for the purpose of collecting medical information critical to the health and survival of the infant. All identifying information that pertains to a parent or individual who surrenders a child is strictly confidential.

THERE IS AN OPTION. DON'T ABANDON YOUR BABY.

Safe surrender sites are hospitals or other locations, typically fire stations, approved by the board of supervisors or fire agency in each county.

Safe surrender sites are required to display the blue and white logo to the right.

The toll-free telephone hotline number provides information and the locations of safe surrender sites. **DIAL**

1.877.BABY.SAF (1-877-222-9723)

OPTIONAL MEDICAL QUESTIONNAIRE

Although a person surrendering a baby under the Safely Surrendered Baby Law will be asked to complete a medical questionnaire, the form is optional and is intended solely for the purpose of collecting medical information critical to the health and survival of the child. Any information that may identify the person surrendering the baby will be removed in order to maintain that person's confidentiality.

CONTACTS

To order Safely Surrendered Baby posters and brochures, please visit SSB Publications at www.babysafe. ca.gov/pg2693. htm. Los Angeles County residents, please visit Los Angeles County Health Services.

For more information on the Safely Surrendered Baby Law, please contact the Child Welfare Policy and Program Development

Bureau at (916) 651-6160.

57217899R00190

Made in the USA
San Bernardino, CA
18 November 2017